AF241942

Books by C.B. Wilson

<u>The Gem Hunters</u>

The Fire Diamond
The Water Diamond
The Ice Diamond (Coming Soon)

<u>Barkview Mysteries</u>

Jack Russelled to Death
Cavaliered to Death
Bichoned to Death
Shepherded to Death
Doodled to Death
Corgied to Death
Aussied to Death
Dachshund to Death
Labradored to Death
Puppied to Death
Retrievered to Death (Coming Soon)

Praise for the Gem Hunters

"Who knew dogs could be trained to sniff out diamonds? Taylor Hunter and her diamond-sniffing doxie are two of the most distinctive characters to arrive in the world of cozy mysteries in quite some time. What a brilliant idea for a new series!" —*Lois Winston, author of the award-winning and bestselling Anastasia Pollack Crafting Mysteries.*

"CB Wilson's *The Fire Diamond* is an engaging mystery filled with sharp twists and unexpected turns. Readers of PI procedurals will appreciate the introduction of Taylor Hunter and her diamond-sniffing dachshund, Glimmer. This promising novel marks a strong beginning to Wilson's Gem Hunter series." —*Ellen Butler, #1 Amazon Bestselling Author*

"A smart and sassy investigative thriller with a cast of delightfully quirky characters and genuine mystery." —*Kirkus Reviews*

With its golden-age mystery flavor, hardboiled energy, and cozy storytelling style, The Fire Diamond is a delight. I highly recommend it to cozy mystery lovers who enjoy international intrigue, engaging characters, full-on excitement, and enough romance to keep things interesting. I give The Fire Diamond five magnifying glasses. —*Don W., Amazon Reviewer*

"Move over Stephanie Plum—Taylor Hunter is the new queen of cozy adventure." —*Lucky, Amazon Reviewer*

"The Fire Diamond, CB Wilson's newest cozy, is a twist-filled mystery that pulls readers into the intriguing world of diamond mining and jewelry heists. Tangled family loyalties, global intel sources, a hunky law-enforcement adversary, and Glimmer, the fearless diamond-sniffing dog, elevate this fast-paced caper. I was guessing to the very end and can't wait for the next installment." —Deborah M., Amazon Reviewer

"If you like mysteries well-seasoned with suspicious deaths, and topped with a sprinkling of romantic tension, this new series will definitely be one of your favorites." —lldawn, Amazon Reviewer

"A sassy sleuth, a diamond detecting dog and enough twists and turns to keep you guessing, this is one whodunit you won't want to miss!" —Ann G., Amazon Reviewer

The Water Diamond

A GEM HUNTERS MYSTERY

CB WILSON

Character List

RECURRING CHARACTERS

Chad the Cad—Hunter's ex husband

Dee the Decoy—Hope's dachshund

Glimmer the Diamond Dog—Hunter's dachshund

Hope Hunter Allegro—Hunter's twin sister

Rocky Rockman—FBI agent and friend of Hunter's

Taylor "Hunter" Hunter—The Diamond Hunter

Le Renard Argente—Hunter and Hope's father

Sophie—Sterling & Sons Insurance Company

Historical Figures

Augustine Viktoria—Last German Empress and Queen of Prussia until 1917 when Kaiser Wilhelm III abdicated

Theodor Seitz—Governor of German East Africa (1910–1918) Prussian

Teutonic Knights—A medieval order of knights originating in Germany & Prussian. This organization fought in the crusades

Administrative Characters

Christian Weber—Teutonic Knights member. Owner, jewelry store in Chicago

Chuck Lenz—Catalina Casino Director of Operations

Ellie Horne—Catalina historian from the Catalina Museum

Waters Family

Melodie Waters—1929 Twin responsible for protecting the Waters' diamonds. Killed in a boating accident in 1929

Walter Fox—Melodie's fiancé

Merle Waters—1929 Twin responsible for protecting the Waters' diamonds. Killed in a flash flood in 1942. Claire's mother

Claire Waters—Merle's daughter. Present owner of the Waters' diamonds

Lionel Waters—Nephew of Waters twins. Cousin to Claire Waters

GREEN FAMILY

Demi Rosewalt—Mother of the Green family

Grandma Jean Green-Allen—Demi Rosewalt's granddaughter. Diamonds in the Sand owner. Casey's grandmother

Lady Byrd—Grandma's sister. Casey's aunt.

Casey Allen—Grandma's grandson

JEWELRY STORE OWNERS

Michael Wise Jr & III—Owners Wise & Sons Jewelry

Tash Foti Wise—Daughter of the owner of Wise & Sons jewelry store

Gemologists Jargon

Art Deco jewelry (1920s–30s) features bold geometric designs, symmetry, and a sleek, glamorous look—often using diamonds, platinum, and strong color contrasts.

Bench jeweler is a craftsperson who makes, repairs, and sets jewelry.

Demantoid garnet is a rare, vivid green garnet prized for its exceptional brilliance and "horsetail" inclusions.

DiamondView unit is a device that uses UV light to reveal a diamond's growth patterns and identify if it's natural or lab-grown.

Duette is a piece of jewelry made of two matching clips that can be worn separately or joined together to form a single larger piece, often a brooch or necklace.

Horsetails are fine, hair-like inclusions in demantoid garnets that fan out from a point, resembling a horse's tail.

Milgrain is a decorative edge of tiny bead-like details used in vintage jewelry.

Standing loupe is a small magnifier that rests on a surface, allowing hands-free close inspection of gemstones.

Prologue

MAY 29, 1929

He's found me. You must protect the diamonds.

No phone rang. No courier arrived. But Merle Waters got the message all the same, her twin's terror knifing straight to her heart. That was the price of their bond. Distance didn't soften fear. It sharpened it.

Some people called it intuition. Others, coincidence. Twins knew the truth. Their connection forged before birth, when one heartbeat faltered and the other felt the tremor. This was no nudge either. This was the psychic equivalent of a hand clamped over a screaming mouth. Someone had closed in on Melodie—someone who knew the diamonds' secret.

Merle didn't waste time. She tiptoed down the hallway, stopping at the farthest door, her knock intense and urgent. Waking Ami at this hour always came with consequences. Tonight, she'd gladly pay.

The heavy door swung open. A small, dark-skinned woman stood framed in the doorway, wrapped in a cape as black as the moonless sky beyond. Her old nanny's eyes narrowed as she studied Merle with the same unnerving stillness that had kept the twins in line for years. Ami wasn't surprised. She'd heard Melodie's silent scream, too. The villagers back in Panama had whispered about black magic. Merle knew better. Ami simply *knew* things others didn't.

"Yu mus' go tonight, chile." Her Creole accent wrapped around the words like a spell.

Merle nodded, fear closing around her throat. There would be a lifetime to regret marrying a man she didn't love, assuming she lived long enough for regrets. She had no choice now.

A single tear tracked down her cheek as her fingers found the leather pouch hidden beneath her traveling dress. The stones inside pressed, cold and unyielding, against her ribs, carrying the weight of secrets that could topple empires.

She steadied her breath. She knew her duty. She knew what tonight demanded.

God go with you, my sister.

The words weren't spoken aloud. They rose inside her like a prayer... and a final goodbye. She would never see Melodie again.

Chapter One

EX-HUSBANDS BELONG IN THE PAST
—WISDOM FROM A JEWEL THIEF

PRESENT DAY

Law enforcement runs in my blood. My great-great-grandfather carved his name into legend by relentlessly pursuing Jesse James across three states. After him came a long line of decorated officers. Medal of Valor recipients. Celebrated detectives. The kind of cops newspapers praised with words like "heroic" and "selfless."

I grew up fantasizing about being *The Closer* or *Rizzoli*. I might be petite, short by anyone's definition, but I made up for it in toughness and determination. I planned to follow in my TV heroines' footsteps until the day I learned the truth about my absentee father.

He wasn't dead or some deadbeat who'd simply walked away. He was a thief. Not your garden-variety smash-and-grab amateur, either, but Interpol's most wanted jewel thief.

The irony wasn't lost on anyone. Especially not the FBI, CIA, or any other agency with initials and background checks. My logical mind, the one that routinely cracked cases before the final commercial break, became a liability. A what's-the-point kind of asset nobody wanted to touch. So, I did what any reasonable person with my particular skill set would do.

My name is Taylor Hunter, and I am a diamond detective.

That's what I call myself, anyway. My business card reads "Specialized Recovery Consultant." That's insurance company speak for someone who does the dirty work they can't. I find lost and stolen diamonds. The ones that vanish without a trace. The ones that make seasoned detectives shake their heads and close case files.

I get called in when law enforcement hits dead ends, and insurance companies get desperate enough to overlook my father's rap sheet.

Because sometimes, the only person who can think like a jewel thief is a jewel thief's daughter.

Friday, 11:30 a.m.

"You're an idiot." My twin sister Hope, two crucial minutes younger than me, delivered her opinion with typical unfiltered candor.

Not that I needed to hear it echoing through my SUV's speakers. In the passenger seat beside me, Glimmer, my long-haired mini-dachshund, released a sharp bark that punctuated Hope's assessment like an exclamation point.

"Are you really so desperate for a distraction that you're willing to work with your ex-husband?"

"The idea sounded better an hour ago when I agreed to take this job." The admission came out more rueful than I'd intended.

"What were you thinking? He's Phoenix PD's *senior homicide detective*." Hope's voice climbed half an octave. "It's not like you two parted as besties. Chad the Cad is a vindictive son of a..." Her huff cut off the rest, honoring her self-imposed cursing ban.

I grinned despite everything. "You'd think he'd refrain from biting the hand that feeds him."

"Good luck with that." Hope's voice dripped with dry amusement. "All the alimony in the world won't soothe his wounded ego."

I pictured her head toss and that knowing smirk playing at her lips. She wasn't wrong. For all Chad's swagger, his pride had cracked the moment I walked out. Sure, we'd both wanted the divorce. But me being the one to actually leave? That had left a mark.

"Sterling & Sons wouldn't have called me if the department had done its job." The words cut deeper than I'd intended.

"My point exactly. He'll be gunning for you with his badge as cover."

"He's a homicide detective." I kept my voice steady. "Stolen diamonds are property crimes. With any luck, we won't even cross paths." Even as I said it, I knew better. Luck and I had long since filed for separation. And Chad the Cad? He had a talent for appearing exactly where he wasn't wanted, wearing a smug grin to boot.

"He'll find a way." Certainty marked Hope's tone. "A theft at the Wrigley Mansion in Phoenix? That's the kind of headline that buys promotions."

She wasn't wrong. Chad collected people like watches—worn for show, wound up when needed, forgotten in a drawer when something shinier caught his eye.

"Who's leading the investigation?" A casual question? My sister never asked casual questions.

"Officer Ortega," I said, though the name felt more like a question than an answer.

"A crony!" Hope's groan hit like a gut punch. "You really are an idiot. And I thought Sophie was your friend."

"She is," I insisted. Sophie and I had shared walls, secrets, and too many bad cups of coffee back in our De Beers security days. She'd seen through Chad's charm long before I did.

The truth was simpler than Hope wanted to hear. Nothing could have stopped me from taking this case. The real mistake? Telling my sister about it. I wouldn't have if I didn't need her help.

I switched lanes on Loop 101 as it curved past Scottsdale toward Phoenix, my focus locked on the road. Not thirty minutes earlier, I'd been home in Sunset Peak, where the only thing drifting across the pavement was a tumbleweed, not a crush of brake lights.

"Standard police work won't crack this one," I said. "The thief walked past millions in easy-to-fence jewels to take the Water Diamond, a single $5 million Art Deco bracelet."

Silence stretched across the line. I could feel Hope's pointed focus on the other end, that old twin-sense humming to life between us.

"You think this theft is about..."

"...the matching piece of the Waters' Duette," I finished for her. Like always. Much to our friends' and family's endless annoyance.

The platinum-and-diamond Duette was a rare Art Deco masterpiece—two separate bracelets that joined to form a single, seamless necklace, their connections nearly invisible. A U.S. diplomat purchased it in 1920 for his heiress wife. After her death, the necklace had been divided—each of her twin daughters inheriting one half, the separation permanent and final.

That division of one necklace, cleaved into two halves, had always intrigued my sister and me. Twins always notice when something meant to be whole was broken apart. To us, the Duette wasn't just jewelry. It felt like the first clue in a much older mystery.

Hope let out a low whistle. "The Deadly Duette. You know the legend. Those diamonds are cursed. Melodie Waters went overboard on a passenger steamer between Catalina Island and the California coast in 1929."

"Her body was never recovered." I kept my voice flat.

"Neither was the bracelet." Hope wasn't letting it go. "Then her twin, Merle, drowned in a flash flood a dozen years later."

"Another freak accident." I cut in before she could start connecting dots that didn't belong together. "This isn't the

Hope Diamond's curse. Just a coincidence wrapped in bad press."

At the sound of my sister's name, or maybe the word *cursed*, Glimmer released a small, uneasy whine from the passenger seat. Her nose twitched toward the desert horizon.

Hope exhaled softly. "The Duette's been split up for nearly a century. Why tempt fate by bringing the pieces back together now?"

Why now was the real question. "There's more to this than a missing bracelet."

"Seriously?" Her disbelief hit like a slap. "You're taking this case and risking a run-in with Chad the Cad over conjecture?"

Hope had a gift for stripping things to the bone. Spoken aloud, my reasoning did sound insane. But I'd learned never to let logic argue with instinct. "My gut says otherwise."

Her sigh buzzed softly through the Bluetooth. "Why is this so important to you?"

"The Waters twins never unlocked the Duette's secret because they couldn't work together," I said quietly. "We can."

A shiver traced my spine. Then came a voice I wondered if I'd ever hear again—low, accented, far too real for a memory. *Every diamond comes with a price, ma chérie. What are you willing to pay for this one?*

Wisdom from my father, the infamous jewel thief? Now that was the real oxymoron.

I knew Hope felt the chill. Twins didn't miss warnings like that. But she hadn't heard Dad's voice. If she had, she wouldn't be hesitating.

"Okay. Fine. I'm in." Her voice shifted, resigned. "I'll pull the GIA report on Merle Waters' half of the Duette. If there's a pattern everyone missed, I'll catch it."

She would. No one read diamonds the way my sister did. Hope saw truth in carbon the way other people saw sparkle. "I'll call you once I'm on-site," I said.

"Better you than me." Another pause. Heavier this time.

"Hunter... be careful. A century-old mystery doesn't tug at twins unless it wants attention. And this one's pointing straight at the Star of the Desert."

A cold ripple ran through me—hers or mine, impossible to tell. "I'm betting it started in 1929 in Catalina. The Arizona connection is just the thread pulling us in."

I ended the call and eased the wheel to the left, turning onto Biltmore Circle Drive from 24th Street. About five hundred feet ahead on my right, the Wrigley Mansion's sign came into view. I slowed, double-checking that I wasn't accidentally pulling into the bank's driveway, then continued over the bridge into the parking lot.

Glimmer stood in the passenger seat, paws pressed against the window, tail wagging. She sensed the adventure ahead.

I put the car in park and stared up. Through the trees, the mansion perched on the hill, the white stucco and red tile roof glinting like a Spanish Colonial crown against the cobalt sky. Built for William Wrigley Jr. back in 1931, it didn't just sit on the ridge; it owned it. Arched windows, Catalina tiles, and wrought-iron balconies. Every detail whispered old Hollywood glamour.

Somewhere inside were answers to why someone would steal the Water Diamond after all these years.

I just had to find them... preferably before Chad found me.

Chapter Two

THE JOB ALWAYS OVERRULES THE
HEART—WISDOM FROM A JEWEL THIEF

FRIDAY, 12:00 P.M.

I locked my Glock in the vehicle's gun safe. Without the familiar weight on my hip, I felt exposed in a way I hated to admit. Still, better that I remove all temptation to shoot my ex-husband should he show up. Sensible, yes, but I missed the reassurance far more than the weapon.

I shaded my eyes against the glare, half-regretting my choice of boot-cut jeans instead of khakis. The heat shimmered off the terracotta path as I walked from the parking lot to the mansion, each click of my designer boots echoing off the steps.

Though far from a fashion enthusiast, shoes were my weakness. My closet resembled a museum of questionable choices: metallic leathers, impractical heels, and colors that could stop traffic. All height equalizers that provided confidence, one inch at a time.

I pulled up the mansion's floor plan on my phone, rotating the image until it aligned with our position at the guard shack beside the side delivery entrance. I noted the two restaurants tucked along the estate's edges and the cluster of special-event rooms stacked like a maze, inviting trouble.

"Come on, partner." I motioned Glimmer to follow. "Let's scope this place out before we head inside."

I slipped past the exterior surveillance camera with a quick detour onto the garden path—less to hide my approach than to test the security system's integrity.

Roses lined the slate walkway, their scent threading through the warm afternoon air as the path curved past a manicured arbor and arched hedges perched on the hilltop. The reason this locale topped every prime wedding list became clear as the valley unfurled below like an Arizona backdrop with Camelback Mountain glowing to the east and the Phoenix skyline shimmering softly through the haze.

Another bank of security cameras caught my eye. The two cameras pointed toward the arbor, focused solely on the mansion's entrances, making the narrow path skirting the perimeter a perfect blind spot.

The Ocotillo fence lining the path looked menacing enough in the afternoon light, all thorns and attitude, but up close it was more bark than bite. Spiky, yes, but hardly a deterrent for anyone determined to get by.

Glimmer didn't even acknowledge the so-called barrier. She leaned in, nose brushing the barbs, and let out a single bark, alerting me to pay attention. That's when I saw the silver glint on a lower Ocotillo spine.

A Wrigley's Spearmint gum wrapper?

I fished a jeweler's tweezers from my crossbody bag. Naturally, the barb still managed to nick my finger as I worked the wrapper free. A careless litter-bug or a clue? Glimmer's low arf snapped that rabbit hole trip. I slipped the gum wrapper into an evidence bag and trailed the dog toward the sleek, glass-walled building jutting out from the mansion's Spanish Colonial frame.

Christopher's was one of two restaurants on the estate, a sleek, modern outpost tucked neatly against the mansion's old-world curve. All clean lines, stone, and warm wood, it didn't challenge the historic architecture. It tempered it. At sunset, the floor-to-ceiling windows transformed the entire dining room into a glowing panorama, as if the desert had stepped inside to watch what happened next.

I'd eaten there once, years ago, celebrating one of Chad's promotions. At the time, I hadn't gotten the appeal of the painfully gourmet cuisine. Even now, I appreciated the farm-to-table thing far more.

The dachshund tossed her head, pointing me toward the narrow gap between the modern glass building and the Spanish stucco, the space capped by an overhead balcony. No need to recheck the floor plan. The restaurant shared the circular drive beside the mansion's main entrance. Which meant we'd approached the Pasadena Room, the room from which the bracelet had disappeared, without anyone the wiser. Granted, an event venue didn't require Level One security, but a 1920s rare jewelry exhibition should've called for more robust defenses.

I paused to study the balcony. From ground level, the wrought-iron railing's star-shaped latticework caught slices of sun and shadow. The balcony doors appeared to be closed, but one of the drapes inside shifted. Just enough to make me look twice. Someone inside watched.

Glimmer stilled beside me, her long ears twitching, nose angled toward the veranda. I felt it too—that prickle in the air, like static gathering before a storm. We were onto something.

I followed her gaze across the drive to a familiar unmarked sedan.

Of course. Chad the Cad's vehicle.

Even from here, I recognized his bad-boy parking style: halfway between official and lazy, just enough to block the entry and mark his territory. A Phoenix PD detective's badge might let him break the rules, but his ego handled the rest.

"Looks like our least-favorite detective beat us to the scene," I muttered, accepting the inevitability without complaint.

Glimmer snorted softly, agreeing.

I crouched near the edge of the path, squinting up at the second-floor balcony again. If I were a thief, and unfortunately, I'd inherited at least a hint of that instinct, I'd have noticed the same thing I saw now. The balcony's railing was old, but its open design made it easy to climb. Christopher's adjacent roofline, with its gentle slope, offered cover to anyone agile enough to scale it.

"Unrestricted access," I whispered. "One decent distraction and you're in and out before anyone notices."

Glimmer pawed the ground impatiently. She'd already scented something. The diamonds, or maybe just Chad. They'd never gotten along. Whatever it was, she wanted to follow it. I glanced from my chunky heels to the low rooftop. If I went for it, I could likely avoid Chad altogether. A good idea, except that sweat coated my hands just thinking about the second-story view.

"Not yet, girl," I said, resting a hand on her back. "We're going in through the front door like civilized people."

Truth was, I wasn't about to give Chad the satisfaction of watching me panic on top of that balcony. My fear of heights had already made that decision for me.

The doxie cocked her head to the left, her look unconvinced.

Together, we walked toward the entrance. The air shimmered, and somewhere behind us, another reflection from the balcony caught my eye, this time just a flash of something I refused to label sunlight. Maybe it was wishful thinking. Or maybe I'd discovered the first breadcrumb in a trail that led straight to the missing bracelet.

"Every diamond..." I murmured, remembering my father's words, "... has a story."

Glimmer's tail wagged once. She was ready to find it.

Whether Chad liked it or not, we were officially on the case.

Glimmer matched my pace as we approached the exterior staircases. Both curved to meet at a landing, boxed in by cascading magenta bougainvillea. Nose up, tail frozen, I tracked Glimmer's gaze to the heavy wooden door, half-expecting someone to step into the pale stone archway. By the time I bent to scoop up Glimmer at the entry, it felt less like arriving and more like crossing a line.

The woman who met us at the door confirmed it. Her tailored blazer and pressed slacks said authority wrapped neatly in hospitality. At first glance, her posture appeared welcoming. Her eyes were not. "I'm afraid dogs aren't allowed inside the mansion." Her pleasant tone stretched thin over steel. I knew the type. Rules and zero flexibility.

Of course. Chad's handiwork. I drew a steady breath. "Glimmer is a working dog. She's here to recover the missing diamonds."

The woman's brow lifted in polite disbelief. "She's not a police dog or a service dog. The rules state..."

My patience snapped. "Glimmer is a search-and-rescue dog. She searches for thieves... and rescues history."

Glimmer's nose twitched eagerly. I'm not sure if my look did it or practicality took over, because the woman stepped aside, revealing Detective Chad Rosas leaning against a carved banister at the base of the sweeping staircase, thumbs hooked in his belt, his badge flashing faintly under the filtered light. The navy sport coat couldn't hide the bulk of his holstered weapon or that same careless confidence that I used to find charming before I learned better.

Hope's "I told you so" rang in my head. "Lowering yourself to property crimes, Detective Rosas?" He looked good. The gray threading through his dark hair only made him more distinguished.

"Nope. For the record, you're interfering in my homicide investigation." His tone stayed neutral as he straightened up, but the smirk pulling at his mouth gave him away. "Still kicking up dust, I see."

My boots clicked on the tile. "Didn't realize killing courtesy called for an official investigation."

He let that one slide. "You're late."

"Your gatekeeper thinks my partner's a liability."

He glanced at Glimmer in my arms. "The dog's your partner now? And here I thought you worked alone."

"She's got better instincts than half your department," I shot back.

His jaw tightened, but the grin stuck. "Always a pleasure."

I studied him. "Let's skip the trip down memory lane, Chad. Why don't you tell me why a homicide detective is parked at the Wrigley Mansion waiting for a diamond investigator?"

The air between us hummed with a brittle quiet loaded with old tension and fresh trouble.

"The night guard was killed in a hit-and-run," Chad said, his voice flat. "White pickup and partial plate that matches a Waters Construction vehicle."

"You think someone in the Waters family stole their own diamond bracelet?"

"The eccentric aunt owns the bracelet. Lionel Waters has money problems." Chad's smirk radiated pure smugness. "Don't need you on this one. Had it solved before you walked through the door."

Of course, he did—neat, clean, and wrapped up. Exactly how Chad liked it. The problem was that it made zero sense. The CEO of the Valley's leading construction company boosting jewelry? "I take it you recovered the bracelet?" I asked, keeping my tone level.

His smile went thin. "Not yet. But I will."

I rolled my eyes, refusing to respond to his jab. "Then you won't mind if Glimmer does a quick sweep. Her track record speaks for itself."

Chad's shoulders set, but he gestured toward the curved staircase. "Be my guest."

Too polite. Too easy. My ex playing the gentleman was reason enough to keep my guard up. I placed Glimmer on the ground. The dog took off, her nails clicking on the tile floor until the carpeted stairs muted the sound as she charged up the steps, her short legs moving with complete confidence. I hustled after her, noting the low banister and shallow steps Wrigley had built for Ada's barely five-foot frame. Not because it suited me—I moved easily enough—but because of Chad. Behind me, he struggled with every step, and watching him do it felt like a small, satisfying win.

At the landing, I looked up. The thirty-foot dome overhead burned like a red-and-gold Moroccan sunburst exploding across the ceiling. Gorgeous. And way too bright for whatever this place was hiding.

Glimmer waited at the top, tail swishing with intent, then trotted ahead down the hall past the elevator and two shallow steps. She vanished into the first room on the right. I followed into the Pasadena Room. Decked out in pure 1920s glamour, the blue-and-gold Catalina tiled fireplace, flanked by twin crystal chandeliers that cast light everywhere, exuded an unmistakable flapper allure, making you half-expect jazz to start playing at any second.

Normally set for formal dinners, the room had been transformed into a 1920s soirée. Mannequins stood where the table should've been, draped in drop-waisted beaded gowns and era-appropriate feather headbands or flashy jeweled headpieces.

My trained eye went straight to the Art Deco jewels. Couldn't help myself. Long pearl strands, complemented by multi-colored jeweled brooches and intricate filigree tiaras cast in rich platinum, made the room appear to be frozen mid-whisper. Center stage, raised on a twelve-inch dais, stood the Waters' display. The prominently positioned bare wrist gave it away long before I could read the placard.

My pulse rate kicked up. A jewel thief walking past all this shine? Not a chance.

My father's knowing voice cut through. *Ma chère, a true thief never lets the heart overrule the job.*

Which made me... not a real thief. I took that thought as a win.

A younger woman observed from the doorway, likely only a

handful of years my junior, but remarkably well-kept. Polished, poised, and dripping money down to her classic pearls. 10mm, I'd guess, their luster showing regular wear. The size of her diamond engagement ring screamed industry connections. The second she smiled at Chad, his good mood made sense.

Her hand extended, the woman approached. "I'm Tash Foti— I mean Wise. The divorce was final months ago."

"Of Wise & Sons jewelry stores?" It wasn't really a question. The woman's legal battles had dominated the society pages for months. A marriage unraveling was painful enough without the court of public opinion weighing in.

"You've heard of us," she added in a breezy trust-fund-baby tone.

Wise & Sons jewelry stores had served the Valley for seventy-nine years, their reputation forged by her family's service to the community. So far, Tash's contribution hadn't quite lived up to that legacy.

"You must be the diamond hunter. I'm the event coordinator for the Daughters of the Pioneers. Naturally, I offered my services for charity," Tash went on, smoothing an invisible wrinkle on her well-cut trousers.

I hid my irritation behind a polite nod, but Chad interrupted before I could respond. "Tash, do you have the box?"

Her attention snapped to him, and her smile warmed instantly. Flirtation or strategy? Hard to tell. With her pedigree, she had both access and the means to make the Waters' bracelet vanish without a trace. And Chad... well, he always did know how to pick complications.

Glimmer's bark drew my attention. Tash passed Chad an inlaid wooden box and bent to pet my dachshund. "She's beautiful, just like my Rusty Boy." Her fluttering eyelashes drew my attention to her striking green eyes.

"This is the Water Diamond's case," Chad said.

I blinked. Chad, helpful? That was rich. Still, I got the

message. He wanted me out of his way as much as I wanted out of this place.

Tash's gaze bounced between us, curiosity lighting up. "Do you two know each...?"

"Here," Chad shoved the box toward me. "Let's see what that diamond dog of yours can do."

My fingers went cold the instant I touched the antique jewelry box, and it wasn't just the temperature. Something else pulsed beneath the surface. The piece was exquisite, walnut and ebony burnished to a dark, liquid sheen. Twin panels of brass and mother-of-pearl mirrored one another across the lid, their perfect symmetry converging at a single onyx cabochon set precisely at the center. The design meant something. I could feel it in my bones.

The hinges creaked as I lifted the lid. Inside, the box was divided into two identical velvet-lined compartments, each perfectly shaped to cradle a matched bracelet. One side bore the faint imprint of recent weight, the other only the ghost of what had once rested there. Even empty, the box still guarded a secret it wasn't ready to surrender.

I set the box on the floor and gave Glimmer a nod. She dropped her nose and sniffed. Her tail flicked once before she started circling, ready.

"Glimmer... hunt."

In a heartbeat, the dachshund shot across the room, paws tapping across the wood floor. She stopped at the balcony doors and scratched at the glass, the same location I'd considered a good entry point from the outside.

I wrestled with the lock until Chad waved me aside. Surrendering to his muscle irked, but I gave in. The door opened with a reluctant click. Glimmer bolted onto the terrace, her nose facing the warm afternoon breeze. She sniffed twice, considering, before making a beeline for the balcony's edge and barking. Her signal.

No need to follow the doxie's gaze over the railing. The guard involved in the hit-and-run accident hadn't walked the bracelet out of the mansion; no one had. It had gone over the side. Someone had either climbed the wall, threading through the camera blind spots to hit this balcony... or someone in the Pasadena room had dropped it to an accomplice waiting below. "This was clearly a professional job," I said.

Chad cursed behind me. He knew Glimmer had just blown his neat little theory to pieces.

I scanned the balcony for additional evidence: no rope fibers, no scuff marks, not even a ripple in the thin film of desert dust coating the railing.

"I'll have the rail dusted for prints," Chad muttered, jaw tight enough to crack a molar.

"Minimum two guys who knew the security system's flaws." I turned back toward the Pasadena Room. "I don't see a camera in here. Did you have a guard posted at the door?"

Tash's hesitant nod set off alarm bells.

I swung to Chad. "You interviewed the guard, right?"

The muscle in his jaw jumped—his tell—indicating that something else had happened. The diversion I'd figured had been employed.

"What?" I pressed. "Was he the guard you found dead?"

Tash's hand flew to her mouth. "Yes. But we also had a brief power outage last night during the event."

Of course, they did. My stomach dropped. "How long?"

"Maybe a minute," Tash replied.

"Seventy seconds thanks to old wiring." Chad's explanation failed my scrutiny.

Tash didn't buy his finality either. She spoke up, contradicting him. "You mean, Mr. Wrigley's ghost, Detective. Apparently, the man liked a good prank. He turns the lights off and on all the time. At least that's what the docents tell me. I can attest to it. Unexplained things happened twice during our setup earlier this week."

"A ghost?" Right. And I was a Hollywood starlet. No matter

what my father claimed, this had his brand of elegant heist written all over it.

Not again. Our last meeting had nearly cost him his life.

"You've been hit by a pro," I said flatly. I turned back to Chad. "Other than the vehicle, why do you think Lionel Waters is your guy?"

"His aunt was planning to will the diamonds to a museum," Chad replied.

"This was to be the bracelet's last showing." Tash shook her head. "Imagine giving away a family heirloom like that."

The way Tash's thumb twisted her engagement ring screamed insecurity. Her nervous habit? "Your ring is an antique cut. A family heirloom?"

Her smile widened. "Why, yes, it was my fiancé's grandmother's ring."

Of course, I had to pry. But it wasn't as if I was jealous or pretending in any way to care who he got involved with. "I'm surprised you haven't had the diamond recut." An old mine-cut diamond sparkled under candlelight. The modern brilliant cut glittered in LED lighting.

"Absolutely not. This ring has been in my fiancé's family for three generations."

I appreciated her sentiment. Every diamond has a story... The older, the more complex and intriguing. "Are you an Art Deco fan?"

"What's not to love about it? It's bold but refined with just the right balance to make an impression." The fire in her eyes told me everything. When you're raised around diamonds, you recognize the same passion.

I even begrudgingly related. The nothing-fussy style drew me, too. I turned back to Chad. "What does the aunt have to say for herself?"

Chad tapped his temple. "She's... not all there."

"Meaning?" I kept my eyes on the small tick in his jaw. Chad's impatience with his own mother's dementia made bias a real possibility.

"She couldn't stay on topic." He crossed his arms. "She lives in the past. Her place is a time warp."

His worst nightmare. I knew exactly where I needed to start once I gathered more information on Tash Wise.

<h1 style="text-align:center">Chapter Three</h1>

BEWARE OF CRAZY LIKE A FOX— WISDOM FROM A JEWEL THIEF

FRIDAY 2:30 P.M.

My dashboard clock flashed mid-afternoon when Glimmer and I finally returned to my SUV. That would be 9:30 p.m. Friday night in London. *Perfect.* Calling Sophie, my Sterling & Sons contact and the best Watson under fire, would cost me big time now. I dialed anyway. Sophie answered after the first ring.

"Good heavens. May I not enjoy a simple evening at the pub?" Her clipped upper-class British tone didn't deter me. She'd been expecting my call.

"You don't drink pints." Fine French Burgundy, yes, and the occasional martini, filthy. My lips puckered. Vodka with equal parts of olive juice ought to be illegal. "I need information from Claire Waters."

"Am I your secretary now?" Her long, measured exhale said everything.

"Do be a dear and ask her yourself."

"Chad said..." I paused mid-comment.

"That cad couldn't tell the story properly if you handed him the script and highlighted his lines."

I bit back a smile. "How do you really feel?" I'd gotten an earful when I'd finally decided to divorce him. I'd never accuse Sophie of British emotion again. "I take it Claire Waters played him."

"Yes, well. Claire Waters is... eccentric," Sophie said carefully. "She served as what you Yanks insist on calling a Deputy Chief of Mission behind the iron curtain and later, as an ambassador during the 1980s."

Sophie's pride echoed something in me.

"Her address is on your phone, if you'd care to look," Sophie added. "You know, the diplomatic corps didn't open its doors to women until the 1970s. Claire Waters stepped out from under her grandfather's formidable legacy and turned her family's diplomatic name into her very own brand of success."

Glimmer's ears twitched when my phone pinged the information's arrival. "Lay out the family tree for me, will you?" I asked.

"The record is as follows..." The family tree flashed on my phone.

"Not particularly prolific," Sophie remarked.

No, it wasn't. This kept the list of possible suspects refreshingly short. More interesting was the family connection. Despite the age gap, Claire and Lionel were first cousins. The real question lingered: did Melodie truly die in 1929?

If not, and that was a very large, very unproven *if*, then that branch of the family could be searching for the Waters' diamonds. Time to start investigating.

"In my opinion, the theft was an inside job. Likely three conspirators. The timing was professional."

Sophie caught my meaning at once. "Not a word from your father since the Peak Diamond's recovery."

Except in my head. He'd survived. I knew it. "Someone wanted the Waters' bracelet specifically. I'm hoping Claire can tell me who."

"Quite. And one does wonder why. It's an extraordinary amount of effort for remarkably little return."

"Unless you have the other half of the Duette," I suggested.

"Proving you have it isn't going to be easy since the first missing bracelet disappeared in 1929," Sophie said.

"True. The photos of the original Duette necklace are low-resolution photos taken back in 1922." A common problem with authenticating Art Deco jewelry since GIA reporting didn't become available until 1955.

"Indeed. It is an Art Deco piece. It stands to reason the patterns replicate in both pieces."

"Under normal circumstances. Do you have the artisan's original drawings?" I asked.

"Oddly, no record of the jeweler exists either," Sophie replied. "Sterling & Sons insured the piece after a GIA grading in 1983."

"This makes no sense. Why wouldn't a jeweler want the prestige associated with a piece of the Waters' diamonds' importance?" I asked.

"Someone paid to keep secrets, perhaps," Sophie murmured.

"Which begs the question—"What is this piece's story"?" My imagination leapt ahead. The Duette's royal aura brought star-crossed lovers or hidden allegiances to mind. Or could it be something more sinister?

Sophie's silence indicated her own agreement. At last, she said, "Very well, let's uncover it. What, precisely, should I be watching for if we're to trace our culprits from within?"

I tempered my curiosity. "Check the Wrigley entry camera for someone going behind the welcome desk between 8:50 p.m. and 9:00 p.m. last night."

Keystrokes clicked softly. "No one was in the vestibule."

"Check the camera feed." Dad had taught me that video wasn't always what it appeared.

"I will confirm. 24th Street traffic cameras for the escape route, is it?"

She had to be looking at a map. "Not this time. I'm guessing the thief took the canal bike trail. He could've exited anywhere along the path."

"A motorbike?"

"Probably. Check the Wrigley security team for unusual cash payments. Whoever lifted the bracelet knew the system's blind spots."

"You seemed to locate them easily enough," Sophie remarked drily.

True, but I knew what to look for. "I also need an address for the hit-and-run victim. And I'll need you to check the traffic cam footage around the site. I want to confirm the truck was from Waters Construction." I rechecked my notes.

"The traffic angle indicates so. Waters Construction reported a stolen vehicle at 6 a.m."

I exhaled. Maybe Chad was right. "What kind of financial trouble is Lionel Waters in?"

"A nasty divorce."

My jaw locked. A man of Lionel's wealth and reputation steal a bracelet to cover divorce proceedings expenses? "Do you know if Claire Waters plans to donate the bracelet to a museum?"

"She's been threatening to donate it to the MET for years."

"Why?"

"Perhaps she intended to protect the piece from the current generation, selling to the highest bidder," Sophie suggested.

Hope and I often bought antique pieces from heirs who valued the payout more than the past. Tash being an exception.

"I'll also send the gum wrapper Glimmer recovered along the escape route to the lab. It might lead to something."

"Spearmint? Perhaps it is the Wrigley ghost."

Glimmer's bark answered for me.

"A shame this isn't FBI jurisdiction," Sophie remarked almost as an afterthought.

My pulse ticked up at the thought of Rocky Rockman. We'd begun as adversaries, but during the Fire Diamond investigation, he'd proved his intelligence and his nerve. I could use both right now.

"I hear Agent Rockman is permanently assigned to the Los Angeles field office," Sophie said.

Her information pipeline never faltered. "It's a long way from Phoenix. And out of his jurisdiction to boot."

"Hardly too far for a weekend rendezvous."

I felt my cheeks flush once again. "I haven't seen him since he transitioned out of Sunset Peak."

"It helps if you meet him halfway."

"In Quartzite? The land of tumbleweeds and jerky?" I replied.

"The actual distance is rather beside the point," Sophie said lightly. "It scarcely matters where you meet. One simply has to make the effort."

"You're one to lecture," I said. Unfair. Sophie's love life tended to be infinitely more complicated than mine. Hope and Gram had said the same thing, and part of me knew they weren't wrong.

So, why was I still hesitating?

No answers came as I turned off 7th Street and into the Camelback Mountain Country Club parking lot. Established in 1899, the club had long been the gathering place for the Valley's most influential families. No doubt Tash's stamping ground. I drove past tall palms, manicured lawns, and the open Mediterranean-style clubhouse.

Oddly, the GPS steered me around the manicured fairways and park-like sprawl of the 18-hole course. Instead, I turned down a street that could have been lifted straight from the 1920s.

Country Club Manor carried that hushed, old-Phoenix elegance, tucked behind hedges and history. Mature trees filtered sunlight over quiet streets lined with Spanish arches, tile roofs, and mid-century lines, each home distinct, yet part of the same story.

Through gaps between the houses, the country club's manicured fairways flashed green against the desert beyond. The neighborhood felt calm, refined, and quietly timeless in the heart of the city.

It seemed fitting, somehow, that Claire Waters lived here in the home her grandfather had built as an anchor for the family who'd moved from one international duty station to the next. I passed the recognizable Craig House, listed on the National Registry of Historic Homes, and parked in front of a mid-sized residence that reminded me of a French country manor, down to the vibrant roses.

As instructed, I followed the stone path skirting the side of the house toward the back garden. Glimmer trotted ahead of me, then veered off in hot pursuit of a fluttering monarch butterfly like it was the crown jewel of the afternoon.

I couldn't help but smile. For all her training, she still enjoyed just being a dog. I envied those moments of pure, uncomplicated joy without calculating the risk.

The dachshund ran ahead as I threaded through hedges tall enough to feel secretive rather than welcoming, following the faint tinkle of running water. The moment I stepped through the arch, an oasis unfolded before me. Sunlight filtered down in slender beams, and butterflies drifted through them, their wings flashing like fleeting prisms, there and gone.

I smiled, even as my instincts stayed sharp. Whimsical places like this had a habit of disguising purpose behind beauty. Heirloom roses in apricot, cream, and deep raspberry climbed trellises and arched over the winding path. Their warm, sweet scent mixed with the color of lantana, milkweed, and purple sage.

At the center, a tiled fountain murmured quietly, droplets catching the light as butterflies gathered along the damp edges. Benches beneath mesquite shade invited me to pause and breathe.

I found my dog stretched across an older woman's lap, a leather gardening glove in her mouth, a basket of tussled cut flowers at her feet. "Miss Waters," I said, not quite sure if a reprimand was in order just yet.

"You must be the gem hunter." Her sharp green eyes locked with mine, holding my attention. "Your diamond dog found me right off." She tugged her earlobe, drawing my eye to a slender diamond drop earring set in platinum, crafted in a clean vertical line, unmistakably Art Deco.

"Glimmer has impeccable taste, ma'am," I remarked.

At first glance, Claire Waters reminded me of my iron-willed grandmother, born in the same era and sharing the same zero-tolerance attitude. But Claire carried ninety-five years with a kind of unapologetic pride. Her wrinkles weren't weaknesses; they were markers of character and courage, the map of a woman who had beaten the odds and carved out success in a world that had never made room for her.

"Do you have any leads on my bracelet?" she asked, her tone matter-of-fact.

"That depends on what you have to tell me," I replied honestly. She'd see right through me anyway, like she had Chad. He wasn't a bad cop; rather, he tended not to dig into the why of a crime.

Claire's crooked smile softened, just enough to signal approval. I'd passed her test, but the feeling of being measured still lingered.

"How'd you fall for Detective Dimwit? The man's a simpleton."

"The shoulders." Thinking back, the swagger hadn't hurt any.

"The tush ain't bad either." Claire's harrumph held a degree of agreement.

I choked. Couldn't help it. Yeah. Claire Waters had grit, all right.

"What did you want to know?" she asked finally.

No reason to hold back. "What your mother knew about her sister Melodie's disappearance."

Claire bristled, disturbing Glimmer, who jumped off her lap and returned to my side.

Claire exhaled. "I was twelve when my mother passed. Why would you think she had told me anything?"

"Your mother and Melodie were twins. She knew ..." I touched my heart. "... if her twin had survived the Catalina disaster. She also knew where she went to hide and why."

Claire went very still.

A flicker crossed her face. Relief, maybe. Calculation, for sure. The subtle shift of someone weighing how much of the truth she could afford to reveal.

As the silence lengthened, I took a lesson from my grandmother and simply waited, my gaze drifting to the frolicking butterflies.

Finally, Claire spoke. "You're a twin. You understand."

My gut twinged not in victory, but inevitability. I had my answer. Details would shorten my search. "My sister is my other half. We don't always agree, but we share a twin telepathy."

Claire's warm smile didn't quite reach her eyes. "I must've been four or five. I remember finding my mother crying. When I asked her why, she said not having Melodie in her life tore her in half."

Four or five? A child's impressionable memory? Or something more? I understood the grief behind it. But the phrasing snagged on something deeper.

"She didn't say death? Or loss?" I asked carefully.

"No. She did not." Claire held my gaze, steady now, testing me again.

Was this the unreliable echo of a little girl overhearing sorrow or the clue I'd been searching for? "Will you tell me her story?"

After a measured pause, Claire gestured to the Adirondack chair beside hers. I sat. Glimmer immediately pressed against my leg and lowered herself at my feet, chin on her paws, ears angled forward. Alert.

Claire raised her head skyward as if asking for forgiveness before speaking. "It's a story of survival."

I'd guessed as much. Survival stories rarely traveled alone. They dragged secrets behind them like anchors.

Claire folded her hands in her lap, her voice thinning with age but not her memory. "Melodie was engaged to Walter Fox," she began. "A prominent rancher who played poker with her father most every Thursday."

She paused for a breath. "She begged her father to call off the wedding. But he said Walter was a good man and he would make a proper husband."

Claire's gaze drifted somewhere far beyond the garden. "My mother always told me Melodie was frightened of him."

"Not nervous?" I asked.

"Frightened." Her emphasis had meaning. "So, she did the only thing a desperate girl could think to do." A fragile smile touched her lips. "She ran away to Hollywood... to star in the talkies."

Quite a risk for a society girl in 1929. So far, my information seemed accurate.

Claire drew in a careful breath, the kind that carried too many years of silence.

"Mr. Fox had someone in the house reading my mother's letters. Eventually, he learned Melodie planned to attend the Catalina Island Casino opening." Claire's fingers tightened together. "He went after her. Told her father he meant to bring her home, but he returned to Phoenix and said he never found her. That was a lie."

Alarm bells rang. "You think he killed her?"

Claire pressed a handkerchief lightly beneath her nose. "I can tell you my mother was afraid of him, too. She said he whipped his horses."

No need to say more. A man's character could be measured in how he treated animals.

"My mother married my father a week after her sister disappeared," she continued. "She told me she had to escape from Mr. Fox."

Footsteps sounded on the flagstone. A middle-aged Hispanic woman in bright floral scrubs approached from the house, balancing a silver tray holding a glass pitcher alongside two frosted glasses.

"Lemonade, Miss Claire. Just the way you like it." She served us with a warm smile, then handed Claire a small Dixie cup, careful and attentive.

"And if I refuse to take these, you'll go straight to Lionel and tattle." Claire's lips pressed into a tight line.

Chad had raised Lionel's name in connection with the bracelet theft. At the time, it had felt convenient. Now, I wasn't so sure. Claire's relationship with her cousin bore investigation.

The aide planted her hands on her hips, shaking her head in exaggerated disbelief. "Miss Claire, my job is to make sure you take your medicine. And I am going to stand right here and listen to every word of this conversation until you do."

Glimmer's ears twitched. So did mine.

I'd expected a fight, not weary acceptance. "The dang things make me sleepy."

The aide's serene smile never wavered. "Be sure to tell your doctor on your next visit."

"Getting old isn't for the meek," Claire grumbled.

There was more to it than that. I saw it in Claire's hunched shoulders. I waited for the aide to enter the house before asking, "Is your cousin..."

"He's a good man. A little too solicitous at times. A body's not made to be fussed over," Claire insisted.

"Think he had anything to do with the bracelet's theft?" I had to ask.

Her emphatic "no" told me everything I needed to know, even before she explained. "He has no motive. I told Detective Dimwit that."

"The divorce..."

Claire folded her hands, a quiet pride softening her features. "Lionel is a Renaissance man. He'll speak of commodity futures over dinner as easily as other men discuss the weather and then saddle his own horse and brush the animal down himself when he returns." She looked back at me, steady and certain. "He protected himself." She sighed. "In my day, marriage was forever. Nowadays... What do I know? I never..."

"Found the right guy." She'd built a remarkable life with little time for herself.

"I made some foolish mistakes. Not why you're here today." Claire sipped her lemonade.

I asked the question I had come for. "Who do you think stole the bracelet?"

Claire tensed, her words measured. "I inherited the Waters' bracelet in 1942. I had many offers to buy it over the years from collectors and museums. In 2013, a man offered to purchase the bracelet. He was different from the rest."

My pulse thumped. "How?"

"He was serious. The others wanted the bracelet for historical or sensational reasons. He had another agenda. Offered me three times what it was worth." She stopped my question with a short laugh. "He was a bear of a man. Tall like your ex."

"Dark hair?"

"Light brown. Gray at the temples. He wore sunglasses. I couldn't see his eyes. Thought he could intimidate me."

Like that would work with Claire. Another man who'd underestimated her. I wondered if it was the story of her life. I could imagine her jumping up on a chair to spit in his eye. "You told him no."

"Right, I did. I told him he'd get it over my dead body. Lionel is with me on this."

Or was he? I cleared my throat. Something wasn't adding up. "Who was the guy who tried to buy the bracelet?"

"I don't know. I refused to take his business card. He said he'd be back, but he never returned." She coughed, a deep, troubling sound.

"The only person who would want the Waters' bracelet that badly would have to have Melodie's half. Or knows the Duette's secret," I said.

Claire neither denied nor confirmed my statement. She also never agreed that Melodie was dead. I went for it. I'd assumed a lot, but it paid off. "Your mother did know where her sister was." It wasn't a question. If Hope vanished, I'd know if anything important happened to her or her daughters.

Claire chewed her lip. Tired eyes seemed to be debating. She finally stood quickly, agile for a 95-year-old, and beckoned for me to follow her. "Come. There are answers and, perhaps, more questions inside."

Glimmer and I followed without a word, matching my stride to hers. Inside, the Mediterranean-style home looked like a nineteenth-century Explorers Club. Dark woods and traditional florals mixed with international keepsakes from Africa, South America, the Far East, and Egypt.

"I feel like I'm in a museum," I remarked.

"My father was in the foreign service like my grandfather had been. He met my mother in 1928 at an embassy party celebrating the Olympics in Amsterdam. You know, my mother and Aunt Melodie grew up all over the world?"

I nodded. If I hadn't, this room would've told me. The sitting room represented a quiet tribute to a well-travelled life—sunlit shelves held travel-worn books and unique knick-knacks. Claire Waters moved more slowly these days, but her hands held steady as she drew a small leather case from beneath an embroidered shawl on the settee.

"This," she said, patting the lid as though it were an old friend, "...belonged to my mother."

The case was worn at the edges, the brown leather softened with age and handling. When Claire released the brass latch, the lid rose with a soft sigh, revealing the black-velvet interior. The items inside hadn't been arranged with a collector's precision but rather nestled the way someone tucks away memories they're not yet ready to part with.

Claire displaced a glass-encased red feather as she eased out a slim booklet tied with a faded blue ribbon. "She kept a diary until the day she died." Claire's thumb brushed the cover. "Every entry was written to her sister. As if she'd listened."

I didn't interrupt. Some silences weren't meant to be broken. It did bring my conversation with my own sister to mind. If the Waters twins had been in sync, why had the necklaces' meaning eluded them? And what did that say about our chances for success?

No comparison. We're too pigheaded to quit. As usual, Hope's encouragement egged me on.

Claire set the diary aside and reached deeper into the case, lifting a small bundle bound with twine. "But these... these were my favorite when I was a girl."

She loosened the knot, and four postcards spilled into her lap like a hand of oversized playing cards, their edges soft and colors muted with time.

"I found these after Mother's death. And I kept them exactly the way she left them. They are all unused and not postmarked. Where or why Mother got them, I have no idea," Claire added softly, tears brightening her eyes. "I can tell you that Mother adored birds. Merle means blackbird. It fit her. She would sit outside and listen to them for hours. She said their song reminded her of her childhood with Melodie in Panama. They grew up with a scarlet macaw in their house named Ruby." Her soft smile had to be a memory.

"That had been quite a life a hundred years ago." My gut

jumped as I touched the first brightly illustrated card. It pictured a larger bird, in the grouse family, I'd guess from the shape. Not particularly interesting.

"It's a white-tailed ptarmigan. They are only found on Vancouver Island in British Columbia." Claire answered my question before I could ask. "I showed the four pictures to a friend of mine in the Audubon Society. He told me the breeds of the birds, but not the secret. The way Mom saved them, I think she believed the postcards were messages from her sister, but my mother lived in Europe. The practical side of me needs to know how Melodie could have possibly sent them to her without leaving a postmark?"

"That's not impossible," I said carefully. "Today, dispatches move through diplomatic pouches. In 1930... did you have something similar?"

Claire gave a soft, incredulous huff. "Well, I'll be. I've been turning that question over in my mind for years, and you settle it in no time."

Her eyes warmed. "If one knew the proper person to ask, a note could travel through diplomatic channels discreetly." She exhaled. "I'm glad she found a way. Mother deserved peace. She never cared much for diplomatic life. After she passed, I traveled with my father and served as his hostess. It suited me." A small pause. "When the Cold War started. I was proud to do my part."

Her fingers rested on a painted card of a macaw with its wings frozen mid-flight.

"I was an only child. I never had a sibling or truly understood my mother's bond with her twin." Her bright gaze lifted to meet mine. "But I believe you do."

My throat tightened. The postcards, the diary, and the weight of the twins communicating in their unique way hung in the space between us. I understood the intent, if not the messages themselves. I've always been good with evidence and patterns I could file away, but emotion, not so much.

Glimmer pressed against my shin, her soft weight grounding me. She gave a low, sympathetic whuff before settling onto her haunches, tail curling around my boot. Her long ears drooped in that solemn way she reserves for human emotions she can't fix.

"She understands," Claire said gently. "Dogs always do."

I glanced down. Glimmer's eyes were fixed on the case, her head slightly tilted, a reminder: I wasn't here just as an investigator. Sometimes my job required a heart, not a notebook.

"Your mother loved her sister," I said, surprised by how raw my voice sounded. "You can feel it in every card."

Claire nodded, her expression softening as if my reaction mattered more than I knew. "She did. I've always believed that love leaves traces. In objects. In people. In the choices we make."

She gestured toward the two diaries and cards, their contents resting like a challenge between us. "Everything you're searching for is there. Know that the diamonds carry a warning. After my grandmother's death, my grandfather divided the necklace, and both of his daughters led tragic lives." She paused, letting the silence sharpen. "So, tell me, Ms. Hunter... do you intend to test fate?"

Glimmer's ears flattened. A low, uneasy sound vibrated in her chest, just loud enough to tell me she sensed something wrong.

"I don't believe in curses." I never had. "Is that why you rarely wore the bracelet? You had plenty of opportunities."

Claire's expression didn't change, but something closed behind her eyes. "Some things are safer when they remain untouched, at least for my lifetime." She paused. "Lionel doesn't share my opinion. You should speak with him before you decide what comes next."

It sounded less like advice than instruction. I nodded anyway. I needed to rule Lionel out as a suspect in the theft, which made the meeting unavoidable.

As I rose to leave, her words slid under my skin. *Some things are safer when they remain untouched, at least for my lifetime.* My twin had said the same thing. I stopped, a chill threading my spine. Was Claire warning me about the bracelets? Or about what happens when two things meant to be separate are brought back together?

Chapter Four

BEWARE OF THE DECOY—
WISDOM FROM A JEWEL THIEF

Even with the trail she'd left behind, tracking down Melodie after a century wasn't going to be easy. Starting at Catalina Island, where her path had vanished, seemed the most productive. But before I chased ghosts across the San Pedro Channel, I needed context. Who was Walter Fox, and why had he pursued Melodie so relentlessly?

I drove past the security guard's hit-and-run site on the way. Nothing stood out. Just a row of anonymous warehouses. Sophie had found no obvious tenants tied to Waters Construction, and no convenient clues waiting for me in the now-shadowed alley. I'd have Sophie dig for hidden connections at a more reasonable hour.

I headed for Lionel Waters' office next. Given the time, I half-expected he'd have already vanished to a golf course. Not Lionel. I met him in the elevator on the way up to the fifth floor, his white hard hat tucked under his arm and a dusting of construction grit still clinging to his scuffed work boots. Tall and spare, his presence commanded without effort or threat. Glimmer stepped forward immediately, placing her paws against his outstretched hand. No hesitation. No warning growl. She liked him.

I found myself looking away from his alert green eyes. Not out of intimidation, but because the framed photographs lining his office walls told me far more about him and his love for his cousin. One photo showed Claire shaking hands with Ronald Reagan, another standing beside Queen Elizabeth.

"They're family milestones," he said simply. "My cousin spent a lifetime navigating rooms most people never see."

"She led an extraordinary life." The word felt inadequate the moment it left my mouth.

"That she did." His voice warmed. "I kept every postcard she sent from her duty stations. I always imagined I'd serve my country as a diplomat myself. That wasn't my path, but it was hers. Deputy Chief of Mission in Poland during the Cold War... and later, a United States ambassador."

Pride edged his smile, quiet but unmistakable. Claire had described him well. A Renaissance man, certainly, but also one who recognized greatness when he saw it.

"Did the Honorable Claire Waters ever tell you the role she played in the negotiations that helped bring down the Berlin Wall?"

I shook my head. I wasn't surprised. I knew there'd been so much more to learn from her.

"She never does," he said softly.

I eased into a leather chair, angled toward the window, Camelback Mountain rising steady and sunlit beyond the glass.

"You don't seem surprised to see me," I observed.

Lionel took the seat opposite mine, the coffee table a deliberate buffer between us. "Claire told me to expect you."

My gut tightened. "And why is that?" Had I been set up? I didn't feel used. Their coordination intrigued me.

A corner of his mouth lifted. "My cousin's diplomatic skills are legendary." His gaze flicked briefly to Glimmer, who had stationed herself beside my chair, alert but at ease. "She believes in preparation. She dislikes being caught flat-footed."

"So do I," I said. "Which makes me wonder why it feels like I've joined a conversation that began long before I arrived."

Lionel didn't answer right away. He leaned back, fingers steepled, assessing me as if deciding how much of the truth I'd earned. Out the window, Camelback's long shadows stretched across the desert, echoing the secrets he kept.

"The diamonds have a history," he said with Orson Welles' finality. "What Claire shared with you is the version the family tells outsiders."

"And the other version?" I prompted.

His eyes sharpened. "Isn't a curse."

Glimmer shifted, her collar clinking softly. She lifted her nose and then fixed her attention on Lionel.

"That's two of you now," I said lightly, though my pulse rate quickened. "Setting the stage."

He didn't deny it. "We needed to know what kind of investigator you were."

"And?" I asked.

"You don't scare easily," Lionel remarked. "And you see patterns others overlook."

I met his gaze. "You've hired others to recover the missing bracelet?"

"No." His reply was immediate. "Reuniting the pieces would be a mistake. Our concern isn't only finding the stolen piece. We need to locate whoever has Melodie's missing bracelet."

"Because they're looking for more than jewelry," I suggested.

His expression shifted a fraction. "Yes."

"And why does that worry you?"

"The real danger isn't what the diamonds did to my family." Lionel paused, deliberately. "It's in the secret they may contain."

Of course, it was. "Which is?"

He exhaled. "I don't know. Neither does Claire. My father's

only warning was to beware if the missing bracelet surfaces and protect ours at all costs."

A dire warning. "Forever?"

"Not exactly. He said, *One day when twin heirs—born of one blood and one destiny—do restore with their own hands the broken chain, shall the world remember its proper order and be made whole once more.*"

"A prophecy?" I echoed. Surreal didn't begin to cover it. "How archaic. What does that mean?"

"Don't know exactly, but the fact that Claire's has been stolen indicates that the Duette's pair is in play."

"Maybe. Maybe not. Who is the man who came to buy the bracelet?"

"Claire told you about him." Lionel shook his head. "His name is Christian Weber. He owns an estate jewelry store in Chicago."

That surprised me. "Did he say he was acquiring it for a client?"

"I believe so, but he refused to disclose the client's identity."

"Did Christian try to intimidate you?"

"He's a bully. But I had no control over the bracelet back then. If it is recovered, I suspect he will be more aggressive when I do, which is likely not long from now," he said meaningfully.

I'd assumed as much. Claire's cough had sounded bad. "What else can you tell me about him?"

"Nothing. I checked into him. His store has been in business since 1947. He wears a large school ring with a white shield and a diamond on it. I couldn't find the college it was from."

A job for Sophie. "Do you think Christian Weber stole the bracelet?"

"Or whoever hired him to buy it. We need to understand why, if we ever hope to learn who that person is."

That Lionel ran a successful company made sense. The man did know how to get to the heart of the matter. I sat back. "What do you suggest?"

"There were notes in Melodie's diaries," he added. "Claire and I never completely deciphered them, but Mr. Fox's fascination with the jewels scared my late aunt, Merle. She may not have understood why, but she knew there was more to the story."

Glimmer stirred at my feet, alert now.

"So," I asked quietly, "...what part do you play?"

"My father lived with Merle and her husband in Germany and London. He attended Eton like his father before the Blitz." He stroked his jaw, looking at me for a moment before rising and moving to his desk. I followed, intrigued when he pressed his thumb on the center drawer. I heard a soft click, and the drawer slid open.

Ah, ma Cherie, do not be fooled by the decoy. Or the show.

My father's words in my head made me look around for the real safe. Two paintings on the walls. No. Lionel would be more subtle. The glassed bar? I noticed streaks in the dust beside the planter. A floor safe. He had been prepared for me.

The ring-sized mini-match to the Duette's walnut-and-ebony case drew my eye. Another piece to the Duette? My curiosity demanded answers, and Lionel knew it. He opened the box and placed a one-inch platinum filigree heart in my palm.

My pulse ticked faster. This mattered. I didn't yet know why, but instinct had always spoken to me before logic caught up. I turned it over slowly, my fingers registering the balance, the intention behind the design. It was a clasp, both functional and sentimental, set with two green stones. Vivid yellow-green. Unsettlingly familiar. Almost the exact shade of Lionel and Claire's eyes.

Rare green diamonds? The sparkle suggested it. Still, something felt off.

I slipped my loupe from my crossbody bag and held the clasp up for closer inspection. The stones answered before my mind fully formed the thought. The fire was too bright. Diamonds scattered light cleanly, confidently. This brilliance fractured it instead, throwing prismatic flashes that danced faster than they should have.

Not diamonds. Demantoid garnets. Stones easily misidentified a century ago. My breath slowed as the implication settled. This wasn't ornamentation. It was a clue.

"They're demantoid garnets or Uralian emeralds," I said quietly. "They've been mined in Russia since the late 1880s." I felt my father's gasp. Not another Russian connection.

Lionel's nod confirmed my conclusion. "According to my sources."

That confirmation sent a chill up my spine because this wasn't just another piece of jewelry. It was a marker. Somewhere, long before the necklace had been split, before the curse took hold, someone had wanted that distinction preserved... without ever being recorded.

"The color looks African. The Russian garnets tended to be emerald colored due to the lack of chromium in the soil."

"So I have been told, but these stones could have been chosen intentionally," Lionel said as his brow arched.

I took his bait. "Why?"

"This color matched Melodie, Merle, and my father's eyes."

"Yours and your cousin's also." I took another look through my loupe. No signature golden, curved chrysotile fibers radiating from the center commonly found in the Russian mined stones. I cautioned myself to be patient. The lack of horsetails in the stone's depth didn't entirely rule out Russian origin. "Demantoid garnets were only discovered in Africa in the 1990s. This..." I rolled the fine platinum across my fingers, feeling the handmade filigree. "...is an early Art Deco design created long before the African stones were discovered."

"You know your jewelry," Lionel replied, clearly impressed.

I turned the clasp again, this time concentrating on the back side. I found the jeweler's mark, worn with age. Two mirrored Ks separated by a star. I switched the magnification from 10x to 20x and saw it—a tiny H.14. The jeweler's internal workshop code for the year the piece had been manufactured.

"This piece was crafted by Kreuter & Company in Hanau, Germany, in 1914." A meaningful confirmation since Kreuter & Company rarely dated their pieces.

"On the eve of WWI," Lionel added. "The clasp was part of the original necklace before our grandfather split the piece. There is no provenance for the actual diamonds beyond the Duette."

The realization settled between us, heavy as the stones themselves. "Then where did the diamonds come from?" I asked.

Lionel didn't answer right away. His gaze drifted to the windows, to Camelback Mountain rising out of the desert, a natural metaphor for misidentification, false assumptions, and hidden truths.

"That," he said finally, "is the question no one in my family could ever answer."

"A piece like this doesn't simply appear in 1921. Not with craftsmanship like this." I turned the clasp over once more, tracing the worn maker's mark with my thumb. "The German atelier indicates this was a royal piece."

"Without a recorded invoice or estate listing..." Lionel exhaled slowly. "Which is why my family told the curse story. It was easier than explaining what we couldn't."

Or what they wouldn't.

"This is impossible. Royal jewels leave paper trails." I met his gaze. Glimmer shifted at my feet, alert now, her attention trained on the clasp as if she sensed the turn the conversation had taken.

"Unless the stones were never meant to be acknowledged. The Russian revolution caused unmentionable upheaval," Lionel suggested.

"It's possible." The sudden lump in my throat expanded. "The Ural Mountains supplied the Russian imperial court with demantoid garnets for years. A private commission could have been routed through Germany before the war. Especially if someone wanted distance between ownership and the origin."

"Or deniability," Lionel added.

"Jewels like this don't vanish by accident," I said quietly. "Someone hides them. Then gives them a new story." And what better cover than a foreign diplomat, someone who could move across borders without question? Which meant whatever these stones were hiding had once mattered very much... and might still.

Glimmer stirred at my feet, alert now, her attention fixed on Lionel as if she sensed the shift. The truth was closer than before.

"My father said Merle believed the diamonds weren't the treasure," Lionel said.

My gut twinged in agreement. "Then they're a clue."

"To what is the question." Lionel asked.

"The bigger question is who wants to collect them now?"

"True." His mouth curved into something like a smile, though there was no humor in it. "Which is why Claire and I are relieved you agreed to look into this."

Relieved or desperate?

I leaned back, the story closing in from all sides. A royal necklace erased from history. A family that had survived by never asking questions—until now. And the second they did, someone else moved in.

"Do you mind if I take the clasp? I want an expert opinion on the garnets."

Without a word, Lionel handed me the walnut-and-ebony box. The gesture felt less like trust and more like consent. He wasn't protecting the mystery anymore; he'd invited me to solve it.

At my feet, Glimmer went still. Her ears flattened as she leaned closer to the box, nose working, as if the wood itself carried a warning.

"Find my cousin's bracelet, Miss Hunter. Whatever the secret, it's time to uncover it," Lionel announced.

Maybe. Maybe not. One thing was certain—Lionel Waters hadn't stolen the Waters bracelet, which made me wonder how

Chad had missed that fact so completely. My ex-husband was many things, but an incompetent investigator wasn't one of them.

45

Chapter Five

BEWARE OF THE STORY BEHIND THE STORY—WISDOM FROM A JEWEL THIEF

I returned to Sunset Peak as daylight drained from the surrounding hills, cloaking the valley in unsettling mystery. Any wonder my thoughts refused to settle? The same questions kept circling with no answers coming despite the number of passes.

Where had the Waters' diamonds truly come from? The stones carried the gravity of royalty, but without a paper trail, provenance could only be a suggestion. And then there was the theft.

Was Merle's missing bracelet an opening move of someone trying to reunite what had been deliberately divided? Or the calculated distraction of a valuable relic lifted for profit and nothing more? Or was it a message that had failed to reach the next generation... lost not to conspiracy, but to time?

If the Waters twins had known the truth, they would not have written it plainly. Twins rarely did. Meaning would be laced into what had been shared without explanation. Which meant the answers weren't missing. They'd been hidden somewhere in those diary entries, waiting for someone who understood how twins spoke when they were keeping secrets.

In other words, I couldn't do this alone.

My twin was already waiting for me at Starlight Estate Jewelers, our family's business on Canary Trail, directly across from Sunset Peak's town center and beside the Old Assayer's Office Museum. A fitting place to untangle a mystery rooted in history, silence, and questionable beginnings.

If anyone could help me decipher what the Waters twins were really saying, it was the one person who had always known what I was thinking before I ever said it out loud.

I pulled into my usual spot behind the shop, easing in beside Hope's SUV, still coated in a fine layer of ranch dust from her drive in. Diagonal across the intersection, I saw the Canary Café, its windows glowing with the late dinner rush. No need to detour there. Hope would have already picked up our usual carne asada nachos and something suitably gourmet for Glimmer. No need for twin telepathy here. Decades of shared cravings guaranteed the outcome.

I unlocked the back door adjacent to my above-store apartment's entry and walked down the staff hallway into the private showroom. I got a whiff of silver polish and desert dust moments before Hope's sunshine-and-rainbows voice floated toward me. "It's about time you got here."

Glimmer shot me her classic *sorry-not-sorry* dachshund look before scampering ahead. Dinner waited for no diamond dog. My stomach growled in agreement.

"You look like you need this." Hope, my mirror image, tonight with a more refreshed posture, handed me a Tajin-rimmed martini glass with my go-to Sunset Peak martini. Shaken citrus-clean, lemon vodka, with a whisper of prickly pear juice. I took a long swallow, allowing the sharp jalapeño garnish to burn my lips and calm the adrenaline skittering through my veins.

As expected, nachos overflowed from a large takeout bowl on the coffee table. Like me, my sister wore dark slacks and a pale blue Starlight Oxford embroidered with our crest. She'd tied her sun-kissed hair, more blonde than brown, back into a neat low ponytail, her hazel eyes alive with that particular spark she got when she'd uncovered something worth chasing.

"What have you found?" Energized, I dropped into the butter-soft swivel chair. Only a handful of elite gem buyers ever set foot in this private showing area reserved to showcase our most extraordinary gemstones. Today, the jeweler's lights glowed at full strength, their crisp, blue-tinged beams sharpening my sense.

"The Waters' bracelet is not a true Art Deco design."

The tortilla chip I'd popped into my mouth lodged in my throat. "What? It was commissioned in 1914. It's also documented as one of the finest pieces of Art Deco design of the period."

"Then someone either changed the diamonds' placement in the bracelet or lied!" My sister doubled down on her opinion. "The design's not symmetrical. There is no apparent sense of order."

I washed the chip down with a healthy swallow of my martini and wiped my salty fingers on my jeans as she handed me the Gemological Institute of America's jeweler's plot drawing. Claire's bracelet lay out in perfect detail before me on a clean white sheet of paper. Rows of small, round diamonds set in neat vertical lines, their pattern interrupted by a scatter of larger, rectangular stones, filled the page. A fine, beaded edge framed the entire piece, in true Art Deco tradition, adding a delicate vintage finish.

"The round diamonds are all 4 mm calibrated within 0.02 mm of each other," Hope continued. "Rare even by modern standards. And look at the filigree. The cutouts are arbitrarily pierced between the platinum design work that is not consistent with Deco artistry." She paused for a breath. "I can tell you that the milgrain is hand-applied. The depth is consistent, and there is no rolling or machine uniformity, indicating it was crafted by a master bench jeweler."

"Kreuter & Co., 1914," I said.

Hope's eyes popped open. "And you know that…?"

She stopped mid-sentence. Like a compass finding north, Hope's attention snapped to the walnut-and-ebony box I withdrew from my crossbody bag. I set it in her hands. No explanation necessary.

Hope inhaled sharply and lifted the lid, the forgotten plate of food cooling beside her. My sister didn't just see jewelry, she felt every smile and tear. Her fingers hovered, then steadied, as if the piece spoke directly to her.

My sister's connection to gems had always bordered on the uncanny. And in that moment, I knew the diamonds told her something unsettling. "This is the clasp from the original necklace before it was divided." It wasn't really a question.

"Yes. Lionel Waters had it. It appears the twins' father gave the girls the diamonds, and his son the clasp that held them together. Interesting symbolism if you ask me."

Hope exhaled deliberately. "This must be quite a secret."

She didn't wait for my response. My sister took the free-standing loupe from the test counter. She closed her eyes first, centering herself, then placed the clasp in the view. At ten-power, the world narrowed to facets and fire.

"Too much dispersion to be a diamond," she murmured. "The light fractures quickly."

She tilted the clasp, angling it just enough for the two matching stones to answer back.

"No horsetails," she said softly.

"Russian?" I breathed.

"The cut says yes, but…" Hope didn't look up. She upped the loupe's magnification. Her brow furrowed almost immediately. "The chemistry is brighter. Yellower than Russian."

"African?" I held my breath waiting for her confirmation.

Hope nodded once. "I know it's impossible. These were set before demantoid had been discovered in Africa. Which means either the timeline is wrong... or African demantoid was discovered long before 1970."

She closed the loupe and finally met my eyes. "Instinct can take us this far. Craftsmanship confirms it. But this?" She tapped the clasp gently. "This requires proof."

"Scientific," I said.

"Trace elements. Inclusion chemistry. Lab work," Hope replied. "If these stones are African and that early, the records aren't just incomplete, they're wrong."

She closed the case with care, as if sealing a confession.

"And once we ask science to weigh in," I said, "there's no putting this story back where it came from."

Hope's expression turned thoughtful. "No. There isn't." She started to pack the clasp into her purse. "I'll send this to the lab in the morning."

"Wait until Monday. I don't want any link between this clasp and the Waters' diamond case. Also, leave it here in the safe."

Hope's sharp gaze cut. "Don't trust me?"

"I don't trust whoever stole the Waters' bracelet. Not with murder one hanging over them."

No argument. Hope returned the box to the counter. "You legitimately ran into your ex then?"

I nodded and offered the *Reader's Digest* version of the afternoon. No need to dig deeper. Hope read between the lines perfectly. "You're wondering how Chad the Cad focused on the wrong guy?"

"Yeah. Granted, Lionel withheld information, but Chad's thorough." I exhaled. "I want to believe someone has deliberately led him in the wrong direction."

"Which means an inside man or woman has gotten to him." Hope leaned back against the counter, waiting for my acknowledgment. Only Glimmer's well-fed, contented snoring broke the silence.

I nodded absently, my attention drifting to Tash Wise. "Chad's not easily..."

Hope studied me for a beat, then sighed. "Okay. Let's say it out loud. Chad's a womanizer."

I snorted despite myself.

"And a sucker for a tight a... rear end." She added quickly, "You're not exactly neutral when it comes to him."

Her comment hit closer than I liked. "You think I'm letting that color my opinion?"

"You are human," Hope said gently. "You want him to be better than this. Or worse. Either way, that's bias."

I reopened the box and looked down at the clasp, the demantoids flashing too eagerly under the light. "If I'm wrong..."

Hope cut in. "Then you adjust. That's what you do." She paused, then smiled, a little crooked. "Dad would've clocked this in under a minute."

That stopped me. Was our absentee jewel thief father talking to her, too?

She dropped her voice, mimicking him perfectly. *A real thief never steals the object,* she said. *"They steal the story."*

I felt it then, the shift as the mystery's pieces realigned.

"This isn't about the bracelet," I said slowly. "It's about what it leads to. Chad's focused on looking for motive and opportunity. He isn't looking for the narrative."

Hope nodded. "And you are."

I straightened, doubt further settling into resolve. "My next step isn't retracing his investigation. It's going back."

"Good. Because whoever wrote this story expected someone like Chad to stop at the surface."

"And underestimated someone like us," I said, reenergized.

She smiled. "Always their first mistake."

It was the perfect lead-in for my next request. I removed the two worn diaries from my backpack. I kept the 1929 to 1931 book and handed Hope the latter. "Claire Waters gave these to me. She claimed it was written in a code she couldn't understand." Or wanted me to figure out on my own.

Hope and I shared a knowing glance before simultaneously

opening the books. Our gasps came in Sensurround. The date was clear. The rest not so much.

> *Avril 1929*
>
> *Klib-la toujou an silans. MF ka gadé mwen.*
> *Sispèk ? Non. Mè i ka veyé.*
> *Chofè-a rapòte vizit Biltmore. Sèvant-la jwenn an plak kwa nwè.*
> *Téléfòn-la montré plis : MF — Chicago — épi Fritz Gissibl*

Hope cleared her throat, breaking our self-enforced silence. "No wonder Claire Waters couldn't read this. It's some sort of French shorthand with insider abbreviations. The club is silent. MF can look after me. Suspect? The driver reported visiting Biltmore. Something about a maid finding a black cross on a plate and a telephone operator?" Hope paused. "If you ask me, no one can solve this without knowing the key."

I leaned back in the chair, letting the coded message settle. While both Hope and I spoke French like natives, our grasp of the many colonial dialects fell far short of UN standards. "Do you think the sketches in the margins mean anything?"

I felt Hope's breath on my neck as she leaned over my shoulder. "They look like birds in flight."

"Merle was a good artist. The roadrunner looks like the real thing," I said.

"I doubt MF and Fritz Gissibl were bird watchers." Hope crossed her arms. "I'm too tired to deal with puzzles."

Renewed energy filled with possibilities. "It's not only about what's being said, but who wrote it. I mean, how is a pampered upper-class debutante communicating with a chauffeur, a maid, and a telephone operator?"

Hope's mouth twitched. "Good point. Class still mattered in

1929. Unless Merle snuck down the back stairs, someone else carried the messages."

Claire would know that answer.

"Someone organized this communication network for a reason," I said slowly.

Hope agreed. "It's as if the Waters sisters expected someone to come after the diamonds."

I shrugged. "A chauffeur doesn't normally file intelligence. A maid doesn't inventory symbols. And a telephone operator doesn't note destinations unless she's been told to do so. Someone trained them, too."

I tapped the page. "*The club is silent*. Melodie was hiding from Mr. Fox. I'd bet MF is Mr. Fox." My gut agreed even if my head questioned the obvious.

"Maybe," Hope said. "But if it were that simple, why bother with initials?"

"This may be nothing more than a diary entry with no attempt at sophisticated modern spy craft," I suggested. "ME could be as simple as me, Merle, referring to herself." Neither of us missed the irony of Mr. Fox watching Merle while she had multiple people watching him.

"What did he do at the Biltmore?" Hope asked.

Like I had all the answers. "We can guess all we like about the initials' meaning. The name Fritz Gissibl is actionable."

Hope picked up her phone without ceremony and started searching. Good thing her daughters had trained her well. Years of watching teenage thumbs fly had its benefits. My sister had become a quiet internet menace.

Her fingers moved faster. She wasn't just searching for a name. She searched for an identity. "Oh."

That single syllable did not bode well. "What?"

"Wikipedia says Fritz Gissibl," she said, "was the treasurer of the Teutonia Society."

My spine straightened. "What is that?"

My twin turned the phone so I could see. "A German-American social and cultural organization back in 1929."

I glanced at the Duette's clasp sparkling in the jeweler's lighting. We'd found the link.

Hope scrolled. "Here's the part I like even less. In the mid-1930s, Fritz became the Nazi Party rep in the US."

My gaze dropped back to the coded line. The maid found a black cross on a plate. It could be a black cross on a shield. The design had religious implications. "The Knights Templar shield was white with a red cross," I said.

She nodded. "The black cross isn't a mistake. It goes back to the crusades, too."

My gut tightened, the way it does when I'm not going to like the answer.

"The shield belonged to the Teutonic Knights," Hope said. "They weren't just monks with a moral mission. They were enforcers. They built fortresses, not churches. That black cross marked territory and represented loyalty, and warning."

She paused, giving the weight of it room to land.

"Eventually, the Knights lost their land," she continued. "But they didn't lose their discipline. Orders like that don't vanish. They go underground. They wait. And when the right cause presents itself, they rise again." Hope lifted her gaze to mine. "That shield wasn't a decoration. It meant obedience without question."

Of course it did. But secret orders and centuries-old shields sounded more Indiana Jones than frontier Arizona

"Teutonic is German," I said evenly, unwilling to dismiss it outright... but not ready to saddle up for medieval crusaders in Phoenix either.

"Technically, yes," Hope replied. "The Order also ruled large parts of the Baltic."

I groaned. That alone meant I couldn't eliminate a possible Russian link. Still, the German connection seemed the most likely, since a German jewelry house had created the Duette and a secret German order seemed determined to reclaim it.

Why? What secret did the diamonds protect?

I looked at the message again, this time focusing on how the writing shifted between languages to obscure the truth. "This wasn't written by a debutante," I announced.

"No," Hope agreed.

I pictured Merle, hiding behind porcelain and pearls, but sharp-eyed, listening from the top of a staircase. A woman raised to be ornamental who had learned, somehow, to protect herself and her family.

"She built a network," I said. "Below stairs."

Hope smiled, but there was no humor in it. "And she trusted them."

"Enough to let them watch the man watching her." A powerful man who believed himself untouchable. I took another sip of my martini. "The question is, who was Mr. Fox and why did he want the diamonds?"

Hope's yawn drew mine. "That search is beyond my ability. It's a job for Sophie's supercomputer."

I checked the time. 9:30 p.m. in Phoenix meant it was 4:30 a.m. the next day in London. Too early to call Sophie. A text would get the process started while I slept.

"Every diamond has a story," I said. "And this one just found its voice."

Chapter Six

SECRETS ARE OPPORTUNITIES WAITING TO BE DISCOVERED—WISDOM FROM A JEWEL THIEF

SATURDAY, 5:30 A.M.

The phone vibrated on my nightstand, ripping me out of an altercation with a bird. Its wings flailing, red feathers flying, and green-yellow eyes burning. My head throbbed in protest—the kind of headache you get when your brain is yanked back into the world mid-screech.

I cracked one eye open and gritted my teeth. My nightstand clock flashed 5:30 a.m. Of course it did. Payback! Sure, I deserved it. Routinely waking Sophie at all hours with questions that wouldn't wait came with a price I'd pay today. She'd even been reasonable to let me sleep until morning, more likely because of my Morning Monster persona. A nickname courtesy of Chad. Any wonder I'd dubbed him the Cad?

Glimmer responded first with a low, irritated growl before disappearing under the covers, wedging herself against my leg, refusing to be disturbed further.

The phone buzzed again. Pale dawn leaked around the blinds, judgmental and rude. I grabbed the phone.

"Sophie," I barked, "if this isn't about the necklace, we're no longer friends."

Glimmer's tail thumped in agreement.

"It does concern the necklace," Sophie stated. "And you'll want to sit up for it."

I did. Beneath the blankets, Glimmer froze. Then her head emerged, both eyes bright now, alert, all business.

So much for sleep.

"Your instincts regarding Walter Fox are, as ever, impeccable," Sophie said crisply. "The difficulty, you see, is that the man does not appear to exist prior to 1925. He simply materializes in Phoenix, flush with cash, and proceeds to purchase respectability by lending to struggling miners."

Her voice cooled. "In five years, he tripled his landholdings most efficiently. And then, in early 1942, he vanished. Quite as neatly as he arrived, leaving behind a daughter and a young son from his second marriage. The nine-year-old boy from the first marriage disappeared with him."

I frowned. "He married twice?"

"Yes," Sophie replied smoothly. "Both wives met with tragic accidents. The first was, by all accounts, a distinguished rider. She allegedly fell from a cliff during her morning ride. The horse returned to the stables without her. Her body was recovered several days later. Their son was two at the time." A fractional breath. "Mr. Fox remarried six months thereafter."

"Only six months," I repeated. "What about a year of mourning?"

"One does admire a man who refuses to linger in grief." Sophie continued, her tone cooling a degree, "His second wife also hailed from a prominent, if financially distressed, mining family. She died of a rattlesnake bite. In her own garden. One assumes the serpent was not invited. Her family subsequently raised the younger children. Mr. Fox appears to change wives with alarming regularity."

I leaned back, a chill threading my spine. "That's not bad luck. That's a pattern." Of course, Melodie and Merle had seen it. Their instincts proved good.

"Both wives moved within the Waters twins' immediate social circle. Proximity, as we know, is rarely accidental. And at the time, you Americans were rather preoccupied with preparing for war. Administrative precision was not always the priority. Records from that period are... conveniently incomplete."

A delicate emphasis. "Merle thought Mr. Fox was German."

"Quite." Computer keys clicked. "Fuchs would be the German rendering of Fox."

I went still. "Could he have been a spy?"

"1929 would be a tad early for that," Sophie remarked. "The Nazi party didn't consolidate power until the 1930s."

"Then why run away in '41?" I asked. "Mr. Fox had made himself a Phoenix fixture."

"Perhaps he completed his task and returned to the fatherland," Sophie replied lightly. "I will check officer rolls, SS and otherwise, under Fox, Fuchs, and Voss."

I hesitated. "The Teutonic Knights were Prussian."

"Indeed." A brief pause. "Curiously, I have found nothing regarding the Teutonic Knights after the fifteenth century."

Which, coming from Sophie, meant something.

"It was a secret society," I suggested.

"Even so," Sophie said, a touch more briskly than usual, "there would be something. Somewhere." Which meant she didn't quite believe the story's clean edges either.

She continued, tone smoothing back into polished efficiency. "Kreuter & Co., the jeweler, is... intriguing. Their archives contain documents proving the necklace's existence. The diamonds are only recorded as provided at the time of order. The inventory supplied was 57 European-cut, 43 emerald-cut, and 2 green diamonds."

My stomach tightened. "Who commissioned the necklace?"

"Only record is the initials TS."

My head went to the obvious common meaning. Thinking about my sister's cursing ban made me smile. "TS? That could be Tom Smith for all we know. We need to know where those

diamonds came from. And why were the demantoids intentionally misclassified?" No excuse. Kreuter & Co. knew better.

"I shall persevere," Sophie said crisply which, in her world,
meant the work was already well underway. "Do try to look
impressed by what we do have."

"I am. How did you find it? Kreuter & Co. closed in 1987."

"One really must be on good terms with the archivist at the
Historical Museum in Philippsruhe Castle, Hanau. It saves an
extraordinary amount of time," Sophie replied.

"Hope will send the demantoid via the usual courier for
testing on Monday."

"I'll advise the lab. The coloration suggests African origin..."
Her tone shift got my attention. "...possibly a clue rather than
camouflage."

"What are you thinking?" I never ignored Sophie's leaps.
They'd saved us too many times.

"The timeline is..."

"Impossible," I suggested.

"Interesting. Perfectly matched, flawless D-color stones from
1910-1920 are virtually unheard of," Sophie said, then paused
long enough that she had my full attention. "There was, however,
a rumor—more myth than documented fact, naturally—that the
German East African diamond fields produced considerably more
gem-quality material than was officially recorded."

My breath caught. I'd read the Stamford University report
too. "Demantoid is mined in both Namibia and northeast
Tanzania today."

"Indeed. Both areas are within the Germans' control. In 1910,
the territory was divided into private mineral concessions and
effectively *sperrgebiet.*"

"Forbidden territory?" My old DeBeers training resurfaced.
"Who controlled the area?"

"The governor of German East Africa, who at the time was
Theodor Seitz."

"TS," I said slowly. "Let me guess. He's of Prussian descent."

"Correct, according to the name search and confirmed by my archivist. Unfortunately, the trail ends there. Theodor Seitz was a relic of the *Kaiserreich*, a monarchist as you Yanks would call him. No evidence he, or his family, served the *Third Reich*."

Sophie let her words sink in before adding, "It is also documented that Kreuter & Co. produced over 700 crown jewels up to the First World War, including a diadem for the German Empress Auguste Viktoria, crafted according to a design by Kaiser Wilhelm II himself. It is highly possible that the Waters' Duette was intended to be a royal piece."

"Or for a royal mistress?"

"Doubtful. According to records, Kaiser Wilhelm II did not have a mistress. The man was considered a conservative prig," Sophie replied.

The weight of Sophie's words settled hard. Even Glimmer reacted to that possibility with a low woof.

A royal German jeweler. An anonymous commission. Flawless old-cut diamonds with no traceable origin. First surfaced at a U.S. Embassy event in London—then hunted a decade later by a German national.

"So, we're looking at a necklace that may trace back to a secret diamond source in Namibia or Tanzania?" I asked.

"I appreciate how absurd it sounds," Sophie said. "Which leads us to the more interesting question: How did an American ambassador acquire a necklace commissioned by a German governor loyal to the Kaiser?"

"And," I added quietly, "why would someone steal it now?"

"I'd speculate that the necklace leads to something," Sophie said.

Silence crackled between us. With only half a drawing in our possession, the chance we'd figure it out had to be zero.

Some secrets didn't stay buried. They waited for the right moment to surface. Or the right person to find it. "What did you discover about Tash?"

"Her legal name is Natasha Wise. She was christened after

Natalie Wood, you know. Her grandfather was acquainted with Natalie's father. Another rather tragic Catalina chapter, I'm afraid."

Another woman who'd been killed in a boating accident. A coincidence? I wondered.

Sophie continued. "She's a marketing executive. Engaged to the proprietor of Diamond Designs, a rather distinguished jewelry design firm in Los Angeles, and I should note, some twenty years her senior. She has no criminal record, and a résumé that positively hums with competence while managing to be entirely overlooked."

Sophie's tone bothered my sleep-lagging mind. "I don't understand." But I did. Tash's situation almost mirrored Sophie's own.

"Hunter," she said at last, "you Americans are endlessly charming in your faith in the value of achievement. That the right person for the job will prevail."

"You Brits are endlessly suspicious of it."

"As well we should be, too." Sophie continued smoothly. "Here is the family line."

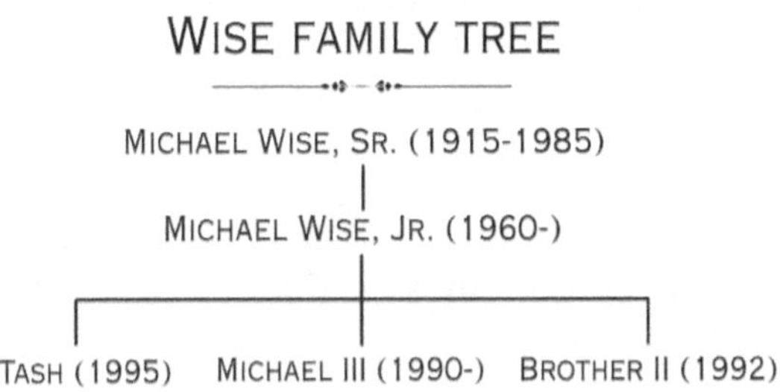

I scrolled through the diagram. Sophie explained, "Tash is the youngest child and only daughter. The family business is spoken for. Her brother will inherit. The younger brother will protect him. The second son always walks two steps behind the heir."

Maybe in old England, though even Prince Harry had blown a hole in that tradition. But here? In the U.S.?

I frowned. Power wasn't supposed to follow bloodlines in this country... but with old money? That world I didn't pretend to understand.

Without pause, Sophie continued. "Tash is merely decorative."

"That's harsh."

"It's accurate."

I glanced at Glimmer, curled beside me, ears twitching. "Still doesn't make her a killer."

"No. But it does make her rather motivated," Sophie replied, her tone measured. "The divorce from Mr. Foti is, shall we say, an undeniable embarrassment. One does not simply endure that sort of spectacle. One must recover from it. Preferably with style."

I could picture Sophie now with her perfect posture, tea untouched, and mind already three moves ahead. "Explain."

"The Wise family operates in a world where influence is inherited, not earned. Tash's marketing role is safe and presentable." Sophie paused delicately. "Unless she forces a disruption."

"Like bringing the fancy jewelry design company to the firm?"

"Not exactly. Marriage alone elevates her socially. It doesn't give her authority."

I got it. "She needs a moment. Something that makes her indispensable."

"Precisely."

I tapped my pen. "Why steal the bracelet? What would she hope to gain?"

"If the Waters' bracelet leads to something bigger..." Sophie took a breath. "Wise is the Americanized version of Weissmann."

My intuition took notice. "Prussian?"

"Indeed. Ms. Wise may know something we do not."

I'd suspected as much when we'd met at the Wrigley Mansion. "But would she kill someone for a promotion?"

Sophie didn't answer right away. When she did, her voice

remained cool, almost sympathetic. "I don't believe Tash thinks in those terms. She wouldn't frame her actions as murder per se. She would consider it an unfortunate consequence."

"That's a yes," I said.

"That's a warning," Sophie replied. "Families like the Wises are very good at protecting their own."

Glimmer lifted her head and gave a low huff.

"Thanks," I said. "I think."

"Oh, Hunter," Sophie added, almost fondly, "one more thing."

"Yeah?"

"Tash doesn't want money. She already has that." A pause. "She wants to be necessary."

The line went dead. I stared at the phone for a long moment before swinging my feet off the bed. I barely felt the cold as they touched the tile.

"Come on, Glimmer," I said. "Let's go meet with a woman who refuses to be nobody."

Chapter Seven

THERE'S ALWAYS A WAY OUT—
WISDOM FROM A JEWEL THIEF

SATURDAY, 10:30 A.M.

Wise & Sons Jewelers occupied a two-story stone building just off Scottsdale Road, the sort of architecture that promises permanence over spectacle. Pale local stone, dark wood beams bracing the windows, and a discreet bronze, Est. 1947, marked the store, as much an institution as the marriage ceremony itself.

Glimmer paused at the threshold, her nose lifted and her ears tipped back. She sensed the nearby diamonds and glanced at me for direction. I gave her the no-worries signal. The dog's dismissive snort seemed unimpressed as she padded forward.

Inside, the jewelry store leaned toward understatement. Several couples lingered over glass cases arranged in tidy compartments, studying engagement rings and diamond solitaires resting on cream velvet. Round brilliants. Emerald cuts. The occasional oval cut. All classics. Everything appeared tasteful, conservative, and entirely lacking pizzazz. No bold statements. Nothing gaspworthy.

Wise & Sons could have used the flattering blue jeweler's

lighting that it had taken me months to convince Hope to install. Here, the stones sparkled politely, their fire subdued by design.

On the far wall hung a large, framed portrait of three men in succession. Based on age, I assumed a grandfather, a father, and a younger man, likely the eldest and current heir to the company. The men stood with the same posture and displayed the same restrained smile, men who expected the world to cooperate with their plans.

Or steal from them. Why else would Wise & Sons post an armed guard at the entrance in one of Scottsdale's safest pockets? The store sold high-end, easily-fenced jewelry, sure, but surveillance cameras already covered every inch of the showroom. Not cutting-edge, but enough to discourage a casual thief.

The real prize had to be behind the steel door that separated the retail floor from the offices. A discreet biometric scanner watched from the ceiling. It logged, time-stamped, and recorded every entry.

Whatever Wise & Sons kept behind that door wasn't meant to be seen or taken.

Tash Wise appeared in the reinforced doorway before I could pinpoint obvious security flaws. "Ms. Hunter and her diamond dog. I assure you that the Waters' bracelet is not here."

Glimmer's head snapped up. She studied Tash with frank appraisal, then sniffed once and turned away, her nose already drifting toward the door leading deeper into the executive suite.

Tash noticed. "Well. That's either good news or very bad for my reputation."

I met her gaze. "She doesn't lie."

Tash's smile held, but something hardened behind it. "Neither do I."

Glimmer let out a quiet huff, then walked past Tash into the private hallway.

Tash played along. "It appears we're going inside?"

I nodded, intrigued by the change in Tash. Yesterday, she'd

been all designer and flash. Today she wore a knee-length pencil skirt and pumps, her hair swept into a soft, conservative chignon.

She gestured for me to follow her through the showroom to the scanning portal, which photographed me as I signed in. Tash's thumbprint on the terminal allowed us entry into the elevator vestibule. Another monitored door blocked access to the back workroom.

We rode the elevator up one floor. When the doors slid open, a 1950s portrait of the store's founder greeted us. His stern gaze deterred Glimmer from leaving my side as we crossed the dark paneled hallway.

"Great granddad was a character." Pride straightened Tash's shoulders. "He was a war hero. Awarded the Silver Star for heroism in the OSS during WWII. That's the prequel to the CIA." She didn't pause for a breath. "He came home from the war and wanted to help GIs settle down and forget the war. He offered them financing to buy their sweethearts' engagement rings."

I looked at the portrait again, seeing past the carefully curated image. This wasn't just a family business built on tradition. It was a legacy shaped by a man who had lived in the shadows and likely brought those same instincts home with him.

"A noble calling." I didn't know what else to say.

We entered the first room on the right. Although the door nameplate read "Tash Wise," the office itself could've belonged to anyone. A solid wood desk and two uncomfortable, hard-backed chairs faced a sun-touched upper window. Only the awards on the wall said anything about the occupant.

Glass shelves held a diamond-shaped crystal from the Gem Awards, a silver medallion from the Couture Design Awards, and a Spectrum plaque for colored stone excellence. Quiet proof that Tash's jewelry designs had been recognized.

"Did you design Wise's new teen jewelry line?" I asked, impressed.

She nodded.

"It strikes a nice balance," I said. "Traditional enough to satisfy parents but modern enough to be trendy."

She smiled. "Balance was always my strength."

I leaned against the desk. "So why don't you advertise your skills?"

Her smile thinned. "I am responsible for..." She folded her hands. "...brand strategy. Charity partnerships. Small campaigns. Nothing that would break a nail."

"But the awards..."

"Remnants of a dream," Tash said. "Proof I once thought the rules might not apply to me."

I studied her flawless posture and the discipline etched into every movement. Sophie's voice murmured in my head. *Tash is decorative. She's meant to remain in the periphery.*

Tash spun her engagement ring a full turn. Someone used to being underestimated apparently didn't quite know what to do with praise.

"I still do good work," she said quickly. "Charity auctions. Fundraisers. Quiet successes."

All safe and behind the scenes. Not nearly challenging enough for the woman sitting across from me. "Sounds like prison," I replied.

Her eyes flicked up. "I call it restraint," she replied. "It's an acquired skill."

Or a flat lie. Sophie may not be right about everything, but she was right that Tash Wise did not strike me as a woman content to remain nobody.

She studied me for a long minute, then said softly, "I admire you. You make your own rules."

"I had no choice," I said. "My father is a jewel thief."

The words lingered between us. We both understood exactly what following the rules demanded and what they took in return.

"The comfortable estate jewelry store wasn't enough for you," Tash said.

"No," I agreed. "I'd rather struggle than allow comfort to become a cage."

Tash leaned back, her fingers laced. "I watch my older brother drive our legacy into the ground every day. He won't listen. He won't change. And no one stops him because..." She gestured toward the photograph on the wall. "...he looks right doing it."

Father. Grandfather. Brother. The future already framed.

"You tried," I said.

"I did. New designs to meet market shifts backed by customer data." Her gaze snapped back to mine. "My dear brother insists tradition doesn't chase trends."

"Then it goes out of business," I said.

A flicker disrupted her composure before settling into determination edged with defensiveness. A really bad combination.

"Then leave," I said. "Take your talent elsewhere."

Her eyes drifted to the awards, then away. "Leaving doesn't erase a legacy or fix it." She twisted her ring again. "I don't want to destroy Wise & Sons. I intend to save it."

That was the dangerous part. People can justify almost anything if they believed it served a greater purpose—especially when it meant saving what they valued most.

I stood. "Careful. Salvation stories get messy."

Tash rose too, smoothing her blouse, her executive mask back in place. "So do theft stories," she said. "Yet here you are."

Touché. "What does your future husband think?"

Her soft *huh* escaped before she could cover it with a laugh, but the truth lingered. Tash wasn't ready to break all the rules yet.

I looked closer, really looked. Tash wasn't nervous. She controlled exactly how much she revealed. Her endgame intrigued me. I pressed. "Why did you take the Waters' bracelet?"

"I didn't." Tash didn't blink. Her hand remained motionless on the desktop.

I believed her. "Then you know who did."

"I don't," she said. "I was instructed to stage the Waters' diamonds prominently in the Pasadena Room."

"Instructed by whom?" I pushed. Getting information felt a lot like pulling teeth.

"A note appeared with my daily mail on my desk. No signature. No return address." She opened a drawer and slid a notecard toward me.

And a fancy one at that, typed on linen cardstock with no identifying embossing or markings. In short, nothing traceable.

"And you followed it?" I asked.

"Of course I did," she replied, her tone brittle. "I assumed someone from the committee had stopped by. And before you ask, no one remembers who left it."

"When?"

Tash checked her calendar. "Two weeks ago."

I filed it away. I'd have Sophie check the store's security footage and delivery logs.

"Why didn't you question it?" I demanded.

"I don't have that luxury." The words slipped out clipped. "I'm second-guessed even when I'm right."

"You're the chairwoman of the event," I said.

"I'm the worker bee," she shot back. "Volunteered to be the fall guy if something goes wrong." She hesitated, then added, quieter, "I'd planned to display the Waters' bracelet in the main gallery, near the piano with the other prominent pieces."

Not as easy a location to lift the bracelet from. "Who knew your layout plans?"

Her mouth tightened. She saw the setup, too. "The entire event committee. It wasn't a secret. Any committee member could've told someone outside our little circle."

"I'll need a member list and contact information."

"I don't think this is going to help, but here." Tash removed a sheet of paper from her desk drawer and handed it to me. "In hindsight, maybe moving the Waters' bracelet saved the other pieces."

"You don't believe that for a second."

Tash's eyes dropped. Just long enough.

I continued my questioning. "Who chose the security team?"

Tash shrugged. "The contract landed on my desk for signature."

"And you didn't question that either?" I pressed.

"No. Because that's how this works." Her jaw set. "But make no mistake. I've been set up. And I don't like it any more than you do."

"You're not naïve, Tash." My voice stayed even, but I kept the pressure up. "You knew something was happening. And you chose to look the other way."

I held her gaze until she couldn't escape it. When she flinched, I pressed my advantage.

"So tell me," I said quietly, stepping closer, "how did you find out about the bracelet's secret?"

Her mouth curved faintly. Not a smile. "The better question is how did *you*?"

Silence stretched between us as thin as a wire. One wrong move and it would snap. "I'm an investigator," I said. Glimmer backed me up with a single, authoritative *woof*.

Tash exhaled. Not surrender, but concession, with perhaps a trace of relief. "I learned about the Knights by accident."

My stomach tightened. "The Teutonic Knights." I didn't phrase it as a question. I needed it to sound like confirmation, not guesswork.

Tash studied me for a moment, then nodded reluctantly. "I was a nosy kid and listened at keyholes."

A young girl in pink pajamas holding a drinking glass pressed against a door came to mind.

"Men came to the house sometimes. Usually late at night when I was supposed to be asleep," Tash said.

"Did you know them?" I asked.

"Some club members and others from the jewelry trade. They met in the basement, in the wine cellar. It was really *Jason Bourne-ish*."

Of course, she'd been a fan of Robert Ludlum's character.

Everyone had been back then. "How did you know these people were Knights?" I asked.

"Dad marked his calendar with a black cross. No names, just the symbol I found online."

Michael Wise was a Knight. Vindication felt good. "What did the Knights discuss?"

"Diamonds," she said with a faint shrug. "Russian stones flooding the market. De Beers. Supply chains. Prices. Boring things."

My stomach tightened. A secret German order of Knights whispering about diamond supply and distribution? How did that relate to the Waters' diamond bracelet?

"One day, a man I'd never seen before came to the house. H-he frightened me," Tash admitted.

"In what way?"

"He wore a ring," she shuddered. "I guess it was a college ring. It was gold with white enamel and a diamond on it. He twisted it like... I can't explain it exactly. I felt like I was watching a gangster movie."

I pictured the scene right out of *The Godfather*. No wonder Tash had been spooked. "American?"

"I think so. He sounded Midwestern. From Chicago, maybe. He looked German."

I kept my expression neutral. Too much interest would ruin the bluff. "Do you know his name?"

"My father called him Christian. Later, I saw the appointment in his datebook. Dad still uses paper, if you can believe it?"

Her eyeroll almost made me laugh. "It must be a generation thing. My grandmother does, too." So did I, but Tash didn't need to know that. "Who was the appointment with?"

"*C. Weber.*"

The same man who'd tried to intimidate Claire to sell the Waters' bracelet ten years ago. "What did they talk about?" I watched her carefully this time, waiting to see whether the answer came from memory or calculation.

"Christian instructed my father to invite Claire Waters to a formal dinner. He was very specific." Tash swallowed. "She needed to wear the Waters' bracelet."

"That's... odd."

"Not then," she said. "Ten years ago, Ms. Waters had just come back after decades overseas. She topped everyone's guest list. She still would if she accepted invitations."

"At ninety-five?"

"She's a remarkable lady." Tash's pride surprised me. "The stories she told were so inspiring. She sponsored my first jewelry design in the Arizona state competition. She told me I'd go far."

"She was right."

Tash's mouth set. "About more than I wanted to believe back then."

I didn't push. Her tight jawline told me I treaded on guarded territory. "Did Claire come to the party?"

"Yes." Tash hesitated. "But she didn't wear the bracelet. She never wore the bracelet."

"Why?" I asked, though I knew the answer. I needed to hear Tash's response.

Her gaze slid away, then back. "Claire said it was cursed. That anyone who wore the bracelet ended up in a watery grave."

The room felt suddenly smaller. Claire hadn't been indulging in superstition. She'd been buying time.

Tash shifted in her chair, fingers brushing the edge of her sleeve. "I thought it was an excuse," she added lightly. "But..."

"But you believed her," I said.

She didn't deny it. "Back then, yes. Now, I believe she was hiding from C. Weber."

"Did Weber attend the party?"

"Yeah." Tash's fingers tightened in her lap. "He wasn't invited. I saw him in the garden, watching. My mother and I handled the seating. He didn't belong."

"Your father caught you looking at him."

She nodded. "I'd never seen him so angry. He sent me to my room. Made me swear I'd never speak of Christian Weber again." Her voice dropped. "He said my life depended on it. I think his did, too."

"That must've scared you." Tash's fear appeared real, yet I still felt she hid something important from me. Or was this what relief looked like, to finally unburden herself to someone who might understand? I couldn't tell. And that bothered me.

"I wasn't a troublemaker back then," she said softly.

Her transgressions could hardly be classified as rebellious. "Did you ever learn why Weber wanted the bracelet?" I asked.

"No. I admit I was curious. I examined the Waters' bracelet before I put it on display. There were no maker's marks or inscriptions. The platinum was unblemished. The stones..." She hesitated. "Flawless, D-color, fine Old European cuts. Unusual for that era and normally reserved for royalty. But royal jewelry is well-documented, and there is no record of the bracelet-necklace combo anywhere."

It kept coming back to that. "What about the spacing? Were any diamonds missing?" I asked.

"No. In my opinion, the spacing appeared intentional, though it's hard to tell why without the second bracelet. Art Deco Duettes were meant to work together. This design was definitely unique."

A notable assessment from an award-winning jewelry designer. "Any engraving beneath the stones?"

"No. I could see straight through to the platinum. I checked each stone for a message. There was nothing remarkable."

I frowned. "Then why would a secret German order of Knights want the bracelet?"

Tash met my eyes. "Because they either have or know where the other half is."

That hit too close to home. "If Weber wanted it so badly," I said, "why didn't he just steal it from Claire?" Unless he had. I made a mental note to call Lionel.

Tash's fingers slid to her engagement ring. Her nervous tell. "I warned her."

She'd broken a promise to her father, risked his anger despite her fear, to protect someone she admired. That spoke to grit.

I squeezed her arm. "There's always a way out. You just have to take the first step."

"I—I can't tell Detective Rosas." She covered her mouth, fingers trembling, almost too predictably. "If the press ever found out…"

"That you have a viable suspect for the security guard's murder?" I finished evenly. "You'll be a hero."

Not in Tash's plan based on her next comment. "You can tell him. Just leave my name out of it. He told me you were married to him once."

"All the more reason to keep me out of it." Something tightened around my throat. A rope, drawing slowly. Had I just been maneuvered? How much of what she'd shared was truth, and how much designed to misdirect?

Tash shrugged, blissfully unaware of the storm gathering in my head. Or perhaps fully aware. Maybe this had been the plan all along, to let me carry her version of events since she couldn't risk telling.

I glanced toward her father's office further down the hall. My fingers itched for a look inside his safe. Not to steal anything, but to confirm if he owned a Knight's ring, too.

Tash noted my interest. "Dad's not here. He's never in the store on Saturdays. His standing tee time at the club is 9:00 with his cronies."

Interesting plan on the busiest day of the week. Which left the real questions hanging between us: Did I believe Tash's stories? Where had Claire hidden the bracelet for ten years? And why bring it out now at a highly publicized event, knowing someone would come for it?

Chapter Eight

SOME THINGS ARE NOT MEANT TO BE SHARED—WISDOM FROM A JEWEL THIEF

SATURDAY, 12:00 P.M.

Before I called Sophie, I contacted Lionel Waters from my vehicle to arrange a meeting with Michael Wise at his private golf club. Since Tash's father, Michael Wise, and Christian Weber were our first credible links to the Teutonic Knights, I finally had a direction worth pursuing.

Sophie jumped on the possibilities after her biased warning. "You don't actually believe everything Tash said, do you?"

"Not everything." Even I admitted that Tash had spoken too freely. "She delivered an Oscar-worthy performance and seemed like she'd been waiting for someone to talk to."

No missing Sophie's hum. "Do be careful, Hunter. Blind ambition is a most persuasive stimulant."

"You make her sound like a psychopath."

"Oh, I wouldn't go that far," Sophie replied. "More like, one understands precisely why the Wise men chose to keep her in such an exquisitely appointed cage."

Suddenly, my struggling working-class beginnings felt just fine.

"Do try not to be noble by contacting Chad the Cad for her,"

Sophie said lightly. "You have an unfortunate tendency to do the right thing."

She made that sound like a character flaw.

"I'd almost like to listen in," Sophie admitted before disconnecting the call.

Of course, she would. I stared at my phone for a full minute before finally dialing my ex-husband. Thankfully, the call went straight to voicemail. While I generally preferred to deal with adversity head-on, in this case, postponement worked just fine.

If he didn't call back, I'd be off the hook. Telling an egomaniac ex-husband that he'd missed a critical piece of evidence in a murder investigation felt less like professional courtesy than career suicide.

I turned onto the palm-lined approach to the Camelback Mountain Country Club and immediately felt the city falling away behind me. The valet appeared from who knew where and opened the passenger door the moment I stopped. "Good afternoon, Ms. Hunter. Allow me to hold Ms. Glimmer while I assist you."

I nodded, too stunned to argue as the handsome young man, a swimmer I'd guess from his muscular build, showed off in a tight polo. Glimmer went to him with no fuss and allowed him to carry her to the driver's side, where he opened my car door.

No valet tag, just a smile as I stepped out of my SUV. "I will have your vehicle washed and waiting when you are ready to depart." With a smart incline of his head, he added, "Have an enjoyable lunch."

The valet placed the dachshund on the ground at my feet and climbed into my Bronco. Standing there, I suddenly realized how out of place I felt. An aftershock from my meeting with Tash? This was the world she lived in, just greener and better watered.

Lionel Waters lounged near the entrance, seemingly watching the day go by at complete ease. Dressed in a crisp polo bearing the club logo and tailored slacks, he undoubtedly wore the same uniform as his father, and his father before him.

Of course, he was relaxed. This place had been built for men like him. It hit me then. This club wasn't just a backdrop for polite conversations over eighteen holes. It was a closed loop. I may not want to understand this world or what it demanded in exchange for belonging, but whatever secret the Waters' diamonds protected had roots here.

Lionel greeted me with a smile that reached his eyes. "If you intend to be my lunch date, Hunter, you'd best act the part."

"Lunch date?" I didn't like where this was going. I never mixed business with pleasure.

"Michael Wise will not speak to an investigator." Lionel winked conspiratorially. "I have a plan. There's a dress waiting for you in the locker room. The attendant is waiting to assist you." He scooped up Glimmer. "First door on the right. Jeans are not permitted in the dining room."

I glanced at my comfortably broken-in pants. "Seriously?"

"Seriously. Both Wise II and number III are on the dining patio holding court. Join us when you're ready."

The dachshund blinked as we both followed Lionel into uncharted waters.

Any doubt that Lionel Waters possessed exceptional taste vanished the moment I stepped into the designer sundress. He hadn't just guessed my size, he'd understood it. The silk skimmed my skin with a whisper-soft confidence that explained, in an instant, why women invested serious money in French lingerie. Luxury wasn't about show. It was about how it made you feel special.

The tailored equestrian print, subtle yet refined, turned out to be just wild enough to suit me. It paired perfectly with my designer boots. Good news, since the skinny-heeled sandals he'd provided had broken ankle written all over them.

I turned once in the mirror. The soft leather envelope clutch completed the look, and with my Glock tucked neatly inside, the bag could double as a blunt instrument. Fashion, after all, should never compromise function.

I strolled past what I would later learn was golf photo alley, oblivious to its legacy

as I made for the lunch patio. My heels clicked across the stone pavers, announcing my arrival where white linens and wide umbrellas contained the murmur of conversations. Privacy here, it seemed, had been engineered.

Lionel sat at a corner table with a complete view of the dining area. I spotted Michael Wise exactly where Lionel had said he would be, half-hidden behind a potted plant, tucked into the opposite corner, the yawning prodigal son at his side, and two men I didn't recognize. I'd never overhear a thing from my location, and if I blinked, I could lose sight of him.

I felt all eyes on me as I took the seat Lionel offered to me, aware I'd have to wait. In this place, timing mattered as much as the questions.

"You look perfect, Hunter." He settled Glimmer into my lap. "She's become something of a celebrity."

The dachshund's head toss agreed. "We're both more comfortable in the shadows," I replied.

"I suspect you rise to the occasion."

I turned away from his searching look, wondering how he seemed to read me so well.

"Regardless, today, you'll need to hold center stage," Lionel stated.

"Thank you for the appropriate armor." I drew his gaze to the dress.

His smile warmed, not flirtatious, more like the approval of a courteous gentleman who knew how to play the game. "I met your father years ago," he said. "At an embassy reception."

I'm sure my jaw dropped. My father's voice echoed in my head as clearly as if he sat across from me. *Ah, ma chérie. Some things are not meant to be shared.*

"What did he try to steal?" I blurted. The question escaped before I could stop it. Was my father tangled in this mess after all?

Lionel dropped the bomb with a laugh. "Your father has

many talents, Hunter. Perhaps one day you'll come to appreciate all of them."

The words hit harder than he intended. Or maybe exactly as intended.

Appreciate him? I barely kept my expression in place. What I wanted was answers—starting with exactly what role my father played in a missing bracelet that suddenly felt a lot less random.

I opened my mouth—and a waiter appeared, immaculate in crisp white, and poured water into crystal glasses. Perfect timing.

Lionel didn't miss a beat. He shifted, smiled, and pivoted the conversation as if he hadn't just detonated it.

My father had always had a talent for intruding at the worst possible moments—even from afar.

I ordered an iced tea and the chicken salad. At least the menu promised chicken. The rest of the description required a Google search and a working knowledge of a foodie's vocabulary.

I felt the daggers before I heard the whispers—eyes drilling into my back, waiting for my reaction. I didn't get the chance to steer things back to my father. Lionel deflected the noise with practiced ease, drawing me into safer conversation. "Ignore them," he said. "They win if they get under your skin."

Said the man who'd fit into all this his entire life.

"And if you keep staring at Wise like that, he'll have to send a drink to our table."

I'm sure I blushed. Any wonder I preferred stealth surveillance? "Who are the men with Michael Wise?"

"One is a club member. I shall have his information forwarded to you. I do not know the other." Lionel smiled. "My apologies for the distance of your table... it would be rather unfortunate if he were to slip away before you had the opportunity to be properly introduced."

"No problem." I placed Glimmer on the ground and reached into my clutch. As subtly as possible, I gestured the dog to run toward Michael Wise's table.

The dachshund took her cue and darted across the patio, tripping a waiter and nearly causing another to spill a laden meal tray. The distraction worked beautifully. Two other dogs barked in solidarity, turning the entire patio into a chaotic scene that had eyes everywhere but on me as I retrieved Glimmer, who practically sat on Michael Wise's foot.

"I am so sorry. I can't imagine what got into her." I didn't wait for an acknowledgment. Glimmer brushed his ankle—just enough cover. Two fingers, quick clip, done. The mini tracker held to his pant leg as I scooped her up, snapped on the leash, and kept moving. No hesitation. No glance back. Nothing to give me away.

Lionel held my chair as I returned. "Nicely done. Your father would be proud."

I paused a fraction too long before sitting. I'd been careful—timed it, masked it, made sure no one watched me. Yet Lionel hadn't just noticed—he'd seen everything.

I settled into the chair, a flicker of unease threading through my composure. Lionel's gaze looked as relaxed as ever, almost bored.

"You have managed to use the club's interest in you to your advantage." No mistaking his pride.

"If we don't get kicked out." I checked the tracker's signal on my phone and texted Sophie the deployed code. Wise wasn't going anywhere without me in hot pursuit.

Lionel smiled. "This club has seen worse. You are quite a woman, Hunter. My wife had a hard time adjusting to the constant scrutiny."

"Soon to be ex-wife, I hear."

"That is correct. It's a shame, really. We got along so well."

"An amicable divorce?" I hated that term. Chad and my divorce had started out that way, until Chad's requests had become outrageous.

"For the most part. The prenup leaves no room for interpretation. She is a successful artist. Frankly, she didn't need me for anything. She did say that she always felt like an outsider."

I related.

"The last straw was when the Daughters of the Pioneers refused to accept her application. Citing that her parents weren't pioneers."

"But yours were."

"I know. Those women will never accept someone who works with their hands." His tsk felt real enough. "How is the investigation proceeding?"

"I have some new information that may be relevant."

He picked up his cocktail glass with practiced ease. "I assumed as much."

"Has Claire's home been burglarized?"

"Not recently."

"Twelve years ago?"

He sat up straighter. "Yes. Twice. We added security. Nothing of value was taken either time."

I smiled, uncertain of whether this secret had been intentional or not. "Where did you hide the Waters' bracelet these last twelve years?"

He sat back again in control. "I think the important question you are about to ask is why she allowed the bracelet to go on display?"

I squeezed lemon into my iced tea. Funny, I hadn't noticed when it had been delivered.

"The Duette's secret can't be unlocked without all three pieces," he said. "My grandmother's agreement with the previous owner was explicit. The three pieces were never to be brought together."

"Who signed the agreement?" I asked, keeping my tone even despite the surge of adrenaline. If legitimate, this document would establish provenance and uninterrupted ownership going back a century.

"Viktoria," Lionel replied. "It's a handwritten receipt dated 9 March 1921."

Handwritten. Potentially binding, if properly executed.

"May I review it?" I asked. "Original ink matters. And verifying the signatures of both the seller and witnesses."

"That may be difficult," Lionel said. "Aunt Melodie retained possession of the document."

Of course she did.

"How do you know about it?" I asked.

"The information is documented in my father's will."

I exhaled, the tension draining out of me. "That's a problem. Without the original document, proving ownership of the bracelet gets complicated. After a hundred years, you'll need to deal with jurisdiction, succession, conflicting laws."

Lionel inclined his head. "You're assuming the person who took it has a legitimate claim."

"No," I said. "I'm trying to understand yours."

"No need," he replied, cool and certain. "My grandmother's word is sufficient."

He looked genuinely affronted as though I'd challenged not a document, but the integrity of his entire bloodline. I changed the subject. "So, the bracelet can't pass to you?"

He shook his head. "No. As Claire's heir, I'm bound by the agreement. Her half must pass to an heir of Aunt Melodie's, specifically one who does not already possess parts to the corresponding bracelet."

"If there are any heirs," I said carefully.

"Aunt Merle was certain there were."

"And twins," I murmured, "have a way of knowing what the rest of the world doesn't."

He inclined his head. "Claire and I have searched for years. Every viable lead circles back to Catalina."

That gave me pause. If Melodie had survived, Catalina should have been the starting point—not the dead end.

"You believed reintroducing Claire's bracelet into circulation would prompt a claimant to surface?" I asked.

He hesitated. "It sounds absurd. But we're running out of

time." His voice dropped. "Claire wants this resolved. She's more of a sister to me than a cousin, you know."

I believed him. "What happens if you can't find an heir?"

Lionel didn't hesitate. "Claire's bracelet must be destroyed. *Melted down* are the document's exact words."

"And the diamonds?"

"They revert to Claire's heir. That's me."

My instincts stirred. This proved that the bracelet's value wasn't the stones themselves. The message had to be in the design. "Are you familiar with the Teutonic Knights?"

He leaned back, took a measured sip of his drink. "They were the German equivalent of the Knights Templar. In the fourteenth and fifteenth centuries, they terrorized villages across Eastern Europe."

"A footnote now," I added, watching his response.

"Not in Eastern Europe," he replied. "The folklore still frightens children."

"And you know this..."

He paused, then continued, almost thoughtfully. "My father was born in Belgium in 1920. Apart from a few brief years in Phoenix, he spent his childhood moving between diplomatic postings. Europe, mostly. He attended Eton. Like his father before him. He later served..."

"Your grandfather went to Eton?" I asked.

Lionel nodded. "Our family started diplomatic service during Grover Cleveland's first administration in 1885."

"That's 140 years."

"Yes. It's a shame Claire is the last of the legacy. My son from my first marriage is a corporate lawyer. I am confident Waters Construction is in capable hands, but he is no diplomat."

"Eton's the school of choice for the British aristocracy," I said carefully.

"And foreign royalty," he replied. "And diplomats. I broke tradition by attending Yale. First in the family to be educated in the States. You know, Claire graduated from Oxford in 1952?"

I didn't, but I filed it away. Something in that lineage mattered. I just couldn't see how yet.

"Your grandmother died when your father was five," I said slowly. "Who raised him?"

The answer, I suspected, was where the real story began.

"Officially," he said, "my grandfather's sister until Aunt Merle married and he went to live with her and her new husband in Germany."

The word *officially* snagged my attention. "Did he have a nanny?"

"Yes. She raised both Merle and Melodie. A French Creole woman from Martinique, I believe."

The light went on, clean and bright.

"Your aunt's diaries weren't written in twin-speak," I said quietly. "The girls spoke French Creole." I looked up at him.

The diaries shifted in my mind, their meaning only a quick translation away. "Tell me about the nanny."

"Her name was Ami. Dad said she was a character. She negotiated like a fishmonger and stirred up trouble like a French courtier. She loved the twins and my father. She even found a scarlet macaw for the girls. That bird cursed like a sailor."

"In French?" The red feather I'd seen at Claire's desk made sense now.

Lionel nodded.

"What happened to the macaw?"

"My dad never got a straight answer. When he returned to Phoenix, both Ami and Ruby, the macaw, were gone. Ami was old, so he thought she might have retired, but she'd never said goodbye. Aunt Merle never said much about it."

A beloved nanny and pet simply vanishing? The thought hurt like a stomach punch. If Glimmer disappeared without a trace, I'd tear the world apart looking for her. Either Merle had mourned in solitude, or she knew exactly where Ami and Ruby had gone.

My salad arrived before I could dig deeper. To my relief, I recognized enough of the ingredients to eat it. I forked a piece of chicken and offered it to Glimmer as the server added dressing and tossed the salad tableside. We'd both survived haute cuisine.

After lunch, Lionel orchestrated the meeting with Tash's father, Michael Wise, with a calm precision I had to admire. Glimmer stayed tucked in my arms as we crossed the dining room, weaving through quiet conversations and clinking glassware.

Michael Wise rose as we approached, his gaze locking onto mine, cool, deliberate, and assessing my value before I'd even spoken. He didn't bother to hide it. If anything, the faint tightening around his eyes said he'd already decided what he thought of Lionel and, by association, me.

"Wise, may I introduce..." Lionel's tone sounded effortless. "Fellow jeweler, Taylor Hunter. I thought you might find a conversation... useful."

Useful. That was a word for it.

"Mr. Wise." I offered a measured smile.

He didn't return it. His gaze moved over me with quiet disdain—cataloging, dismissing. "Hunter, is it?" Wise's attention flicked back to Lionel, not me. "My daughter tells me you're a detective."

There it was. The judgment. The real question—did he object to what I was... or what I might find?

"A diamond detective. Recovery specialist." I kept my voice even. "Freelance."

Glimmer's low growl threaded the silence—quiet, precise, enough to draw a few curious glances. Wise ignored it. Ignored her. Ignored me.

Instead, his attention shifted briefly to the man slouched beside him, his son, Tash's brother, who sat like a dead weight in his chair, eyes dull, posture loose. Drunk enough not to care. Or too far gone to notice. Either way, Tash had reason to worry.

Wise's gaze snapped back to me. "You will keep my daughter out of the Waters bracelet theft." Wise nudged his son, already disengaging. "We have another engagement."

Not a request. A warning. A threat. Maybe both.

I held Lionel's gaze as they walked off. One rigid with control, the other barely upright. A respected jeweler and his liability.

Message delivered. He'd intended to make me feel small. It didn't work. If anything, it did the opposite.

Men like Michael Wise didn't waste time on irrelevance. Which meant I wasn't the problem. I was the threat.

And now I needed to know why.

Chapter Nine

CODED MESSAGES ARE CREATED TO BE BROKEN—WISDOM FROM A JEWEL THIEF

SATURDAY, 4 P.M.

I called Hope the moment I slid into my car. "The twins spoke French Creole," I said before she could greet me.

"Well, that explains the odd translations," Hope replied calmly. "I'll start on the translations..."

"Ami was from Martinique," I cut in.

"I'll see if her family name is in the diaries. And what her profession was before becoming the girls' nanny."

I paused. "Why?"

"I've done more research, and the French ran a decent informant network in South America around 1900 to 1910. The Waters were high-placed American diplomats in the Panama Canal zone with a bright future," Hope explained.

"Ami brought the girls a scarlet macaw," I added.

I heard keys clicking. "A bird wasn't unusual for diplomats to own in the Canal Zone."

"Except this macaw swore like a French sailor."

"Oh." Hope stopped typing. "A nanny from the docks of Martinique? That makes Ami..."

"… a spy," I finished, the words settling with uncomfortable clarity.

"You think she and the twins' mother worked together?" Hope asked.

"Who would suspect the wife of a respected American diplomat? Moving from post to post, above suspicion every time."

"And she pulled her children into it?" I felt Hope's outrage.

I didn't like it either. "Think about it. Ambassadors' kids grow up together. They blend in. They learn the local language easily." I let that settle.

"And kids have no filters. That could've been us," Hope added quietly. "Only Dad's version of international relations involved breaking and entering."

If Ami had been quietly feeding information to the French, then the girls would've grown up fluent in more than Creole. They'd have learned how to listen without reacting. How to remember without writing. How to pass a message without knowing it was a message at all. That kind of education didn't fade with age.

"If the French had been watching in the 1910s, they wouldn't have stopped in 1920 or 1930. Not with Germany regrouping and empires realigning," Hope added.

I glanced at the passenger seat. Glimmer watched me steadily, head tilted, as if she sensed the shape of the problem even if she didn't know the words. "If Melodie and Merle had been assets, then the two pieces of the Duette have to be a signal of some sort, and someone, somewhere, still understands what it means." Families like the Waters didn't just stumble into secrets. They inherited them.

"That would depend on who the twins' mother worked for," Hope said.

I tightened my grip on the steering wheel. "I'll be back in Sunset Peak in an hour. I'll meet you…"

"Go back to your place and relax. I'll come by later, when Sophie has your trip to Catalina finalized. She's already working on a timeline of the twins' father's diplomatic postings. I know what to do. I'll forward the translations as I complete them," Hope said.

I wanted to argue, but Glimmer's yawn triggered my own. It had been a long day.

Another call beeped in. "It's Chad. I need to talk to him," I said quickly and disconnected before Hope could tell me yet again what an idiot I was. When a confrontation with my ex-husband felt easier than one with my sister, it was officially time for me to rethink my career choices.

"I'm returning your call. What do you want?" Chad snapped. The accusation in his voice made me regret answering almost instantly.

Glimmer lifted her head from the passenger seat, a snarl on her lips. Chad's voice always did that to her.

"Consider this call a professional courtesy." I kept my tone level.

A pause. "You have my attention."

"There's another player. About ten years ago, a representative connected to the Teutonic Knights..."

"Knights?" he scoffed. "What is this, medieval cosplay?"

"No," I said calmly. "And here's what I have." I laid out the facts I'd gathered, carefully omitting the third piece of the Duette, the German provenance, and Claire's health. "I don't think Lionel Waters is involved. I think..."

"You're too close," Chad cut in. "You really think I wouldn't find out you had a fancy lunch with Lionel Waters at the Camelback Mountain Country Club today?"

Glimmer's growl deepened in her chest. Chad had eyes on Lionel. *Wonderful.*

"I cornered Michael Wise," I said. "He's tied to the Teutonic Knights."

"And why would Wise & Company's president want that bracelet?" Chad demanded. "He has a vault full of diamonds."

That was the question. "I don't know yet," I admitted. "But

it's not about the platinum or the diamonds. It's something else. I know it."

"Yeah, yeah. You can quit the dramatics," he said dismissively. "A Duette that leads to some lost treasure. Too bad the other half is sitting at the bottom of the ocean."

"The San Pedro Channel," I corrected before I could stop myself.

Glimmer's low, decisive arf warned me to shut up too late. I'd already said too much.

"Whatever. You're in Fantasy Land, Taylor. Let the professionals do their job."

I didn't bother replying. I ended the call. I knew better. I really did. At least, I'd accomplished the goal. I'd handed him a potential new suspect he wouldn't be able to ignore once the name crossed his desk. Whether he acknowledged it or not was his problem.

The knot in my chest didn't loosen. Chad dismissed things he couldn't control. But he'd gone quiet when I corrected him about the San Pedro Channel, and that told me more than his bluster ever could. I wasn't just a nosy insurance adjuster anymore. I was ahead of him. And Chad the Cad hated nothing more than being one step behind.

I turned onto Carefree Highway, the afternoon sun flashing off oncoming windshields on the divided roadway, when the hairs on my nape tingled. Someone was following me.

I checked the rearview mirror. The BMW and the pickup truck looked normal enough. The dark SUV hanging two car lengths back, exactly the distance I'd been taught to maintain when tailing someone, didn't.

I took a sharp turn onto a side street without signaling. The SUV continued along Carefree Highway. I memorized the license plate and texted it to Sophie before my hands started to shake.

Had Wise ordered my surveillance? If so, my performance at the country club had rattled him more than he'd let on. Or fooled him less. I pulled up the tracking dot's location on my phone.

Michael Wise was at his Scottsdale jewelry store. Odd for a Saturday, according to his daughter, but not impossible.

A hawk suddenly circled overhead, spiraling in the thermal. My pulse spiked before it banked away toward the desert. Was this bird for real or one of the FBI's surveillance drones, clever little machines disguised as birds, that had been deployed during the Fire Diamond investigation? Rocky had called them efficient. I'd called them unsettling. I couldn't look at the animal the same anymore. After you've been hunted once, even nature feels tactical.

Dad had also inserted himself into my life plenty of times over the years, always uninvited, and never openly. But overtly following me didn't feel right either. That Glimmer snoozed on the passenger seat unbothered made me wonder if I was being paranoid. Or maybe paranoia was what kept you alive.

I texted Hope, though she already knew what had happened and what the next steps were. Sophie's message arrived in my inbox just as I parked behind my apartment above our jewelry store. I glanced at the list of eight royal women named Viktoria who'd been alive in 1921.

Auguste Viktoria, the dethroned German Empress and Queen of Prussia. Dead by April of that year.

Princess Viktoria of Prussia—Kaiser Wilhelm II's sister.

Princess Viktoria Luise—Kaiser Wilhelm II's daughter.

Victoria of Baden, Queen consort of Sweden.

Princess Viktoria of Hesse and by Rhine, sister to the Russian Empress.

Victoria Melita of Saxe-Coburg and Gotha, once a duchess, once a Russian grand duchess, twice displaced by history.

Princess Viktoria Adelheid of Schaumburg-Lippe.

Victoria Eugenie of Battenberg, Queen consort of Spain.

Mostly German bloodlines from fallen empires, threaded with enough Russian connections to continue to keep a possible link to the Russian Revolution in play. These were women who had stood at the center of power and somehow survived its collapse.

Any one of them could have owned the Duette and passed it along. But why not record it? And the big part that didn't fit: how did diamonds so intimately associated with imperial Europe end up the property of the wife of a then-insignificant American diplomat?

No answers forthcoming, I turned off my SUV and smoothed my skirt before reaching across the console for Glimmer. Lionel had insisted I keep the designer dress he'd purchased for me despite my protests. Jeans-and-boots girls don't have much call for fancy dresses, but he'd outlasted me. The Camelback Mountain Country Club's unwavering scrutiny hadn't helped my case any, either. Public arguments rarely did.

Glimmer's patience had reached the breaking point, too. She wriggled free, hit the pavement, and bolted. Not toward her usual patch of gravel, but straight for the back door. She paced, whining, until I unlocked the door. She then shot past me right up the stairs, barking.

My adrenaline spiked. Had that SUV I thought had been following me beaten me to my home or was someone else waiting for me? My heart slammed in my chest as I slipped my Glock out of my clutch. I knew exactly what they'd be after. It was time to get the Duette's third piece to a safer place than our store's high-security safe.

I followed silently, taking care that my boots made no sound and motioning Glimmer to be quiet. She froze, trembling, every muscle coiled, teeth bared toward the landing above.

We'd lost the element of surprise, but had trapped the intruder. My right forefinger remained on the trigger as I dialed the local police with my left thumb, my ears alert to any sound. Before the call connected, the door swung open.

Chapter Ten

THE PERFECT HEIST IS STEALING
SOMETHING THAT IS NOT MISSED
—WISDOM FROM A JEWEL THIEF

SATURDAY, 7:00 P.M.

Glimmer launched through the gap, tail whipping back and forth like she planned to clear the way with sheer force. I followed, my weapon trained, focused... until a familiar voice cut through the pounding in my ears.

"Don't shoot the chef." His voice slid over me... low, familiar, and intimate in a way that went straight to my core. If that hadn't stopped me, the sight of him would have. Rocky Rockman filled the door frame, dark hair rumpled like he'd run his hand through it one too many times, broad shoulders stretching the fabric of his polo. Silver eyes locked on mine, sharp and heated, as if he really liked what he saw.

"W-what are you doing here?" My voice betrayed me, breathier than I intended. I'd given him a key. I just hadn't expected him to use it.

"Trying to figure out what you did with my girlfriend." His gaze dipped slowly, deliberately, before returning to my eyes. "You look beautiful."

My pulse stuttered. It had been three weeks since I'd seen him.

He looked... rock solid and sexy. The kind of man who made a woman acutely aware of the space between them.

Then the scent reached me. Warm dark chocolate and chilies simmering in mouthwatering mole. I licked my lips as I eased the Glock back into the clutch, suddenly hyperaware of my bare arms, the way the silky dress skimmed my hips, and how exposed I felt standing there under his gaze. We'd never named what this was between us. We'd agreed to no rules, no promises, no tidy definition to lean on. Just chemistry for as long as it lasted. But this...

Teenage jitters still sparked through me, ridiculous and thrilling, my body reacting before my brain could catch up. "You said you had a case."

"I do. I missed you." His fingers traced my jaw, slow and deliberate, tilting my chin until his mouth found mine. The kiss was warm, unhurried, electric.

"I..."

Glimmer chose that moment to ram my calf, knocking me straight into him, and barked as if she'd just solved the world's problems.

Rocky's laugh broke against my mouth as he caught me with one arm and bent to scoop Glimmer up with the other. She rewarded him by enthusiastically washing his face, tail thumping against his chest while he scratched behind her ears.

"Traitor," I muttered.

He grinned at me over the dachshund's head, his eyes still liquid silver. "She has excellent timing."

Jealous of my own dog, I cleared my throat and stepped back just enough to breathe. The air still felt charged, as if we'd only paused something, not ended it.

"Chicken mole?" I asked.

"Exactly the way you like it." He set Glimmer down, but his hand lingered at my waist, his thumb brushing the fabric of my dress as if testing whether I'd pull away.

I didn't.

"Well," I said lightly, though my pulse said otherwise, "we'd better dig in."

He smiled slowly, knowing. "Careful," he murmured as I stepped past him. "That sounded like an invitation."

And just like that, the door closed behind us, leaving the question of us still unanswered, humming between heartbeats, waiting for the next excuse to surface.

"How long have you been here?" I asked.

"A few hours."

"Why didn't you call?"

He avoided my eyes, setting two bowls on the counter and spooning steaming dark-brown sauce over brown rice like this was any other night. "How was your day?"

"Fine." I stared at him. This version of Rocky, home-cooked dinner, easy smiles, and familiar hugs, felt off.

"Can't I ask?" He glanced up, his expression almost wounded. For a split second, I nearly let it go.

I didn't. "You're not a surprise kinda guy," I said quietly. "So why are you here?"

He straightened, shoulders squaring, warmth snapping into something harder.

"Chad called me."

Of course, he had. Rocky's connection to my ex-husband had made our encounter during the Fire Diamond investigation tense from the start. Our divided loyalties and professional posturing had nearly gotten us both killed. I hadn't trusted him then, but he'd earned that trust since, proving himself solid, careful, and reliable. Which somehow made this worse.

"About what?" I asked, folding my arms.

"About the Duette. And about you." His tone had turned pure FBI now.

That tightened something in my chest. Not fear. More like annoyance edged with something hotter. Glimmer chose that moment to abandon me, curling at his feet and fixing me with a look that suggested I was being unreasonable.

"So," I said, lifting my chin, "you flew in from Los Angeles to do what exactly?" I let my gaze sweep him, slow and unimpressed. "Keep an eye on me?"

I stood, hands settling on my hips. "I don't need a keeper. I'm perfectly able to take care of myself."

"Over the last six months, the FBI has recorded five thefts involving Art Deco jewelry." His soft tone knocked the righteous fury right out of me.

I dropped into the chair. He wasn't here to manage me. He was here to help. Why did I always overreact around him? "What were these thefts?"

He glanced at his phone, scrolling. "Two museum pieces. One from a private collection. One taken during a charity exhibition."

My stomach tightened. I leaned back and reached for my fork. The bite of spicy chicken gave me a moment to regroup. "What exactly was stolen?"

"A single bracelet in each case," Rocky said. "Targeted and deliberate." His gaze lifted to mine. "The thief bypassed pieces worth significantly more."

That did it. I set my fork down slowly. Patterns meant intention—and intention brought my father to mind.

"How were the museums hit?" I asked.

"During open hours. The thief created a diversion, cut the glass case, and vanished. All video surveillance was corrupted."

"Suggests a bold and highly organized criminal." The thought unsettled me.

"It was well-planned and precisely executed," Rocky agreed.

I liked collaborating with him. He dealt in facts. Not fluff.

"You think the Waters' diamond theft is connected?" I asked.

Rocky didn't answer.

"Jewelry is a common theft item, easily fenced and of high value with little risk unless the piece happens to be memorable. Hope and I get a handful of hot items a year at the store. We usually get a police alert. I haven't seen anything about this..."

"You'll have to ask your new chief," Rocky said, the implication landing exactly where he wanted it.

I agreed. He'd run circles around Sunset Peak's latest hire. "Let's skip the politics. What do the cases have in common?"

"The thefts were surgical," he continued. "By the time anyone realized something was missing, the pieces were already gone." He paused, then added, "The FBI traced every bracelet back to the same German jeweler—Kruetz & Co. Manufactured between 1915 and 1919."

He had my undivided attention.

"Chad couldn't find a listed craftsman for the Waters' bracelet." His gaze held mine, waiting.

"It's a match," I said. "Don't ask."

Rocky gave a single nod. No pushback. I'd always respected that about him. The man understood boundaries, especially when they involved client privilege. Those arguments never ended well anyway.

"An hour ago," he continued, "Chad called and asked me about Christian Weber." His voice dropped. "That's when I knew our cases weren't just similar."

I leaned back, the pieces sliding into place. "They're connected." I let him digest that before asking, "Who is Christian Weber?"

"A jewelry collector, of sorts," Rocky said. "He runs an estate jewelry shop in Chicago. Inherited it from his uncle."

"Legitimate?" I asked.

His mouth twitched. "Nothing we can prove otherwise. Not yet. His associates are a mixed bag of..."

"Intimidators and hackers," I finished.

Rocky gave a short nod. "He's on Homeland Security's radar for antiquities smuggling."

So, definitely not a Boy Scout.

"What was his uncle's name?" I asked.

He glanced down at his phone. "Voss."

The word hit like a spark. "Fox. In German."

"Prussian to be exact."

Adrenaline surged as the pieces snapped into alignment. Christian Weber wasn't circling the Duette by accident. If he was tied to Mr. Fox, then he'd known about the bracelet long before it ever resurfaced. And that meant he hadn't just found the trail. He'd been waiting for it.

Rocky lifted his long-neck Dos Equis and took a slow drink. "Care to share?"

I nodded. There was no point holding my cards now. Despite my instinct to always keep information close.

"Have there been any murders tied to the thefts?" I asked.

"No," he said. "No weapons, either. The MO is a simple distraction, and the piece vanishes."

I leaned back. "Like the work of a master thief."

Our eyes locked. My father's name didn't need to be spoken. It hovered there anyway.

Rocky finally looked away. "The value doesn't support that," he said. "Not on its own."

"The value isn't the point," I said. "The thief is hunting for the other half of the Waters' bracelet."

Good news. Maybe. It meant Melodie's bracelet remained unaccounted for.

I walked Rocky through what I knew quickly: the Waters' family tree, Merle's diaries, the gaps that didn't make sense. I told him about the Teutonic Knights, about Tash's unease, and about Christian and how his name kept surfacing in places it didn't belong.

Rocky didn't interrupt. He just listened.

"I'm waiting on Hope to translate the diaries." I exhaled, feeling the clock start to tick. "If we're lucky, there's something in there that tells us where the original necklace came from."

"What does the Duette lead to?" Rocky asked.

"I don't know exactly. We're tracing the mineral composition of the demantoid garnets. It doesn't fit chronologically or geographically." I chose my words carefully. "Is the FBI taking jurisdiction from Phoenix PD?" No denying the little leap of anticipation at the thought of working this puzzle with Rocky again.

"Not yet. Phoenix PD wants the hit-and-run arrest first."

That deflated me. "Is it even connected?" I asked. "It doesn't fit the pattern."

Rocky gave a measured shrug. "The security guard assigned to guard the Waters' diamond ends up dead in a vacant industrial complex hours after the theft." His voice stayed even. "That suggests it does."

I didn't want to agree. But I did.

"So, what changed?" I asked quietly. "What pushed this from theft to murder?"

"Don't know. Your involvement changes the rules further," he added. "You're in danger."

"Chad told you that? He must want me off the case more than I'd thought."

Rocky exhaled, slow and controlled, the sound of a man who'd been carrying this longer than he wanted to admit. "Weber knows it, too. Anything in his way is eliminated."

A sane person would be concerned. I grinned. "I can take care of myself," I said. "I know how to use a gun."

Glimmer chose that moment to bark, sharp and indignant, planting herself between us like a furry line of defense.

I gestured weakly. "And I have an attack dog."

Rocky's mouth twitched as Glimmer lunged for his ankle with more enthusiasm than threat. He shifted easily out of reach, one hand dropping to steady her. "And," he said, quieter now, eyes lifting to mine, "you have a boyfriend who intends to keep both of you alive."

No joke this time. Just a promise.

My stomach bottomed out. "You could've said that when you walked in."

"I suppose I could have." He circled the small table and ran his finger along my jawline. "Make no mistake, Christian Weber doesn't tolerate loose ends. And right now, you're standing between him and something he wants."

Glimmer pressed against my leg beneath the table, grounding me.

"And now?" I asked.

"Now we protect you and try to find the missing half of the Duette. We also make sure Christian Weber never gets close enough to choose how this ends."

For once, I didn't argue. Living another day sounded like a great idea.

Chapter Eleven

THE PAST DOES NOT PREDICT THE FUTURE—WISDOM FROM A JEWEL THIEF

Merle's diary translations arrived just as I dried the last dinner dish. For an ultra-organized guy, Rocky had a knack for leaving chaos behind. How many pots did it take to cook mole? Not that I complained too loudly. House rules had him making the after-dinner coffee anyway. Besides, two in my current one-butt kitchen made the task a Twister game.

My printer hummed softly across the living room while Rocky poured coffee into two of my Starbucks international mugs. A silly tradition, maybe, but I collected one from every country I'd traveled to, twenty so far—seven in the original classic design, the rest in the brighter, cartoon-style versions. Rocky chose my favorite without asking.

I watched him for a moment, drawn to the easy normalcy—and the deep sense of rightness his presence stirred.

I set the stage as Rocky sat across from me at the table, all business. "Merle wrote this entry in 1929. At the time, her twin, Melodie, hid from Mr. Fox in Los Angeles. Meanwhile, Mr. Fox

watched Merle, waiting for her to give away her sister's location."
I lowered my eyes to the page and read.

April 20, 1929

*CI looks lovely. Cats in the ladies'
room? Your part was too small, but you
looked beautiful. Auntie says you're too
thin. MF comes every Thursday now.
Father demands I show MF my diamonds. I
hear Mother's warning. He knows the
truth. I feel it in my bones.*

*Ruby squawks at him. She will not sing.
Ami has nothing more to add.*

"CI is Catalina Island," I explained. "Melodie filmed several
early talkies there. MF is Mr. Fox. Ami was their nanny. Ruby is
their macaw." I glanced at Glimmer curled on the chair between
us, eyeing us both. Any wonder I felt under scrutiny. Animals had
a sixth sense. What Ruby's reactions told, I could only guess.
Rocky didn't nod this time. He stayed very still. "Go on."

May 1, 1929

*My heart breaks. Father demands your
return. MF is here every day now. He
watches BR. He says very little. Ruby
will not eat. I am ready. Our time is
almost up.*

The pattern snapped into focus. Mr. Fox didn't rush. He
waited, tightening the circle, day by day, like a big cat waiting for
the right moment to pounce. Had Melodie's disappearance been

planned? Forced by the man in relentless pursuit of the diamonds?

"Melodie was lost at sea on May 30th. The next entry is the day after her disappearance," I said.

May 31, 1929

It's done. I am safe on board a ship. You must call me Mrs. Richmond. B has agreed to a stop in Switzerland. Keep your diamonds safe. Some day we will be together again.

I turned the page, my pulse steadying as the pieces locked into place. "Merle knows her sister is alive. She married Byron Richmond and took her young brother with her to Europe. The family was posted in Germany until 1933."

I read on, the entries becoming more telling.

September 1929

Message received. The diamonds are safe. We have done our job. Germany is unsettled. The Knights are many here. Network in place. I will keep watch. Be safe.

"After that, the language is more cryptic. She didn't stop," I murmured. "She just moved the information gathering operation."

Rocky leaned forward, forearms braced on the table. "Spying?"

"Intelligence gathering." The phrasing mattered. "Merle built a network of people no one would notice."

"Why?" he asked slowly.

I didn't answer right away. My eyes drifted to the margins of the page, where Merle had drawn a familiar symbol—a white shield with a small black cross, no larger than a thumbnail.

"Because they knew someone was coming." I closed the diary, my fingers lingering on the worn leather cover.

"The real question isn't why Melodie disappeared. It's why she and her sister sacrificed so much to protect the diamonds," Rocky stated.

I admired how he got right to the point. "I need to find Melodie," I said simply. I'd known from the start this would be my task.

I reached for the postcards Claire had given me. They mattered—I could feel it. "Do you know a bird expert?" I asked.

Rocky's arched brow answered without words. Of course, he did. He even had the contact on speed dial. Who knew an FBI connection came with benefits?

Rocky snapped a few photos and sent them off. Then we waited. It felt like forever, though it was probably only a few minutes before his phone rang.

"Thanks, Professor." Rocky switched the call to speaker.

A rough, gravel-edged voice filled the room—older, definitely over sixty, with a distinct East Coast nasal tone. "Any time, Rocky boy. How many times have I told you that birds tell stories?"

Rocky glanced at me. "Often. Let's hope you're right in this case."

"I am. The first is a white-tailed ptarmigan. They're only found on Vancouver Island, British Columbia. The goldfinch is Washington State's bird. The third is a cherry-headed conure, also called a red-masked parakeet. And the last is a macaw." The voice paused, then returned, sharper now, energized. "Those red-masked parakeets are interesting. There's a well-known feral population in San Francisco. And that macaw. It's a hybrid of an Ara macao and an Ara ararauna, commonly called the Scarlet and blue-and-golds. The bird is called a Catalina macaw since it was bred there. Hmm. I'd say these postcards map a route. Canada to Washington... down to San Francisco... ending at Catalina."

My gut tightened as I looked down at the postcards again: Melodie's journey? Could each card be that breadcrumb she'd shared with her twin—a message sent without words? That would mean the cards weren't souvenirs. They were a cry for justice.

I explained my theory after Rocky thanked the professor and hung up. "What I don't understand is why go to Vancouver? Why not disappear into the noise of 1929 Los Angeles?"

"You said Fox found her on Catalina Island," Rocky said.

I nodded.

"If he was watching the steamers, she'd need another way off the island."

"She could've hitched a ride on a private boat," I suggested. "She'd filmed there. She'd had plenty of opportunities to make friends."

Rocky leaned back in my café chair, his broad shoulders nearly swallowing the narrow backrest. "In 1929, Prohibition was still the law. Catalina was a rum-runner's haven, supplied by Canadian motherships."

"How do you know that?" I asked.

"I'm FBI."

Like that explained it. I folded my arms.

"My uncle lived in Los Angeles. I visited Catalina every summer. My favorite summer was the one I spent a week at the Boy Scout camp on Catalina at Cherry Cove."

Of course, he really was a Boy Scout. Firsthand knowledge beat anything I could pull from a book, too. "You think Melodie escaped on a smuggling ship?"

"Think about it... She knew how to build networks. Befriending the local smugglers made sense. They could've known someone who could help her disappear."

My instincts agreed. Melodie's trail didn't end at Catalina. It started there.

"Finding her after all these years will be next to impossible," I said.

"Maybe not." Rocky slid a finger across the remaining postcards. "Vancouver, Seattle, San Francisco, and back to Catalina. She came full circle."

"That makes no sense if she truly feared Mr. Fox," I said. "He didn't leave Phoenix until 1942."

Rocky turned the remaining postcards over one by one, studying them the way he approached crime scenes, with a patience and methodical focus I admired and wished I could match. "Perhaps she no longer considered him a threat."

Rocky frowned and pulled out his phone. "Catalina Island," he murmured, scrolling. "Bird sanctuary... here. The Catalina Bird Park opened in the mid-1930s. They kept exotic birds. Get this. They bred the first Catalina macaw from a scarlet macaw and a blue and gold macaw."

My intuition took notice. "The twins' macaw disappeared with Ami right after Merle left for Germany."

Rocky acknowledged my comment, but continued reading, his attention focused on the screen. "Avalon," he continued, "has bird tiles on shop fronts, walkways, and in public spaces." He looked up. "I remember them." He showed me the images from the web.

I recognized the tiles instantly—not because I'd seen *these* before, but because they carried the same design elements as the tiles at the Wrigley Mansion in Phoenix. Hand-painted ceramic. Catalina clay. Heavy glaze. Colors chosen to survive salt air and time.

I stepped closer, unwilling to miss a single detail.

The first panel showed two parrots, their bodies angled toward each other as if caught mid-conversation. One was pale, its colors soft greens and yellows. The other scarlet and cobalt with flashes of gold. They weren't mirror images. They were opposites sharing a branch. Balance through contrast. Was the artist trying to tell me something?

I felt the familiar prickle between my shoulders. Paired imagery always drew me. In jewelry, in history, and in families.

The next tile tightened my chest. I'd seen the imagery before. I reached for Merle's diary and skimmed a few pages. My ah-ha moment came a minute later with heart-pounding clarity. "Look."

Rocky whistled. Merle had drawn the same two scarlet macaws pressed so close their feathers overlapped.

Rocky typed on his phone. "The *Catalina Double Scarlet Macaw* was created by the Catalina Tile Company in the early 1930s."

"Merle's drawing is from September 1929." I scanned the next few pages. "Here's the green parrot." I showed him the drawing, details exact. "And the twin toucans with the outer green border."

"All dated 1929?"

I nodded. Merle had designed these tiles. I was sure of it. But the timing didn't track. Merle had been in Europe in the 1930s.

I took another long look at the macaw tile. The bold reds, yellows, and blues drew the eye, but the tile itself felt kind of unsettling in the way the birds seemed to peer right through you. These birds appeared to be guarding something.

Intrigued, I turned to the green parrot. It perched alone, hunched, head dipped, gaze turned inward. The bird felt... lonely. On the next tile, two toucans, their oversized beaks cutting through a sky washed in lavender and yellow, faced the horizon together.

A thought clicked into place. Was I reading too much into this? Rocky was definitely going to think I was crazy. "These tiles seem to tell the Waters twins' story," I said quietly. "First, they are together. Then divided. Then, standing guard over a necklace they were charged to protect."

He didn't laugh. He folded his arms and studied the sequence again.

"The twins came from a long line of tile makers..." I let my thought linger before I asked, "Which artisan created these tiles?"

Rocky referred to his phone. "The Catalina Tile Company

doesn't credit a single artist. According to this, the designs came out of the company's in-house studio, which was a team of artisans."

"There has to be a list of the employees," I muttered.

"Maybe," he said mildly. "The problem is that most of the Catalina Tile Company's design logs didn't survive after the plant shut down in the late '30s. When the Great Depression hit, operations slowed, and records vanished."

I glanced back at the tiles. "Someone has to know."

"The Catalina Museum has Catalina tile experts..." Rocky suggested.

My gaze dropped back to the cards. Not exactly messages, but possibly proof of life and place. If I was right, Melodie left a trail only someone who knew what to watch for would recognize. Time for me to pick up the trail on Catalina Island.

I leaned back slowly, my heart still racing. "Why would Melodie go back to Catalina? It seems too risky."

Rocky's eyes lifted to mine. "Perhaps she left something behind."

Before I could noodle that idea, an alert pinged on my phone. *Tracking signal lost.* Michael Wise's dot vanished from the map, as if it had never existed.

A curse just slipped out. "He found it." The hair at the back of my neck prickled. The room suddenly felt too open, too exposed.

"Who found what?" Rocky asked, his gaze keen.

I started to speak but stopped. Placing a stealth tracker was not something you admitted to a lawman, especially one on the same case. I wasn't getting away with a brush off, either, I realized. "I, uh... I tagged Michael Wise at the club."

"You what?"

Rocky had heard me. The sudden anger in his silver eyes said so. I stepped backward, not in fear; I needed to get my facts straight.

"You could've jeopardized our investigation," he finally said.

"Not mine. In all fairness, I didn't know you were involved."

"Tell that to the judge."

"I don't live under the same rules you do. My job is to recover the stolen bracelet by any means I can," I replied.

"Without breaking the law."

I nodded, crossing my fingers anyway. Some things were better left unsaid. I operated in the gray area. He couldn't. I changed the subject. "Do you want to know what I learned?"

Rocky nodded.

"Michael Wise went from the golf club to his jewelry store, then to a cigar shop and home. The signal vanished at home."

"It could be as simple as the shirt went in the washing machine," Rocky suggested.

I conceded the possibility with a nod. "Except I tagged his pant leg."

"A pant leg? How did you do that?" A wry smile tugged at his lips as he scratched Glimmer's head. "I see. She's making you a delinquent now, too. Isn't she?"

How did he always know? "Glimmer's a great wing woman." I rolled my eyes at Glimmer's head toss. "I still feel like someone's watching me." I moved to the cabinet tucked beside the window. Opened it and pulled out a pair of night-vision glasses.

Rocky's brows shot up. "Please tell me you don't just keep those lying around."

"I don't," I said, handing him a second pair. "I keep them ready. Look."

He hesitated, then lifted them to his eyes. His posture stiffened. "The car across the square with its lights off. There's someone inside."

"Watching." I texted Hope before the thought could settle. *Use the safe entry.*

Rocky lowered the glasses slowly. "I can't decide if I'm impressed or deeply concerned."

"Both," I said. "You should be."

The door behind us opened without a sound. Rocky spun

just as Hope stepped in, dressed head-to-toe in black, hood up, the silhouette unmistakably female. She held a small dog carrier as if it weighed nothing.

"How did you get here?" For an FBI undercover investigator who prided himself on controlling every variable, the last five minutes had rattled him.

Hope brushed a cobweb from her sleeve with a shiver. "Old bootlegger's passage. Runs from the assayer's office next door straight into this building. Remind me to burn these clothes." She set the carrier down and met my eyes. "There's a suitcase in my car for you. Sophie has a plane waiting at Scottsdale Airport. You'll fly to Burbank tonight. Drop the demantoid garnets at the lab in the morning. Then you go on to Catalina."

I nodded, though a knot tightened in my chest. The plan snapped into place with brutal efficiency.

Rocky stared between us. "And me?"

Hope tilted her head. "You get to choose—escort or decoy."

"You two are switching places?" His tone made the idea sound ridiculous.

Hope's smile agreed without words. "I'm sure you've seen *The Parent Trap*? I liked the original with Hayley Mills. Hunter liked the remake. I think it was..."

"Dennis Quaid," I replied. "And the wine." Our repartee wasn't helping. Rocky wasn't amused.

"Relax. We've done it for years," Hope said calmly. "You're one of the few people who can tell us apart."

Rocky rubbed his jaw. "What about the dog?"

Hope unzipped the carrier. A blond dachshund slipped out, nearly Glimmer's twin with the same alert eyes and confidence. She stretched, shook, then Glimmer met her with a decisive head-butt. Tails wagged in perfect sync.

"Meet Dee," Hope said. "The decoy. She's Glimmer's shadow in training."

Rocky leaned back, stunned. "You two have this all figured out."

"Twins are double trouble," I said, though the words rang hollow.

"Tell me about it," Hope replied dryly. "I've got two of my own." She let that sit for a minute before adding, "You've got forty-eight hours, sis, before my husband calls uncle."

"The man's a wimp," I shot back. Hank was still in the doghouse after working with his old gambling ring. The fact that Hope had forgiven him at all still surprised me.

"I'm starting to understand how he feels," Rocky muttered, raking his fingers through his hair. Then his gaze sharpened. "What exactly is your plan?"

"Are you coming with me or staying?" I asked.

"Since we don't know how long our friends have been watching," he said, "I leave as planned. Commercial back to L.A."

Always practical. Disappointment hit harder than it should have. "I know you're right."

"Of course I am," he said. "That's not the question. What's your plan in Catalina? What are you looking for? How do you execute?"

All good questions. I opened my mouth and stopped.

"You don't know." Rocky exhaled. "Good looks and intuition won't stop a man like Christian Weber."

I swallowed. Doubt crept in, unwelcome but familiar. I'd leaned on instinct my whole career, trusted that inner nudge to steer me clear of disaster. But Dad's revelation of how he'd watched me from the shadows, helped when I needed it, and pushed when I hesitated, still echoed. Had those instincts really been mine... or his all along?

We'd stopped his nemesis together to recover the Fire Diamond. Dad didn't need to protect me anymore. If he ever truly had. And if he was still out there after the injury, I was afraid for him. Afraid that whatever came next would reach him before I could.

"You're right," I said with manufactured bravado. "I have the clues to pick up Melodie's trail."

"Which will be hard enough to follow without someone hunting you," Rocky said. Glimmer tilted her head, unimpressed. Even she seemed unconvinced.

"What about jurisdiction?" I asked.

"There's... an ethics issue."

The words hit me harder than they should have. "How's that?" I asked, a thread of unease working its way in.

"We..." Rocky pointed at me, then back at himself. "...can't work together."

"Why? We work well together. And we already..."

His brow lifted just enough to stop me. Heat crept up my neck. Right. *That.* I folded my arms, trying to look less disappointed than I felt.

"Find me an actionable link in Catalina," his voice softened, "and I'll figure something out."

Rocky Rockman. The man who followed rules like they were carved in stone. And yet... the way he looked at me suggested he might be considering bending one.

Our eyes locked, the moment stretching. Too much unsaid. Behind us, Hope cleared her throat loudly and announced something about walking the dogs. A second later, she vanished.

I took a deep breath. "This is my life."

"You're good at it." Rocky's fingertips skimmed my lips. "Be careful."

His kiss lingered longer than he did, a next-time promise already a casualty of circumstances we couldn't or wouldn't control. Story of us, really. We excelled at the almost, the moments loaded with everything we didn't say, that meant too much and got us nowhere.

Building a "we" took more than chemistry and proximity between crises. It took two people willing to stop choosing the exit. I wanted to believe "we" were possible. But wanting had never been our problem. Everything that came after was.

Chapter Twelve

HOW YOU GET THERE MATTERS LESS THAN THAT YOU ARRIVE— WISDOM FROM A JEWEL THIEF

SUNDAY, 1 P.M.

Glimmer pressed tight against my leg. I stroked her ears and murmured reassurances as we flew over the San Pedro Channel toward the mountain silhouette barely visible through the thick marine-layer haze.

I settled back into the Beechcraft King Air's leather seats. A big upgrade from the Twin Otters Sophie and I had flown across Africa. Not that I complained back then. Those stripped-down workhorses had their own appeal. They didn't care if the runway was more suggestion than fact. The King Air couldn't compete with a flashier Lear, but it delivered enough comfort for two passengers who needed to arrive clear-headed and ready to work.

As we approached, the island rose from a blur into sharp ridges and sunlit cliffs. It seemed to have its own eco system away from the mainland, a magical clarity, so to speak. The pilot banked, revealing Avalon tucked into its crescent harbor, the white curves of the Casino gleaming at the shoreline, Wrigley's mansion standing guard above pastel buildings and scattered boats. It looked idyllic, probably exactly what Melodie had seen when she'd stepped off the boat in 1929.

Avalon during Hollywood's heyday must have been something else, with movie stars arriving by steamer, jazz spilling into the night, and illicit cocktails flowing. After reading more of Merle's diary, I understood why Melodie risked returning. She'd been happy here. Some places let you hide in plain sight. Others call you back with memories stronger than fear, and you go anyway, despite the risk.

As the King Air skimmed past the harbor and climbed inland, the island turned rugged and quiet. The Airport in the Sky appeared at the last moment atop a 1,602-foot-tall mountain, our pilot informed me, located 10 miles from Avalon. The narrow airstrip had been constructed by leveling two adjacent peaks and then using the debris to fill the gaps. Except for another Beechcraft parked beside an aluminum stand-up hangar, we were alone as we touched down.

Before the rotors' thrum-whup-whup-whup faded, a dust-coated white SUV rolled up. A woman stepped out, wearing dirt-caked hiking boots, khaki pants, and a long-sleeved shirt. Her expression stayed neutral, but her posture carried a trace of irritation, the look of someone who'd been volunteered for a job she considered beneath her.

"Taylor Hunter?" she asked.

Best I left my who-else-did-you-expect remark unsaid. "Hunter, please. And this is Glimmer, the diamond dog."

The hiker's mouth twitched as she glanced at the yawning dachshund. "Seriously? That dog finds diamonds?"

"That she does."

"If you say so." She folded her arms, her skepticism clear. "You've got friends in high places. I was ordered to assist you however I could."

Sophie, call in favors? We'd decided I'd go in under the radar. "You can start by telling me who you are."

"Sorry. I've only just arrived from the interior myself. Ellie Horne. I'm a historian at the Catalina Museum. My executive director requested I assist you."

"Are you a Catalina tile expert?"

"We have an extensive collection at the museum. I'll connect you with the right people."

Ellie waved me toward the SUV. I followed until Glimmer's low growl stopped me mid-step. My guard came up fast as my gaze swept the surroundings. No one around. No cameras. No movement. Nothing obviously wrong.

Then I found the bumper sticker. A Siamese cat, stretched in full smug glory. *Catitude.*

I nearly choked on my chuckle. Glimmer didn't dislike cats so much as she believed the question of dominance required regular revisiting. No time for debate today, I tucked the dachshund under my arm and climbed into the passenger seat. My dog struggled at first, finally settling into my lap with a healthy dose of dachshund attitude.

Ellie pretended not to notice. She reached behind the seat and handed me a small, corrugated shipping box. "This arrived on the ferry from Long Beach for you."

I didn't need to open the package. The weight felt familiar and comforting at once. While California's concealed carry laws didn't allow me to carry a weapon even while on a case, a taser was allowed. This one had a few extras that were not specifically forbidden by the penal code.

We left the Airport in the Sky, the SUV threading through rolling hills and low scrub that fell away into steep drop-offs. Ellie turned tour guide as we passed Black Jack Junction, then Middle Ranch—something about eucalyptus trees and the first Mrs. Wrigley planting them for shade. I nodded. The words registered somewhere behind the noise in my head.

Something or someone was coming. I couldn't name it. Couldn't shake it either. That particular twinge in my gut I'd learned not to ignore. With every curve toward Avalon, another slice of pristine coastline appeared, a reminder that Catalina's beauty came with conditions.

As we passed the zip line and began the descent into town, tile roofs poked through the canopy about the same time the afternoon sun sparkled off the harbor.

Ellie finally asked the question that had been on her mind since we'd met. "Are you really looking for diamonds lost at the Casino opening almost a hundred years ago?"

I met her eyes in the rearview mirror. "Lost," I said carefully, "is one word for it." Glimmer shifted in my lap, ears alert.

Ellie cleared her throat. "After all this time, how do you expect to find them?"

That question I wished I could answer. "Retrace steps and hope for a link from the past that shows me the way today." Spoken aloud, the chances for success seemed impossible. I didn't begrudge Ellie an eyeroll.

She exhaled instead, affected by my honesty. "You're going to need all the help and luck you can get. Avalon might be a small town on an even smaller island, but it isn't exactly an open book. I see why my boss asked me to assist you. I'm an islander." She must've read my confusion. "A third-generation Catalina resident."

A glimmer of hope lit. Trust Sophie to find me a guide to navigate this small town's politics. I just needed to convince Ellie that the quest was worth it.

"What exactly are we looking for?" Ellie asked.

"A starlet who disappeared at the casino opening. She supposedly fell off the SS Catalina."

"You're talking about Melodie Waters. My great-grandfather worked on the steamship. Her disappearance was the only safety issue in the ship's 50-year history. Am I to understand you think she didn't drown?" I'd sparked Ellie's interest.

"That's what I'm here to investigate."

"Did Ms. Waters stay at the St. Catherine?" Ellie asked.

"The hotel she stayed at had cats in the ladies' room," I replied.

Ellie smiled for the first time, brightening her whole face.

"That'll be the Metropole. The wallpaper is iconic. Mrs. Wrigley…"

Like that said it all. "Can you make me a reservation and see if I can stay in the same room Melodie stayed in?" I asked. No particular reason why. Just a feeling.

"The hotel has been renovated dozens of times since 1929. I hardly think anything would be the same, including the view."

"The feeling will be," I replied.

Ellie shrugged. "I assume you'll want to tour the Casino."

I nodded.

"The 2:30 backstage Casino tour is generally sold out when the cruise ships are in town. I'll see if I can get the Casino's Director of Operations to take you on a private tour. If anyone can help you, he can. He lives in the upstairs apartment overlooking Avalon harbor and is the resident expert on everything past and present that occurred there."

"I bow to your expertise."

She smiled. "Anything else you'd like to see?"

"The old aviary."

"That's easy. Why? There's not much there anymore."

"I'm interested in the bird tiles."

Ellie nodded. "OK. We'll park near the Metropole and drop your bags at the hotel. You can look around while I work on your room."

I didn't grasp the significance until we approached Avalon and the SUV eased through the tight curves carved into the hillside where homes clung to the slope, stacked and staggered wherever the rock allowed. The road remained no wider than the winding stretches we'd driven from the island's center. Here, golf carts and the occasional four-wheel-drive truck hugged the curbs, making it nearly impossible for two vehicles to pass.

When Ellie parked on Marilla Avenue, just shy of Casino Way, I understood why. From there, Avalon belonged to pedestrians. Even golf carts only went so far. If I wanted answers, I'd have to walk the rest of the way myself.

The fountain at the roundabout gave me my first taste of the island's indigenous Catalina tile. Both the gloss and pattern reminded me of the tile style I'd seen throughout the Wrigley Mansion in Phoenix. I needed to find the murals.

To the left, the Casino arch framed the iconic Casino—bright, unmistakable, and despite its name, never a gambling hall, but a grand dance and entertainment venue. A green fence split Steps Beach from the walkway. Shops curved along the harbor, striped awnings shading their glass fronts. Music drifted from the Green Pier, and beyond it a cruise ship loomed, dwarfing the smaller boats clustered in the harbor.

While the waterfront buzzed with tourists wandering wide-eyed, I saw the undercurrent right away, subtle but clear. Locals didn't linger. They met Ellie's eyes, nodded, and moved on. No small talk. Avalon might look welcoming, but outsiders stayed on the edge. If I wanted answers, I'd have to blend in—something I should've warned Glimmer about.

She sensed something the moment we reached the harbor walkway. Her subtle snap to full alert, ears forward, tail rigid, nose sorting through everything the breeze carried off the water, told me she was tracking. I held her in check and followed her line of sight, looking for whatever drew her attention.

"Just so you know," Ellie said, unaware, "dogs aren't allowed on the beach or inside the Casino."

"She's a working dog," I replied automatically.

"She's not a police dog or a service dog. You'll need to request an exception," Ellie replied.

Dog-friendly apparently had its limits. I'd deal with the Casino access later with charm, credentials, or outright persistence. Glimmer needed to get in there, so I had to make that happen. But first things first. "Where did the steamships arrive in 1929?"

Ellie frowned, then gestured to the building directly in front of us. Sailor's Delight Ice Cream with its hanging cone, the Blue Water Grill, and the waterfront all resided there. "Two thousand passengers arrived on every ferry. The pier would've been packed with porters, luggage, and crowds pouring off the ships. Coin divers would've been in the water, too."

We paused at the low wall above the sand and water. I'd come to Avalon with one goal: to stay unseen. I would've chosen shadows over scenery, somewhere I could watch without becoming part of the view. But Avalon didn't offer much privacy. Tourists crowded the rail, arms stretched high, phones angled toward the harbor, toward each other, toward anything worth posting. Maybe toward me.

Every lens felt like a risk. Every click shaved seconds off the window I had to track Melodie without company. Glimmer wasn't comfortable for a different reason, though. She tugged at the leash, restless, her nose scanning the air as if she'd found something. And the last thing I needed was for anyone to notice.

"Not now," I murmured. Glimmer ignored me.

She somehow caught me off guard, slipped free of my hold, and bolted, straight for the stairs leading to the beach. Before I could react, she bounded down, hit the wet sand near the waterline, and started digging, fast and furiously, sending sand flying like debris from a hurricane as a small crowd gathered, whispers rippling outward. *What's the dog doing?*

Ellie swore under her breath. "This isn't... you need to control your dog." She'd seen the uniformed deputy coming our way, too.

Great. Less than an hour on the island, and we were already being noticed. I didn't stop Glimmer. With all the phones focused on her, we'd already been spotted. Whatever she found had better be worth it.

As the deputy approached, the dachshund's nose disappeared into the hole in the sand. Then she stopped, sat back, and barked once.

"She's found something. Hang on a minute," I said before I joined the dachshund on the sand. I dropped to my knees as she plunged her head back into the hole, her front feet vanishing up to her shoulders. When she emerged, she dropped something heavy and bright into my palm. The crowd sucked in a collective breath as I brushed away the sand. An elegant single, one-carat, give or take, emerald step-cut diamond ring set in a simple platinum setting sparkled between my forefinger and thumb. Nothing particularly unusual about it. Brides chose the traditional rectangular cut all the time. Why had Glimmer focused on this particular ring? What was she trying to tell me? The question tugged at me until the light caught a faint inscription inside the band.

"Forever one. Casey."

The deputy's jaw dropped. So did Ellie's. "I take it you know the owner," I said unnecessarily as I handed him the ring.

Suddenly, not only was Ellie a believer, but everyone else was too, and our stealth visit to Catalina Island, thanks to the camera-ready cruise ship visitors, had just gone viral. Whoever had stolen Merle's bracelet now knew exactly where I was and what I was looking for.

Chapter Thirteen

NEVER DISCOUNT LUCK, JUST BE
PREPARED FOR THE CONSEQUENCES
—WISDOM FROM A JEWEL THIEF

SUNDAY, 1 P.M.

By the time I settled into my suite at the Hotel Metropole, Catalina had already made up its mind about Glimmer and, by extension, me. People whispered and pointed at us as we walked toward the hotel. Others stopped us. They all had one thing in common: they needed something recovered.

Going viral didn't happen in a matter of minutes. The attention surprised me until Ellie explained that the diamond ring Glimmer recovered belonged to a beloved islander, who'd lost it while proposing to his girlfriend six months ago. The shock wasn't that Glimmer uncovered it. It was that no one else had. For weeks, that same beach had been combed, metal detectors sweeping grids mapped like crime scenes, and still it stayed hidden. Diamonds, in my experience, were like that. They surfaced when they were good and ready. In this case, I called it karma. Glimmer-style.

Good thing, because Catalina had unwritten rules. A *local* lived here but wasn't an *islander*, whose family had lived here for generations. The distinction mattered. Fortunately, I'd landed with the islanders, the ones who remembered and who didn't

121

forget favors or slights. Which meant if Melodie had left anything behind, I'd be aligned with the right group to find it—if they chose to share.

Inside the Hotel Metropole, our popularity continued. The hotel manager personally greeted us at the door. "You're the dog who helped find Casey's grandmother's diamond ring." The sandy-haired man's comment got my attention, but he'd continued before I could question him further. "We take care of our friends here." Glimmer acknowledged the comment with regal calm.

The manager dropped his voice after sharing a knowing glance with Ellie. "I understand you would like to stay in a specific room. Our hotel historian is searching our registration archives for the exact room as we speak. If you don't mind waiting..." He motioned a waiter to hand me a glass of champagne. "Please have a seat. It shouldn't be long."

Ellie departed to commandeer a golf cart, Catalina's answer to Vespas in Rome, promising to return shortly to escort me to the old aviary. Bubbles tickled my nose as I sipped the drink, fully aware of the eyes on me as I explored the elegantly modern lobby. The Hotel Metropole certainly defined boutique-elegant with polished wood floors, framed black-and-white photographs, and a bifurcated staircase that split into two directions at a central landing, updated just enough to be comfortable without completely vanquishing the ghosts. The banister even felt smooth beneath my hand, worn by generations of guests who'd climbed it with trunks, hatboxes, and dreams. Somewhere beneath the modern lighting, this place managed to be a retreat where people came to disappear for a while.

A few minutes later, the manager returned, announcing his success with a broad smile and a keycard. I thanked him. "The ring Glimmer recovered, you said it was a family heirloom?"

He nodded. "His grandmother's diamond. She gave it to him for his future wife."

"The setting was modern."

The manager shrugged. "I'm sure Grandma will love to meet Glimmer and thank her personally. Her shop is on the harbor toward the Green Pier."

Was this anything or just a lucky find? My intuition told me nothing as I followed the bellman to my room. Whether the room had actually been Melodie's mattered less than getting into her head, understanding why she'd loved this island and what, despite the risks of being found, had drawn her back.

The newly refurbished waterfront mini-suite offered a spectacular view of the Casino from its private balcony. I stood out on it despite the cool afternoon breeze, my gaze scanning the harbor, habit more than paranoia. Boats rocked gently below, enough pirate flags flying from masts and outriggers to kick up my pulse rate. Tourists drifted along Casino Way toward music and activity. But beauty had edges here. And I felt them. For a moment, I could almost see Melodie, the rising starlet, standing here, watching the same water and weighing her choices.

As I closed the balcony door, I knew the Teutonic Knights were coming. I could feel it. Whatever the Waters' diamonds led to had to be big enough to bring this long-quiet group out of the shadows.

I'd come to Catalina to find answers that someone was willing to kill for. Now, time was the enemy. I removed a nondescript baseball cap from my carry-on bag and pulled it over my eyes as I rested a hand on Glimmer's back, drawing comfort from her steady warmth. We'd faced this kind of danger before, just never with so many curious eyes watching.

"Okay," I murmured. "Let's get started. We don't have much time."

Glimmer opened one eye, tail thumping once. *Ready.* I hoped it would be enough.

Ellie met us at the Metropole Café. "No time to stop. The Casino's Director of Operations is waiting to give you and Glimmer a private tour before the afternoon crowds show up."

I scooped up Glimmer with my free hand and climbed into a

four-seater golf cart that had seen better days. Whatever color it had started life as had disappeared under a fine coating of island dust.

Ellie handed me a deli-wrapped hoagie. "You'd better eat fast." A half-eaten sandwich in her left hand, Ellie grabbed the wheel. The golf cart lurched toward Casino Way. She swung around, shot under the Casino archway, and gunned it straight for the landmark.

I managed two bites of the turkey sub and slipped Glimmer a prime piece of meat before Ellie skidded to a stop at the entrance.

The Avalon Casino rose before us like an Art Deco treasure. White walls curved into a perfect cylinder. "Twelve stories." Ellie's voice slipped into docent mode. "Built in 1929. The curves aren't decorative. They guide the eye upward." She pointed toward the pillared crown. "That balcony? Fourteen feet wide, wrapping the ballroom. Untouched since opening night."

Her finger lifted higher. "And the cupola. Twenty-five feet above the roofline. Before the war, it glowed with a neon ring. A beacon for the guests." She paused. "Now it's just one bulb. Still does the job."

The Casino stood against the afternoon sky, iconic and immovable, as if it had decided long ago it would outlast everything around it. But it wasn't the architecture holding my attention today.

"The murals are beautiful," I said.

Ellie's smile agreed. "There are nine, designed by John Gabriel Beckman, the same artist who worked on Grauman's Chinese Theatre."

I didn't doubt it. The brilliant blues and greens in the underwater scenes that covered the loggia walls featured swimming fish, swaying California kelp forests, and divers floating amid marine life, all frozen in eternal motion.

"The Casino Mermaid, unlike the Art Deco panels surrounding her, is pure Art Nouveau. Notice the flowing lines and vibrant tiles. The mural was finally tiled in 1986, fifty-seven years after Beckman first designed it."

The whole thing screamed glamour from another era, when people dressed up to see a movie and didn't mind the twenty-six-mile boat ride to get here.

I blinked as we entered the dark entry hall. Glimmer's nose sniffed like mad. Thousands of people had been here. Did she sense something, or was it the man in the entry? In the dim light, he looked familiar enough to make me do a double-take. For a split second, I caught a flicker of a Brad Pitt moment—the kind where he steps through a doorway all quiet confidence and effortless control.

Up close, though, he was simply a well-put-together man in his prime, lean, athletic, and dressed in a fitted dark shirt and tailored slacks. His easy smile and relaxed posture carried the kind of ease that made you look twice... and wonder why.

He stepped forward and extended a hand. "Chuck Lenz. At your service."

"Thank you for seeing us." I took it, noting the strength in his hands.

"My pleasure." He crouched down to pet Glimmer. "You're our little heroine, aren't you? Found Casey's ring. The affair was..." he shook his head, "...for the best."

"I don't understand."

"Casey's girlfriend decided not to marry him when he lost the ring," Ellie replied.

"That's harsh."

"She turned out to be a... It doesn't matter. The ring has been recovered thanks to you." Chuck scratched Glimmer. She gave him her most flirtatious head tilt, ears perked just right.

I smiled. Buttering up the guy who could help us never hurts.

He straightened and got down to business. "Ellie mentioned you're looking into the woman who drowned back in '29. You think she might have lost something here at the Casino?"

"Maybe," I said. "I'm hoping you could tell me how someone

might disappear if they were being chased. Inside the building, I mean."

He stroked his jaw, thinking. "No one was chased on opening night. At least not that made it into any official record or newspaper account. Over ten thousand people showed up for the festivities. If someone was running, they would've been noticed."

"But with that many people and no surveillance cameras..." I let the thought hang.

"We had spotters." He pointed upward. "Up in the rafters with eyes all over the ballroom. They watched for any shenanigans."

The word choice made me smile. "Seriously? Shenanigans?"

"Morality back then was stricter than today," Chuck said like a man who longed for the return of Victorian high collars. "Wrigley didn't want any scandalous behavior in his Casino. The spotters made sure couples kept things appropriate on the dance floor."

I thought of Hope's constant battles over the twins' school wardrobes. Times had definitely changed. "How did they watch without being seen?"

"Binoculars from hidden compartments built into the architecture. I'll show you when we get upstairs." He glanced down at Glimmer, who sat at my feet. "How does this work? Do we just let her roam around, or...?"

I smiled at his concern. "Don't worry. She won't tear through the place like a bloodhound on a scent trail." I ignored both Chuck and Ellie's raised brows. "She only hunts on command. Most of the time." No denying my dachshund's impromptu beach dig this afternoon. "Some stones just want to be found," I added lightly. "Think of her as a very well-behaved tourist right now."

"Good to know." Chuck opened the heavy wooden door into the theater wider. "Let's start with the theater level and work our way up."

We stepped into the Avalon Theatre, and I stopped short.

Even though I'd known what to expect from photos, the sheer glamour took my breath away.

Red velvet seats arranged in perfect rows beneath a domed ceiling that soared overhead like the inside of a cathedral. Black walnut paneling lined the lower walls, while murals swept across them in geometric patterns and vibrant colors, depicting scenes from Catalina's history, interspersed with figures that seemed to dance in the half-light.

"Impressive, isn't it?" Chuck said. "First theater in the world built specifically for talkies. Wrigley spared no expense."

Ellie added additional historic details. "There are 1,184 seats. The place was designed with acoustics so good that Radio City Music Hall copied them. There are no speakers either. The ceiling's shape carries every whisper to the back row."

Clearly, this wasn't just a movie house. It was a statement that didn't hold Glimmer's interest at all. Her nails clicked on the polished floor as she sniffed the space with professional interest. She only started pulling on the leash when we reached the ballpark-style ramps leading to the upper level.

"Wrigley borrowed this design from his baseball stadium," Chuck said. "No stairs meant thousands of dancers could get up and down without creating a traffic jam. Imagine getting ten thousand people up there."

The enclosed space felt utilitarian compared to the glamour below. Just smooth concrete underfoot and institutional beige walls. The steady upward grade made my calves burn.

"How many of these ramps are there?" I asked.

"Six total. We're climbing the equivalent of twelve stories." He glanced back at Glimmer, who was trotting ahead with her nose working overtime. "Is she picking up anything?"

"Not yet." We rounded the final turn into a small lobby area just below the ballroom level.

"Here's where it gets interesting." He pushed open the door, and we stepped into the Casino Ballroom.

I stopped. Glimmer stood beside me.

"Twenty thousand square feet," Chuck said. "World's largest circular ballroom. No support pillars anywhere."

The space opened up around us in a massive, perfect circle. Rose-hued walls rose to an eighteen-foot arched ceiling where five enormous Art Deco chandeliers hung like crystal constellations. The dance floor stretched before us, an intricate pattern of maple, white oak, and rosewood that gleamed under the soft light.

"It's floated," he continued, walking onto the floor. His footsteps made almost no sound. "Engineered for elegance. Built on cork strips. Muffled the sound of three thousand dancers so the moviegoers below wouldn't hear a thing."

I moved onto the floor. Solid, but with the slightest give.

"See those?" He pointed to raised seating areas that ringed the dance floor. "Perfect vantage points. Downstairs..." he gestured toward the exit, "...the Marine Bar served soda. Not a drop of alcohol. Wrigley's rules."

"And Prohibition," Ellie added.

French doors lined the entire perimeter, leading to what had to be the promenade.

"The spotters," I said. "Where were they?"

He pointed to shadows near the ceiling. "They had binoculars trained on the floor at all times. Watching for couples getting too cozy, people causing trouble, anything out of place."

"You're right." I agreed. "If someone ran through here..."

"They would've seen and reported it." He crossed his arms. "Which is why I find your theory interesting. Because there's no record of anything unusual that night. Not in the ballroom, anyway."

I looked at Glimmer. "Let's see what she finds."

Glimmer's front paws vibrated against the floor. Not from the ghostly echo of thousands of dancers—she'd locked onto something real.

I pulled the Duette's clasp case from my crossbody bag and held it to her nose. "Glimmer, hunt."

Chuck and Ellie went still, watching as the dachshund shot

forward like she'd been fired from a cannon. Her nails clicked rapid-fire across the polished wood as she crisscrossed the circular room, her nose working overtime, picking up traces invisible to the rest of us.

The dog covered the perimeter. Doubled back. Zigzagged through the center.

Then she stopped dead in the middle of the dance floor. The dachshund rose onto her hind legs and barked—one sharp, definitive sound that ricocheted off the fifty-foot ceiling like a whole pack had spoken.

"She found something," I said unnecessarily.

Footsteps echoed from the hallway. Staff, I guessed based on their uniforms—appeared in the doorway. Ellie's whisper hadn't drawn them. The bark had. A sound that probably had never been heard in here.

Chuck stared at Glimmer, then at the exact spot where she stood, his excitement deflating. "We've renovated this flooring at least a dozen times over the years. There's nothing underneath."

But Glimmer stayed up on her hind legs, nose pointed upward, body quivering with certainty.

I followed her gaze to the center lighting fixture directly above us. Not a chandelier like the five hanging in the room. An Art Deco centerpiece carved from wood with four lights suspended from it, geometric and elegant. The kind of thing you'd stare at while dancing, mesmerized by the rotating colors.

"It's not below," I said. "It's above."

Ellie shook her head. "That's impossible. The center fixture was replaced in 1936. Melodie Waters drowned in '29."

I watched Glimmer. She hadn't moved. Hadn't dropped to all fours. Her focus remained locked on that fixture.

"Glimmer can distinguish diamonds in a fifty-foot radius," I said. "What she's sensing might not be inside the fixture itself. It could be near it, behind it, or above it. But I can tell you with certainty there are diamonds up there." I glanced down at my dog, still statue-still on her hind legs. "And she's never wrong."

At least, I hoped not.

Chuck turned to Ellie. "You're right about most of the lighting being replaced. I'd never question your knowledge of Casino history." He looked back up at the center fixture. "But those original tube lights have never been changed. We've never disturbed the housing to replace the bulbs."

Perfect. What better place to hide a stolen bracelet than somewhere nobody could reach?

But the question gnawed at me: Why hadn't Melodie retrieved it? Was I wrong in believing that she'd returned to Catalina? Unless someone or something had stopped her. "How do we get up there?"

Glimmer dropped to all fours and did. She stayed at my side as we crossed the ballroom and exited a door to the right side of the stage. We walked to a plain brown door with a posted no tres-passing sign. The door had no door handles, just a simple padlock. Not my security-minded self's favorite deterrent, but something.

A concrete staircase rose into darkness.

"Not many people know this exists." Chuck switched on his cellphone light. Ellie and I followed, illuminating the area with our own phone lights. "It accesses the roof's structural supports above the ballroom ceiling."

"How could Melodie have gotten up here?" Ellie voiced my exact question.

"I'm asking myself the same thing." Chuck swept his light across the beams. "This access wasn't public knowledge."

"Unless someone told her," I said.

He stopped at a broom-closet-sized opening cut into the framework. From here, a narrow gap in the ballroom ceiling offered a perfect view straight down to the dance floor below.

"One of the spotters' stations," he said.

Ideal work for a voyeur. Even in the dim light, I could see the geometric pattern of the floor far below. Every couple who'd ever waltzed across that polished wood had been visible from up here.

"Surveillance, 1929," Ellie murmured. "Not so different from today."

"Except today we record it," I said.

Chuck nodded. "Any one of the spotters could've told her about this place or shown her the way up. Maybe even helped her hide."

Which meant Melodie hadn't acted alone. She'd had someone on the inside... someone who knew the Casino's secrets, who had access to places the public never saw.

Suddenly, it all made sense. Mr. Fox had found her. She'd slipped away from him in the crowd, but for some reason was afraid to go for the exit. "Do you have a list of the spotters that night?"

Ellie shrugged. "I have no idea. I'll check the records."

We climbed single file into the rafters, Chuck, me with Glimmer tucked under one arm, then Ellie. The air grew warmer and stuffier. When we emerged at the top, Chuck swept his light across the space.

I stopped and stared.

Above the elegant fifty-foot dome that ballroom dancers had admired for nearly a century was a completely different world. A complex lattice of beams crisscrossed the space like a giant game of pick-up sticks. Thick structural supports, painted rust-orange, ran diagonally and horizontally, creating triangular patterns that recurred into the shadows. Metal pipes, ventilation, and electrical conduits snaked between the beams in parallel lines.

"It's like the skeleton of the building," Ellie whispered.

"Exactly what it is," Chuck said. "Steel frame, wooden supports. This is what holds up the ballroom floor, the ceiling, the roof above us."

I didn't look down. Not once.

The urge clawed at me anyway, insistently sending a prickling sensation through my toes that made my breath hitch. Not quite pins and needles. Worse. Sheer awareness.

Fifty feet of empty air waited below the narrow catwalk. I

locked my gaze on the beam ahead and kept moving, each step deliberate and controlled. My pulse still ran too fast.

Heights and I had a deal—I didn't acknowledge them, and they didn't get inside my head. Tonight, they pushed their luck.

I set Glimmer down on the narrow catwalk. The space between beams dropped away into darkness, straight down to the ballroom ceiling below. One wrong step and she'd go through.

"Glimmer, hunt," I ordered.

The dachshund didn't hesitate. Nose to the ground, she picked her way along the narrow walkway with the confidence of a dog who'd been trained on uneven terrain her whole life. I followed, refusing to let the drop exist at all.

The center light fixture had to be somewhere in this maze. And if Melodie Waters had hidden her half of the Duette bracelet up here in 1929, she'd walked these same beams.

The question was: Had she walked back out?

Anticipation surged as Glimmer made a beeline for the Casino's center point, her sharp bark echoing through the rafters.

I followed, still refusing to look down as a tingling crept into my toes, that familiar warning I ignored on principle. Focus forward. One step at a time.

Chuck hurried after her, waving Ellie and me back as he crouched beside the light fixture housing. He brushed away at least an inch of dust. "I can't imagine how she got a bracelet inside this. The casing's solid metal, and the opening's barely wide enough for the bulbs."

I leaned over his shoulder, carefully keeping my gaze fixed on the metal, not the drop below. He was right. The gap couldn't have been more than half an inch. No way the entire Duette bracelet could fit in there.

But Glimmer was never wrong.

"It's something," I said, uncertainty creeping into my voice for the first time, "connected to Melodie Waters."

Chuck took me at my word. He pulled a multi-tool from his pocket, selected a thin blade, and carefully scored along the seam of the casing. The old metal resisted, then gave way with a screech.

Ellie aimed her phone light into the opening. The reflection nearly blinded us.

"Diamonds," I breathed. Relief hit hard, strong enough to quiet the tingling in my toes. For a moment, the drop below didn't exist. Only the stones. Not the platinum bracelet. Just the stones.

"Don't touch anything yet," Chuck said, his voice steady despite the slight tremor in his hands. He pried the casing wider, revealing the interior. "We need to document this. And we need to be extremely careful. These have been sitting in here for almost a hundred years. The setting, if there is one, could be fragile."

"Photos first. Every angle," I said.

"I'll film." Ellie moved her phone slowly over the opening. Inside the narrow tube housing, I could see loose diamonds, four in different shapes, catching the light like trapped stars. They sat wedged between the electrical conduit and the metal housing, deliberately placed where they wouldn't interfere with the fixture's operation but would stay hidden.

"She broke the bracelet apart," Ellie suggested. "And took out the stones."

"It looks like it. Wait, what are the dark smudges on the stones?" But I knew even before I handed Chuck my industry fine-pointed tweezers from my toolkit and slipped on blue plastic gloves, forcing my focus on the task. Anything but the open space below, hovering at the edges of my awareness.

"I'm going to extract them one at a time." He tested the tweezers. "Someone needs to spot me and catch them in case I drop them."

"Lock the tips when you clasp the stone." My voice stayed steady as I forced myself to step closer, cupping my hands, ignoring the empty drop below, even as my toes flexed to somehow attach to the narrow footing.

He worked slowly, the tweezers' narrow tips reaching into the gap. The first diamond came free with barely a sound. It was a step-cut emerald stone. The moment the stone fell into my palm, I had my lighted loupe ready. The stone was D-color, maybe a carat, similar to the ring Glimmer had found earlier. "This isn't dirt. It's dried blood."

"Blood!" Ellie looked horrified. "How did she get the diamonds out of the setting to hide them?"

A good question. "Unless she banged her wrist on the beam while escaping." Ellie's light beam flickered around the nearby beams while Chuck extracted the remaining diamonds. Three old-cut rounds, also caked with dried blood. Definitely a match to the stones in the Waters' bracelet that had not been seen since 1929. One thing was certain: Whoever had put them in the light casing didn't want these to be found. Getting right back to: If the Waters didn't want the Duette reunited, who did?

"Only four stones?" Ellie asked. "Where's the platinum setting, the clasp..."

"Somewhere else." I closed my fingers around the stones. "Melodie hid them separately. Safer that way if someone ever did get the bracelet."

Chuck sat back on his heels. "So, the question becomes... where's the rest of it?"

I looked down at the diamonds in my hand. Cold and flawless. Not worth a fortune on their own, but with the bracelet... clearly worth killing for.

Chapter Fourteen

PLANS ARE MADE TO BE CHANGED
—WISDOM FROM A JEWEL THIEF

I stood in the Casino lobby, finally back on solid ground, my breathing easing as my adrenaline faded. Chuck and Ellie disappeared into his office to call the sheriff. I pulled out my phone and dialed Rocky. He picked up on the second ring.

"I have four of the Waters' diamonds with what looks like dried blood on them. Can you take jurisdiction before the L.A. Sheriff does?"

No small talk. Rocky would know the moment his phone lit up that I'd found something.

I imagined him pinching the bridge of his nose while he processed my information.

"Yeah," he said after a beat. "I've asked another agent to officially lead the investigation. After I pass on your information, I'm certain he'll agree with your assessment."

"Does that mean you're off it?" The question slipped out before I could stop it. I felt the loss already. I'd admit it. I'd gotten used to him being there.

"No," he said. "I'm the subject matter expert. I'll make the call." His voice lowered slightly. "Then we'll discuss Glimmer digging up rings on public beaches."

"That wasn't in the plan." The dachshund's find had gone viral faster than I'd imagined.

"Never is with you. What else have you got?" Rocky asked.

"Just the diamonds hidden in the Casino. I'm headed to the old Bird Park now. When can you get here?"

"In a few hours. Watch yourself. We don't know all the players yet."

He disconnected before I could respond. The Teutonic Knights couldn't possibly be on the island this quickly. I texted Hope anyway: *Need you here. Twin thing.*

When I looked up, Ellie stared at me. Not alarmed exactly, but more than a little interested.

"The sheriff wants us to drop the diamonds at his office," she said carefully. "But I imagine you've handled that."

I nodded. "FBI will take jurisdiction within the hour. I'm happy to wait in his office until it's official."

Ellie shook her head. "I told him as much." Her gaze flicked past me, then back. "Hunter... what is this really about?"

"Not here." From what I'd learned, the Casino had a way of holding sound in the most unusual places. I motioned toward the exit.

Glimmer launched herself into the golf cart before I could, tail high, claiming territory. I nudged her aside and slid in next to Ellie.

"The diamonds we found are part of a Duette," I said quietly as the golf cart rolled forward. "Two bracelets designed to lock together and create a necklace." I watched Ellie from the corner of my eye. "One was stolen from the Wrigley Mansion in Phoenix the day before yesterday. A man was murdered over it."

"Murdered?" Her breath caught. She turned to me, real shock breaking through her composure. "And you think someone here was involved?"

The right question. I didn't answer immediately. Because beneath her concern, real and unmistakable, I felt something else. Recognition in the way her eyes sharpened when I'd said Duette.

Ellie knew more than she was letting on, which was good news. That meant Melodie had left a trail. The question wasn't about the diamonds in the Casino anymore. It was whether I could trust the woman beside me to help uncover the rest, or if she'd been protecting this secret long before I set foot on Catalina Island.

"We have enough daylight to reach the old Bird Park." Ellie's gaze stayed fixed on the path ahead.

"Perfect."

I felt the diamonds' cool, constant pressure against my skin in the hidden body pouch I used whenever I was on unfamiliar ground. The stun gun rested at my hip, familiar and ready. Ellie didn't concern me, at least not physically. The unknowns did. Who else on this island knew about the Duette? And how far would they go to keep it buried?

The golf cart hummed uphill past storefronts, giving way to stucco cottages and iron gates. Bougainvillea spilled over walls in reckless pinks and purples. Eucalyptus trees leaned overhead, shedding ribbons of bark like a snake's skin.

We climbed Metropole Avenue, banked right onto Banning, then made a sharp turn onto Avalon Canyon Road. The air turned cooler, thick with fog.

"See that gate?" Ellie slowed as we passed a weathered entrance shaded by large eucalyptus trees. "That's all that's left of Catalina's Bird Park. It houses a preschool now."

The old arched gateway, across the street from the Catalina Island Golf Course, sat back from the road, its tiled roof darkened by fog and time, Spanish curves softened into shadow. Eucalyptus trees towered overhead, pale bark peeling, branches rustling in the light breeze.

Beyond it, the remains of the aviary, once Sugar Loaf Casino, rose in rusted arcs, a vast circular skeleton half-swallowed by fog. Steel ribs curved where dancers once moved, and thousands of birds later filled the air. Today, locked gates and cheerful signs marked it as a preschool. This place wasn't abandoned. It had gone quiet.

I looked past the overgrown plants and rust. Hard to imagine what Ellie described next: the biggest bird park in the world in 1929, nearly eight acres holding eight thousand birds. Free admission because William and Ada Wrigley simply loved birds.

"MGM recorded bird calls here in 1939 for *The Wizard of Oz*." Excitement edged Ellie's comment. "Those creepy noises in the Haunted Forest were Catalina's birds."

"What happened to it?" I asked.

"Pearl Harbor. The island closed during WWII, and tourism never fully recovered. The park shut down in 1966. The birds were relocated to the L.A. Zoo."

I stared at the quiet grounds, fog drifting through where wings once beat. Only the bones remained, breathing freely in Descanso Canyon. Catalina had a way of doing that. It let the past walk alongside you, just close enough to make you wonder who else had stood right here, watching the fog roll in, thinking they were alone.

"I'd like to see the bird tiles, especially the double macaws," I said.

Ellie's forefinger scratched her thumb—her unconscious tell? My gut took notice.

"We need to walk from here." Ellie's tour-guide-smooth voice took over. She pointed to a well-worn path. "The plaza fountain is now in front of Pete's Plaza Café. We should meet there for breakfast."

I nodded. Along the outer wall, cracked stucco and vivid tile panels showed parrots frozen mid-call, their colors tiled brightly against the gray.

"These were made at the Pebbly Beach tile factory in the 1930s. The signature colors are Toyon red, Mandarin yellow, pearly white, and obsidian black. The Toyon was created by mashing the Catalina Island Toyon plant's bright red berries."

My critical gaze settled on the tile's composition. Every angle and curve matched the sketches in Merle's diary. She had either been or knew the artist. The question was whether the birds were just decorative or had they been posed? I traced the seams with my eyes, noting repetition, placement, what was centered, and what was not. Why these birds? Why here? Maybe the tiles were just cheerful remnants of a vanished attraction. Or maybe they were meant to signal something, waiting for someone patient enough to notice what didn't quite belong. Unfortunately, these tiles weren't talking to me at all.

Ellie's next comment crushed that idea. "This tile, like the other bird tiles, was made in the Cuerda Seca style by installing six tiles together to create a single picture. The artist of record was Roger "Bud" Upton."

I looked at her sharply. "I thought you said Catalina Tile staff artists created the bird tiles."

"They created the tables and consumer tiles in the mid to late '30s."

A dead end? I pivoted. "Tell me more about the Catalina Macaw." Ellie's finger-scratch again. I'd hit a nerve.

Ellie smiled faintly, the way locals do when a visitor finally notices what's been hiding in plain sight. "They were bred at the Bird Park. A hybrid, a mix of scarlet and blue-and-gold macaws. They named it after the island because that's where the breeding program took off. Caretakers lived on-site. Some were islanders, some brought in specifically to handle the exotic birds."

My intuition took notice. Could it be that easy? Melodie loved macaws...

"I know where you're going, and I can tell you that there was no woman involved with the birds' care or the breeding process. It wasn't done back then."

"Women took many men's jobs during the war..."

"Not here."

That hit like a punch. "What about twins on the island?" Not that twins were necessarily hereditary, just more likely and definitely generational in our family.

"I-I don't know."

"I think you do." Confronting someone in the middle of nowhere broke my promise to Rocky to be careful, but I couldn't help myself. Glimmer even agreed. She shook her head and stepped between us, my guardian angel at work.

Ellie's hesitation confirmed my suspicions. "What do you know?" I asked.

"I want to help you, Hunter, but you're looking for something that's not here," she stated. "Larry Green arrived in Avalon in 1935. He was a widower with two children. They were twins. A boy and a girl. He was a veterinarian and avid birdwatcher who cared for the birds at the sanctuary. He owned a macaw."

My pulse thumped. "Did this macaw speak?"

"Don't they all?"

Not all in French profanity. Ellie's omission defeated me. Someone would've remarked on that. "Did he stay on the island during the war?"

"No. He enlisted. Spent some time training here on the island before shipping out. I don't know where."

My excitement dropped a degree. "How old was he?"

"I don't know exactly. Middle-aged."

"Who cared for his children while he was overseas?"

"A nanny at first. Then his sister moved in here. She was wheelchair bound but kept up with them. When he returned from the war, he worked on the breeding program."

Maybe I was wrong. Could Mr. Green have been Melodie's husband? If so, what had happened to her? Did he even know about the bracelet's secret?

"Tell me about the bird tables," I said.

"Not much to tell. They were commercial artwork. Green's sister could've been a contributing artist. Back then, there wasn't much work for a disabled person."

Merle had been a good bird artist... Too many pieces didn't fit. Merle had been lost and assumed dead in 1942. If she had survived, what would have caused her to abandon her own daughter?

"What happened to the Green children?"

"The son moved off the island. Someone said he worked for the FBI. I don't know for sure. The daughter stayed. She was a good artist. She sold paintings and cared for her father until his death in 1980."

Ellie had answered my questions, adding nothing more. "What did Mr. Green do after the Bird Park closed?"

"He went to work at the L.A. Zoo until he retired."

"And the daughter, did she marry?"

"Yes. She married the Harbor Master."

"Are you telling me she still lives on the island?" That would make her an islander like Ellie.

"No. She died in 2008."

Of course, she had. She'd be almost ninety-something now. Ellie's grasp of dates astounded me. It was as if she knew these people personally. "Children?" I asked.

Ellie about scratched her thumb raw. "Three daughters."

My patience slipped as the evening fog swirled around my feet. This was about islanders. "You know I'm going to find out..."

Ellie nodded, resigned. "The oldest daughter owns a jewelry store in town. Her husband is a boat captain and tournament fisherman. I went to school with her daughter."

"Why hide this?"

"I wasn't." Her voice dropped. "The ring Glimmer found was hers."

The pieces slid together. Glimmer hadn't found just any ring —she'd found part of the Duette and Casey was part of it.

"Is Casey on the island?"

"No. He lives in L.A. His grandmother picked up the ring from the police station."

The pieces fell tentatively into place. I had planned to ask to test the diamond, but I doubted I needed to. Glimmer had been drawn to the ring because it was part of the Waters' Duette. The dog's senses always astounded me. This one especially so. The real question was whether Melodie's heirs dismantled the bracelet or Melodie herself? No matter what, I'd led the Knights directly to them.

"I can't believe Casey and his grandma are connected to Melodie Waters." Ellie looked shaken. "If what you claim is true, it means an islander's been hiding something for decades."

Or protecting something bigger. And what better place to hide than a remote island where nothing sinister ever happened?

I tempered my response for Ellie's benefit. "They may not be. But they know something about the diamonds from the missing bracelet." A Sophie deep-dive into Larry Green was in order. I checked the time. Midnight in London wasn't too bad.

I looked back at the double macaw tile—twins, mirrored, watching something just beyond the frame. The tiles might not be talking. But the island was.

Chapter Fifteen

THE TRUTH CANNOT BE HIDDEN ONCE
REVEALED—WISDOM FROM A JEWEL THIEF

SUNDAY, 7 P.M.

I met Rocky for dinner at the M Restaurant, the Metropole's coastal Italian spot facing Crescent Street. In the 1920s it had been all formality and fanfare. Now it favored linen-draped wrought-iron tables and easy outdoor views. Some things hadn't changed. Dinner at the Hotel Metropole still moved at an unhurried island pace. The soft glow of lights and muted clink of silverware carried as much meaning as the conversations drifting past.

I felt exposed sitting on the main street, nothing between us and the world but glass and a salt-heavy breeze. Anyone watching would know exactly where I was. Still, with a rugged and armed FBI agent across from me, I felt protected. Even if he drew attention dressed in a tourist's Hawaiian shirt and Dockers.

I'd traded my dusty jeans for clean black ones and a long-sleeved shirt. The sixty-something degree damp air still made me shiver and clung to my skin like a reminder. Catalina didn't let you forget where you were. Or who might be watching.

Glimmer didn't mind the attention. She craned her neck to

peer around the heater, her small body half-blocking the view, as if she were deliberately creating a pocket of privacy. From behind her, the whispers and sidelong looks faded, leaving us momentarily hidden in plain sight.

I rolled my eyes. The lifted chin and self-satisfied stillness promised pure dachshund attitude, which I'd need to deal with later.

For now, I sipped a Buffalo Milk, Catalina's signature cocktail. Usually a martini drinker, the mix of vodka, Kahlua, crème de banana, and half-and-half felt like part of the island bargain. Too sweet for my taste, but an indulgence you tried once, just to say you had.

Across the table, Rocky drank a local Catalina Brewhouse beer, far too relaxed for a man trained to notice everything.

"How did you get here so quickly?" He'd been waiting when Ellie dropped me off in the hotel's lobby.

"I hitched a ride with an LAPD helicopter."

This said a lot about his ability to initiate interagency cooperation in the current atmosphere inherent between local and federal agencies. "How'd the deputy take your taking over the case?" I asked.

"On the surface, not happy, but I couldn't help but feel he was relieved."

"A conspiracy of silence," I murmured. He'd heard me, alert as always.

"Small town," he replied as if that explained away my frustration.

I waited for the server to take our order before speaking. "Casey's diamond is from the Duette." I let that sink in. "The cut and color match the emerald cut I found in the casino." Glimmer's woof added her certainty, too. "I suspect that's why Glimmer found it."

Rocky took a long swallow of his drink. "Likely why Casey's grandmother whisked the ring away and is conveniently not available."

"You've already tried to examine the ring?"

He nodded. "I'd guess someone warned her I was coming."

"The deputy?" I asked.

"Or the Catalina dispatcher protecting their own."

"She's possibly a descendant of Melodie Waters."

Rocky said nothing. He didn't have to. I knew that arched brow look. The man trusted facts: intuition didn't work for him. "Do you think Melodie dismantled the bracelet?" he asked.

"I don't know. The stones I found at the casino could've been dislodged accidentally if the setting had hit a hard surface, like the beams in the immediate vicinity."

"The blood on them certainly suggests that possibility. I'm surprised the diamonds weren't damaged."

"Diamonds are the hardest substance known to man. Platinum would fail long before the stones." I paused. "That's the irony. If the goal were to keep the Duette's secret buried forever, dismantling it would be the best solution."

I swirled my drink. "But I don't believe that was ever the intent. The Waters were entrusted with the Duette for a reason. Which tells me there is a moment, some specific scenario, when its secret is meant to resurface."

Rocky considered the liquid in his glass. "I'll send the stones for DNA testing. Maybe we can identify familial matches."

"My results will be faster." Tested on arrival at the lab, to be exact. Sophie's influence ensured that.

"My lab is better. The sample is nearly a hundred years old." He leaned back, already braced for an argument.

"The Casino's environment was cool, dry, and dark. The stone's integrity should be intact." I reached inside my blouse, acutely aware of the sudden stillness across the table, of his gaze warming my skin as surely as a touch. My fingers hesitated, then steadied, though my pulse didn't. I placed a small evidence bag in his hand, the single diamond catching the light.

"In the name of cooperation..." I said.

"You have four stones." His voice remained dry and professional to the last syllable. His eyes didn't. "What else do you need?"

I'd given in too easily, and we both knew it. He read me far better than I liked.

"One of Larry Green's children may have joined the FBI," I said. "Mid-1950s, most likely."

"Before DNA," Rocky said.

"I know. But there would be fingerprints. Blood type. A service record. Something. The last name was Green."

He leaned back, studying me in that unhurried way that always felt like a slow unraveling. "What's really worrying you?"

I shifted beneath his gaze, heat climbing where caution should have lived. "That the time to solve this case is running out fast since I've led the Teutonic Knights straight to Melodie's half of the Duette."

Rocky didn't dismiss my concern. "We have eyes on Christian Weber and his known associates. And I didn't come alone. The ferries are being watched. So are new private boat arrivals and air traffic, too."

I'd assumed as much. I glanced past him at the neat rows of private boats rocking gently in the breeze. "That's not really help-ing." Anyone with a purpose could reach the island if they wanted badly enough. "The Knights are coming for the diamonds."

"Then tell me," Rocky said evenly, "who do you want me watching?"

He would, without hesitation, if I asked. That was the prob-lem. I didn't know yet. I needed to know far more about Larry Green before I pointed Rocky in any direction that mattered.

"Casey's grandmother is a brunette," he added. "Dark eyes."

Unlike Lionel and Claire Waters, who had light hair and green eyes. Doubt slipped in, unwelcome and persistent. Was I wrong about the connection?

I let my gaze drift beyond the table, past the present, and into another time entirely. I imagined Melodie seated at a formal table nearly a century earlier, a crystal glass in hand, posture perfect, and her eyes sharp, watching...

Styles had changed. Technology had leaped forward. Life moved faster now.

But people hadn't changed at all. They still kept secrets.

Chapter Sixteen

TWO HEADS ARE BETTER THAN ONE
—WISDOM FROM A JEWEL THIEF

MONDAY 6 A.M.

Glimmer's German Shepherd-sounding growl pierced my consciousness and sent me into fight or flight mode. I palmed the stun gun conveniently stashed beneath my pillow, rolled to the far side of the king-sized bed, and hit the floor, my knees braced beneath me as I prepared to defend even before I opened one eye. My heart pounded in my chest as my gaze swept the room. No one at the door. The curtains appeared undisturbed.

My dog blinked at me from the foot of the bed, her woof in sync with another trill. My phone! I cursed under my breath. Predawn barely blurred the edge of the curtains. It had to be Sophie. Twice in three days? She must have a death wish. "I swear I'm turning my phone off at night," I snapped.

"I'm afraid then I shall be forced to switch it back on. You can't escape me, Hunter. Not when I have information."

My head pounded, adrenaline and melatonin warring for victory. "Wait. What? Let me at least..."

A knock at the door interrupted Sophie's laugh. "Room service. I'll leave the coffee at the door, ma'am."

Good thing. Pajamas weren't my thing.

"Let it never be said I don't take proper care," Sophie said.

Glimmer growled my answer for me and rearranged the fluffy comforter into a fresh nest. I grabbed a white terrycloth hotel robe from the closet, padded across the cold tile floor, and cracked the door open. No one in sight. I lifted the silver tray off the cart, blocking any sudden exit.

I poured the coffee from the silver pot, dark and black, exactly the way I needed it, and took a long swallow.

"Human?" asked Sophie.

"Yeah. This better be good."

"Larry, Lawrence Green, was born in 1905 in San Francisco. Married a woman named Demi Rosewalt. Here's the Green family lineage."

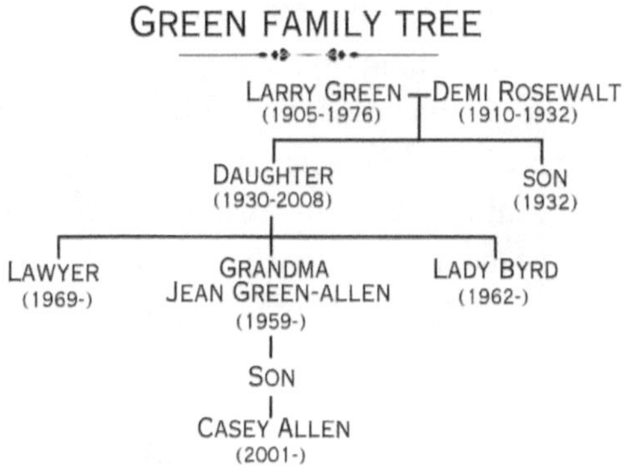

The graphic helped. Spoon-feeding me information worked best early in the morning.

"No genealogy on Demi, but the records are from 1930. Not certain how terribly precise they are," Sophie admitted. "They did have two children. Demi died in '32 in a fire. Larry was, in fact, a veterinarian who worked at the San Francisco Zoo. A friend of John Muir's, it seems. He would have been an excellent hire for the Wrigley Bird Park experiment."

My headache took another crack at my patience. "No connection to Melodie Waters?"

"Not that I have found. Dr. Green had no links to the diplomatic corps or any of the Waters' posts. What doesn't quite track is that Dr. Green had three brothers, and his wife was an only child."

"Then who was the sister that came to live with him?" I asked.

"My question as well. I've found no record of a nanny or housekeeper for Mr. Green, either in San Francisco or on Catalina. Nor that he owned a macaw. He was awarded the Army Silver Star for his work during the war. After some digging, I confirmed he was an officer attached to the signal corps."

"What's the signal corps?" I asked.

"Army cipher and radar service," Sophie explained.

"How would a veterinarian know anything about that?"

"The man cared for animals. The Signal Corps' Pigeon Service was rather a prestigious duty, particularly in Europe," Sophie said. "The Corps used over fifty thousand birds who delivered messages at a ninety percent rate. Dr. Green could easily have overseen breeding programs, disease control, and/or veterinary protocols. Managing the entire communications network would require someone with both veterinary expertise and an understanding of military operations. Quite distinguished, actually."

"Is there any evidence Dr. Green had military training?" I asked.

"No. In times of war, many are called to a higher duty," Sophie replied.

I let it go, but the unease lingered. "I don't understand why a vet would leave a job at the San Francisco Zoo for a bird park on a remote island in the first place?"

"Perhaps he needed an escape after his wife passed?" Sophie suggested. "Not uncommon."

"With two small children? You'd think he'd stay near family."

I pictured Sophie's shrug. We both liked facts over conjecture.

In this case, no proof existed either way. Nothing to disprove the theory. Nothing to confirm it.

"His son, Louis Thomas Green, retired from the FBI in 1980. His daughter, Jean, married the Catalina harbor master. Everyone calls her Grandma. She's Casey's maternal grandmother. The family has roots in Catalina, dating back to Dr. Green's relocation there. The family still owns the original home."

"How is Ellie connected?"

"Fourth generation from another family rooted on the island. I should hope she could assist you," Sophie said.

"Yes. She's been full of information. Not all of which I believe."

"Quite." Sophie's comment lacked surprise. "Provincial thinking. That did enter my mind."

"Possibly. *Why* is the question?"

"You aren't one of them, despite Glimmer's assistance. Or you're mistaken about the Catalina connection."

"Glimmer isn't wrong about Casey's ring," I insisted.

"Casey's grandmother owns a jewelry store. Perhaps she can better answer where the diamond originated?"

My gut took notice. "Is she the oldest of three sisters?"

"Indeed. The middle sister is a veterinarian who also runs a bird rescue with her daughter."

We were getting somewhere. "Is the vet's daughter also...?"

"No. The elder veterinarian did well for herself. Her daughter is a trust fund baby. Unmarried. Quite the Audubon activist. Something about Least Terns in San Diego. The youngest sister is a DOJ attorney."

Of course, there was one in the family. "What about the other branch? Dr. Green's son?"

"Military aviators. Three generations of Annapolis graduates."

"A distinguished family," I said. "Doesn't explain why one diamond surfaced in an engagement ring."

"If four diamonds from the Duette had been dislodged after a mishap, perhaps additional stones had loosened and fallen out when Melodie made her escape. She also may very well have removed all the diamonds from the setting and used them as currency to facilitate her departure."

More unanswerable speculation. "Any signs of Melodie in Vancouver or San Francisco?"

"No," Sophie said. "Finding a woman bent on disappearing before formal identity verification existed is rather difficult."

"What would an injured debutante cut off from her family's money do?"

"Marry, of course, someone well-removed from her social circle."

"Or take a job as a nanny," I suggested.

"Not likely. That would potentially put her in the same sphere she wanted to hide from."

"A teacher or secretary then?" I suggested.

"She would require credentials."

"Not too difficult to forge back then. Melodie spoke French fluently."

"Hunter, you're reaching. The most straightforward answer would be to sell the diamonds one at a time."

Of course, Sophie had a point. I just didn't want to believe it. The Waters' family pride, at least on Lionel and Claire's side, would never allow it. The answer had to be who'd entrusted the Duette into their care. "Anything more on the diamonds' origins?" I asked.

"The demantoid garnet is definitely African, Tanzanian most likely, as you suspected. You and your sister are as reliable as the science."

"From German East African territory?"

Sophie's agreement sent possibilities running through my head. German-mined diamonds, created into a necklace by a German jewelry maker on the eve of WWI? This had to be a piece intended for the Kaiser's House of Hohenzollern, yet it ended up in the possession of an American diplomat.

Possible scenarios raced through my head. Not a prayer that

I'd get more sleep. Instead, I dressed warmly and dragged Glimmer from under the comforter. Despite her objections and pure doxie attitude, I knew a morning walk would clear both our heads.

The fog had thinned overnight, retreating just enough to give Avalon back its edges. I walked the Crescent Avenue promenade slowly, the harbor stretched out beside me in softened blues and silvers. Boats bobbed, their hulls emerging and disappearing as the mist drifted. The air smelled of salt, kelp, and a hint of eucalyptus that must've carried down from the hills with the faint promise of morning.

Shop windows remained dark, except for the coffee and pastry shops that buzzed with life. I stopped in front of Casey's grandmother's island jewelry store, Diamonds in the Sand, apropos if you ask me.

The jewelry store occupied the corner of Whittley Avenue and Casino Way, prime real estate for catching tourists streaming off the Green Pier and heading to the Casino. Framed in brick, void of Catalina tile accents, windows displaying their wares dominated the storefront. Its displays had remained out overnight, not locked away in a safe, suggesting the merchandise catered to creating memories rather than to investment. Turquoise, opal, and chalcedony set in silver, accented chunky fish-and-octopus bracelets and sand-dollar pendants. A rotating stand of charms retold Catalina's story in tiny steamers, miniature Casino buildings, and bison.

No need for caution. Except the tiny red lights indicated 24/7 HD surveillance from multiple angles with pan-tilt-zoom cameras. I shielded my eyes with my hands, cutting the glare as I peered inside. Night vision and facial recognition technology appeared to be at the backroom entry, identical to what I'd seen at Wise & Sons. First class security for products worth more on an insurance claim than on the sales floor?

I texted Rocky. This was no coincidence.

Somewhere behind me, a door opened. Then clicked shut.

The soft sound, not particularly threatening, still made the fine hairs along my neck stand on end. My hand slid to the stun gun beneath my sweatshirt on my hip. Ready.

I adjusted my pace toward Marilla Avenue, pretending I hadn't noticed a thing until Glimmer halted so abruptly she nearly tripped me, darting sideways to the base of the building. A low woof rumbled in her chest as she nosed along the stucco.

"What?" I whispered.

She ignored me.

The flash of silver caught the light before I fully registered it. My stomach tightened. I crouched. A foil gum wrapper, Wrigley's Spearmint, lay half-tucked against the foundation, too clean to have been there long. A carelessly discarded wrapper wasn't evidence. It was litter. Or was it? Since I found another at the Phoenix Wrigley Mansion, too.

I slipped the wrapper into an evidence bag and continued up Vieudelou Avenue toward Mrs. Wrigley's Chimes Tower, telling myself I wanted to admire the view, but it was more than that. I wanted the high ground to see who else moved below.

Glimmer quit about halfway up Chimes Tower Road. Honestly, it wasn't that steep. The mini dachshund planted her front feet and splooted onto the pavement, her four legs sprawled in opposing directions. I would've left her there as any spoiled child deserved, but the clock tower rose above the eucalyptus trees just ahead like a steady sentry. I scooped the dog into my arms and carried her the rest of the way. As I drew closer, the tower's cream-colored walls caught the early light, the clock face pale and watchful.

I remembered what Ellie had told me the first time I'd heard the Westminster chimes. "Mrs. Wrigley built them. She wanted to add character to the island. But it was practical too. Only the rich wore watches back in the 1920s, and visitors needed to know when to catch the steamer home. The chimes told time every fifteen minutes. Seven in the morning until ten at night. Now they ring eight to eight." She'd paused. "Only half of the 440 chimes Deagan produced still operate."

Yet the unmistakable sound still reverberated across the bay. Apparently, time on Catalina wasn't something you could ignore.

Glimmer draped across the back of my neck as I made my way down the hill. The fog had lifted just enough to remind me that clarity didn't mean safety. It only meant you could finally see where you were standing.

My stomach growled when I reached Crescent Avenue. Breakfast at Pete's would give me a chance to eat and to see the tile fountain that had been moved from the Bird Park. Not that I expected an epiphany. The tiles weren't speaking to me. I wondered if they were relevant at all.

A steady stream of people brushed past me on the harbor walk. The early boat from Long Beach had docked, bringing tourists and island workers into town from the ferry pier. Couples, families, and day-trippers hauling backpacks, all ready for adventure.

I scanned faces out of habit. Looking for threats.

The bump came from behind. Light, seemingly accidental. Glimmer's warning growl and the tug on my crossbody bag came half a second later.

I was back in Africa, where street urchins with quick hands and quicker feet roamed freely on the filthy streets. The memory surfaced sharp and clear. My hand snaked out before thought caught up. It was muscle memory, the training so ingrained that I caught a wrist mid-motion. Small. Delicately boned. The fingers clutching my bag zipper went rigid.

Glimmer launched. Fourteen pounds of teeth-clamping fury.

A scream cut through the wispy fog. High-pitched and way too young.

Chapter Seventeen

PROTECT YOUR FLANK—
WISDOM FROM A JEWEL THIEF

MONDAY, 8:30 A.M.

I spun the thief around. Not a street kid. A girl. Fifteen, maybe sixteen, dark hair pulled into a tight ponytail, wearing an oversized hoodie that hung on her, still creased as if it had just come off the rack.

Her eyes were wide with shock and something quieter. A sense of inevitability, as if she'd already seen too much and knew how this would end.

"Let go." Her voice cracked. "You're hurting me."

I wasn't. I didn't loosen my grip. Glimmer teeth had locked on her pant leg. The dog growled yet maintained her hold on the denim.

Bystanders slowed and watched us. A woman clutched her purse closer.

The girl's free hand reached into her pocket.

"Don't." My voice came out flat. Her hand froze.

We stood there, Crescent Avenue's morning foot traffic flowing around us, trying not to stare while the fog muffled everything except the sound of her now-panicked breathing.

"Who sent you?" I kept my tone even.

Her eyes darted left, then right. Looking for a way out that didn't exist.

"Nobody. I wasn't... I didn't..."

"Try again," I said.

The calculation in her eyes shifted. From escape to negotiation. "You're Hunter." Not a question.

My grip tightened. "How do you know my name?"

She swallowed hard. "Everyone knows. You're the one looking for the diamonds."

"Who told you that?"

She clamped her mouth shut. She weighed her options. Deciding how much truth would buy her freedom.

Behind us, a man's voice called out, "Everything okay over there?"

I didn't turn—didn't look away from the girl's face. "Fine," I replied. "Just a little misunderstanding, which way school was this morning."

The girl's expression shifted again. Recognition dawning. She understood what I'd just done. I'd given her an out she didn't deserve.

"Last chance," I said quietly. "Who sent you?"

Her lips pressed into a thin line. Glimmer clamped down harder on the pant leg, her eyes alert and ready to pursue if needed.

"C-Casey," the girl whispered finally, "sent me."

The man who owned the ring Glimmer had recovered? I released her wrist, and beneath my thumb, I saw a faint shield tattoo as she stumbled back. I caught her hoodie, stopping her fall as she rubbed the red marks my fingers had left. Her eyes were still locked on mine.

"What exactly did Casey want you to do?" I asked.

"See if you had the diamonds." She backed up another step. "That's all. I swear."

"And if I did?"

"Text him." The girl's hand moved slowly toward her pocket. She pulled out a phone. Cheap. Probably a burner.

I held out my hand. "Give it to me."

"What? No..."

"Now."

She hesitated, then placed the phone in my palm. Her fingers trembled slightly.

I unlocked it. One contact. "C." Three messages in the thread. All from this morning.

Boat docking. Target walking down Casino Way. Move now.

Someone did have eyes on me. I looked up. The girl tried to back away. Glimmer's growl stopped her.

"Why did you think I had the diamonds on me?" I felt their presence pressed against my waist.

"They're not in your room, and you don't have a safety deposit box assigned at the Metropole."

My jaw locked. Again. It took a second to conquer the too-familiar surge of anger before her words sank in. Someone with detailed knowledge of the hotel was also involved.

"Tell Casey I want to talk." I held up the phone. "I'll return this when we do."

She nodded sharply. "Get the dog off me." Her tone suggested she'd been cornered by an attack dog. I reached into my crossbody bag as I kneeled and attached a dot-tracker to the hem of her pants, making a show of calling Glimmer off.

The moment the dog stepped back, the girl turned and darted toward the Casino. Like she could escape on an island with ferry service as the primary exit. I didn't pursue. I'd gotten what I needed.

Glimmer whined softly.

"I know." I pocketed the girl's phone and checked the tracker's signal on my own. The steadily moving red dot had just passed the Casino. Rocky was going to love this. "Casey or whoever "C" is just made this interesting."

The fog thinned slightly. But the morning felt colder than before. If "C" really was Casey then he was involved with the Knights. Did that make him a good guy or bad?

159

Chapter Eighteen

THERE IS A FINE LINE BETWEEN RIGHT AND WRONG—WISDOM FROM A JEWEL THIEF

MONDAY 10:30 A.M.

Rocky met me twenty minutes later at Pete's Avalon Plaza Café on Sumner Avenue, as I was sharing a ham-and-cheese omelet with Glimmer. I'd claimed one of the red chairs beneath the awning, my back to the stone wall.

I slid the wannabe pickpocket's phone across the table beside his steaming coffee cup. "She's headed back to the ferry landing."

Rocky shook his head as he dropped into the chair across from me. Today's loud Hawaiian shirt practically blinded me. The look said tourist. His piercing gaze said *watch out*.

He sipped the coffee. "We'll keep an eye on her once she's on the mainland."

"What do you have on the security company protecting Grandma's store?"

"Just like you suspected," he said. "They specialize in low-priced security for small to mid-sized independent jewelry stores and estate jewelers."

Glimmer stole a strip of ham off my dangling fork. "Same monitoring structure between Casey's grandmother's store and Wise & Sons?"

Rocky leaned back, casual to the point of performance. "Appears so."

"That's not a coincidence."

"That was my thought."

I lowered my voice. "What about Christian Weber's store?"

"Protected by them, as well."

There it was, the click of alignment. The kind you only feel right before the floor tilts.

"At Wise's store, I thought the system was about paranoia. Now I'm wondering who's watching."

"Owners who like control," Rocky said.

"Or the Knights spying."

Rocky studied me over the rim of his coffee mug. "You're thinking access."

"I'm thinking feeds," I said. "Facial recognition means cloud integration."

"I'm working on the warrant," he said evenly. "The connection to Christian Weber is thin."

I bit back my objection. I admired his by-the-book attitude. It was also infuriatingly inconvenient. "Casey's grandmother is in danger. She's been watched for a long time."

Spied on like a goldfish in a bowl, actually.

"I know," Rocky said. "We haven't located her yet. Ellie claims she doesn't know where she is either."

No doubting his thoroughness. "Grandma may already be off the island," he said. "She has access to private boats."

She hadn't run. There were too many safe places to lie low on the island. The question was why she didn't want to be found. I reached into my bag and retrieved the evidence bag containing the gum wrapper. "Glimmer found this outside Grandma's store."

Rocky scrutinized the contents. "It's a gum wrapper."

"Wrigley's Spearmint," I added.

He eyed me speculatively. "This is the island Wrigley built. I bet they sell a fair amount in town."

"True, but I found the same brand wrapper on the thief's escape path at the Wrigley Mansion in Phoenix."

He leaned forward, interest engaged. "Why did you...?"

"I sent it to my lab long before you were involved."

He exhaled. "You should've given it to Chad."

I rolled my eyes. "I should have fingerprint and DNA answers later this morning."

Rocky rotated the plastic evidence bag. "If there are answers to be found."

"*Touché*. Have you questioned Casey?" I asked.

Rocky glanced at his watch. "Our team is arriving about now."

I looked past him, toward the bird tiles that had brought me here. Unlike the tiles at the Bird Park, this one talked to me. It seemed to point inland, maybe telling me where I could find the next clue.

After breakfast, I returned to the Metropole via Crescent Avenue specifically to walk by Diamonds in the Sand. The closed sign remained on the door despite the buzz of cruise ship shoppers relentlessly hunting for the perfect souvenir. Grandma's absence concerned me. Was she hiding from me or someone else, or had she already been found by the Knights?

I waved to the hotel's front desk manager and waited for a response before heading up the left staircase to my room. Glimmer ran ahead, pausing at the door, the grumble of a low woof hurrying me along. She leaped past me as I opened the door.

"You know how much I hate that sweatshirt." As expected, Hope sat on the sofa, her laptop dominating the coffee table, only half-hiding her all-black attire. More burglar than cat, I figured no one had noticed her arrival. Me on the other hand...

"Colorful and memorable," I replied easily. "You should've seen Rocky. We were a neon sign at Pete's this morning."

Hope smiled as Glimmer jumped into her lap.

"You missed the pickpocket on the ferry," I remarked.

No excuse from my sister, just the truth. "I watched for threats. You're on your own with annoyances."

That comment hurt. "Easy for you to say." I slipped into the chair beside her. "The pickpocket said Casey sent her."

Hope folded her arms. "Interesting. I met Casey. He didn't seem like an annoyance."

That got my full attention. "You *met* him."

"With Sophie's help, I laid in wait for him last night." Hope shrugged. "He works in sales for a pottery manufacturing company in L.A. Glazes, kilns, supply chains. Knows his margins."

"And?"

"And he's very happy he lost the ring before he could propose." Hope tilted her head. "Said marrying that girl would've been a mistake."

I frowned. "That doesn't exactly scream revenge."

"Not in the least," Hope agreed. "It screamed relief."

"Did he say anything interesting?"

Hope paused. "Nothing incriminating. Plenty revealing."

"Is he a Knight?" Crazy as it sounded, I had to ask.

Hope lifted one shoulder. "Not sure. He didn't flash a shield ring or swear an oath. But he asked careful, leading questions."

"What about a tattoo on his wrist?"

Hope scratched her chin. "I didn't see one. I take it the pickpocket had a tattoo."

I nodded. "If Casey isn't part of this, then someone is using him to gain information."

"Which means you are correct that Casey's family is in danger."

I asked my next question. "Did you see anyone else?"

Hope smiled, the particular smile she used when she knew she was about to win the point. "I met Casey's grandma's middle sister."

"The vet?"

"That would be Lady Byrd. In addition to a lucrative

Newport Beach veterinary practice, she runs a 501(c) bird sanctuary, home to parrots and macaws. You know, the loud ones with opinions. I met her at the sanctuary."

I blinked. "You didn't…"

"…adopt a macaw?" Her half smile told me nothing.

"Did you?" Glimmer lifted her head and stared too. My sister's soft spot for all living things made any animal rescue trip a threat.

"Of course not. I did ask for one that spoke French. She suddenly remembered a meeting. Her daughter escorted me to the exit. She has green eyes. Reminds me of the demantoid," Hope added.

"Just like Lionel and Claire's eye color."

Hope nodded. "She's, uh, passionate. The kind of woman you'd expect to chain herself to a tree to make a point." Hope's gaze drifted, amused. "She told me about her great-grandpa's macaw."

"One that spoke…?" I prompted.

"French," Hope said. "Fluent enough to swear in it. Apparently, great-grandpa reprimanded the bird in French whenever it got mouthy."

I blinked. "Of course he did."

"She said the bird sounded… *racy*." Hope shrugged. "Her word. I'm guessing tone, not vocabulary."

I rubbed my temples. "I'm impressed. All that before getting on the ferry."

Hope's smile flashed quickly and unapologetically. "I multitask well. Sophie says that Grandma and her sisters all live comfortably, but within their means. Only Lady Byrd has any real money. And I don't see her as a jewelry fiend."

"A reluctant participant?" I asked.

"I'd guess she's big on responsibility. So, an inherited problem would be important to her."

My thoughts drifted to Lionel and Claire, passionate defenders of a history they barely understood. "If I'm right, one of the sisters has the bracelet. Most likely Grandma, since she's the oldest and gave Casey a stone."

Hope exhaled slowly. "If protecting the bracelet was the goal, separating a single stone makes no sense. I'm wondering if each daughter has a part. That would be the ultimate way to protect it."

A fleeting sense of loss tightened my chest. "Lionel's biggest concern is the legal requirement to destroy the setting, not the diamonds. It makes me think that the setting is the key."

"Lionel and Claire Waters are second generation," Hope said gently. "Grandma and her sisters are third. Casey is five generations removed from where this tale began. You also don't know that Melodie ever passed the story on."

I hated it when she pointed out the obvious. I needed to believe Melodie had told someone. That the truth hadn't vanished with her.

Hope reached for the remote and sent the murder board up onto the hotel's large-screen TV.

"Let's assume," she said, "someone remembers more than they're admitting."

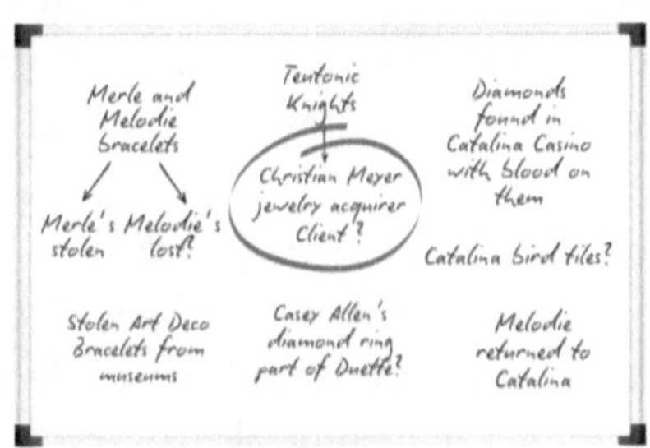

The visual always helped, but in this case, even after an hour rehashing the clues, I had no idea where to find Grandma. Hope reached for her phone.

"I'm calling Sophie. Maybe she has an idea."

I didn't argue as Hope's call connected.

"I'm here with Hunter at the Metropole," Hope announced. "We're trying to figure out where Grandma is hiding."

"It's always reassuring to see the two of you aligned," Sophie said, briskly setting sentiment aside. "If I may be blunt, I'd suggest Grandma is hiding in plain sight."

"Why is that?" I asked. Though I agreed. Rocky's team watched the island.

"Grandma's husband was a boat captain—one of those positions that appears benign until one considers access."

"Meaning she likely has access to a boat," I added. Rocky's opinion as well. "That could get her off the island."

"Not necessarily. She has friends quite capable of keeping her out of sight until her sisters arrive," Sophie said.

A valid point, but... "The island is seventeen square miles of mostly wilderness. If she pops a tent somewhere in the interior, I'll never find her."

"I should think the sisters are drawing together," Sophie said. "The solicitor sister took emergency leave this morning, and the vet's husband owns a fishing boat which departed from Newport Beach a few hours ago."

Meaning they could've already arrived on Catalina Island. "What's the boat's name?" I asked, already texting Rocky.

"*Bury*," she replied, the faintest note of satisfaction coloring her tone.

"What kind of name is that?" Hope asked.

"An anagram for Ruby," Sophie and I answered together.

Sophie chuckled softly, the sound she made when the pieces slid neatly into place. "Frightfully old spy craft. Very nineteen-thirties indeed."

"That makes Demi Rosewalt..." I reset the letters in my head.

Hope typed feverishly on her laptop. "Melodie Waters," she said triumphantly.

My gut took notice. "I need to find Casey's grandma."

"Indeed, you do. Someone attempted to erase her store's security footage last night..."

"...but they weren't good enough." I finished Sophie's sentence, now fully alert.

I pictured her slow smile. "Heaven forbid. A blond man entered her store and confronted her."

"Send me the link." I trusted Sophie's assessment, but putting a face on the enforcer helped. Or a shoulder and a linebacker-sized one at that. Although he stood only slightly taller than Grandma, I'd guess he dealt in intimidation.

Of course, I didn't recognize him, but familiarity tugged at me. "What are they saying?" A video without audio never tells the whole story.

"I'm afraid my lip-reading skills are rather poor," Sophie replied.

As were mine.

"Let me draw your focus to the ring on his left hand."

Shield-shaped, white enamel with a black cross. "Ha! Told you the organization existed."

"I never doubted you. I simply needed more to work with." Sophie's words lingered to my dismay. Innuendo never held up in court. "Grandma convinced them to leave a few minutes later, but surveillance lost him a block away."

"Can you get a clear visual of who is waiting outside the building?" I asked.

Sophie manipulated the image. Each enhancement helped, but in the end, the picture remained blurry. "The enforcer has a leader."

My breath caught. The Knights were officially here. "I led the Knights right to them all."

"Technically, Lionel and Claire drew you in," Sophie replied.

Rocky had done an excellent job defending and denying my role too, but responsibility still stung. "It's late in London. You could've texted me all this. What else do you have?"

"Well, consider this a warning. Information has emerged connecting Christian Weber to blood diamond trafficking," Sophie replied.

My stomach bottomed. Anyone associated with legitimizing diamonds mined in war zones and sold to finance conflicts needed to be taken out of the gene pool. I heard my father's warning as if he'd been beside me. *"Take care, ma chérie—these are men with no scruples."*

Hope grasped my arm. She'd heard dad's warning, too.

"What does that say about the Waters' diamonds?" my sister asked.

"They lead to something rather important."

"We need to know where they came from." As I said it, I knew I wasn't going to like the answer.

Chapter Nineteen

INFORMATION GATHERING IS PARAMOUNT
—WISDOM FROM A JEWEL THIEF

MONDAY 2 P.M.

"Casey is missing."

Rocky's call caught me flat-footed. "The only lead we have to his disappearance is a witness who says a person dressed in black entered his condo around seven forty-five last night."

Hope stiffened beside me. I felt her anxiety like static in the air.

I wasn't followed. I wasn't careless. I know better than that, Hope insisted without words.

Rocky confirmed her statement. "My team also found a black SUV parked down the street on Ring cam."

"Someone was watching Casey's place." Guilt hit fast and hard. Had I just put my sister in harm's way, too? Had she been followed to Catalina? I hadn't meant to… but intent didn't matter much when people disappeared.

Casey had joked about losing the ring. About mistakes narrowly avoided. And now he'd vanished. "Any ransom demand?"

"Not that we know of," Rocky said evenly. "But Grandma's sister, the veterinarian, has her boat moored in Hamilton Cove."

Just past Descanso Beach, tucked into the rugged hillside, away from Avalon's tourist area. It was the kind of place that advertised privacy and delivered it. If you wanted to disappear without technically leaving the island, that would be a good place to go.

"You just confirmed what Sophie already told us," I replied. "And there's more." I laid out the threats against Grandma and the whispers tying Christian to blood diamonds.

Silence. The wrong kind.

"Say thank you," I said, unable to keep the edge completely out of my voice. "Sophie's information should be enough for the warrant."

Hope's brow lifted in silent warning. *Defensive*, she was telling me. Maybe she was right.

But every time Christian's name surfaced, my gut reacted. And if the *Bury* sat quietly in Hamilton Cove, it wasn't there for the view.

"Did the pickpocket get on the ferry?" I asked.

"Yes. I'll have a team on her as soon as she arrives in Long Beach," Rocky replied.

A knock interrupted our conversation and gave me the excuse I needed to hang up. I reached for my stun gun, the feel significantly less comforting than my familiar Glock. I met Hope's eyes and jerked my chin toward the bedroom. She slipped behind the door without argument.

I checked the peephole before I touched the handle. Ellie, shifting from foot to foot outside, could be the break I'd been waiting for.

Glimmer pressed close to my leg. Her tail didn't wag as I opened the door. "Come in. I was just thinking about you," I said, like that was the whole truth.

Ellie swallowed hard as she entered. I closed the door and clicked both bolts behind her. No smile greeted me, just the straight line of her mouth and tight shoulders, like she'd rehearsed what she was about to say and hated every word. "Grandma wants to see you." Her voice dropped. "She says you caused this."

Glimmer let out a sharp woof from behind my leg. I didn't respond to the accusation. Some secrets couldn't remain hidden forever, no matter how hard the protectors tried. "Where is she?"

"I'll take you to her. Grandma said we need to be careful."

"I have a plan." I didn't raise my voice, yet Hope heard me.

She emerged from the bedroom as if she'd been lounging poolside all morning, dressed in a bathing suit, a gauzy cover-up, and oversized sunglasses perched in her hair.

"I'll spend the afternoon at Descanso Beach," she said brightly, adjusting her tote over one shoulder. "Try not to get caught before dinner. I'd like to finish my book before heading home."

Ellie stared at her. Then at me. Then back again. "There are two of you?" she breathed.

"Yes," I said evenly. "The only reliable way to sneak out when you're being watched."

Understanding dawned slowly, and with it, alarm.

"You think someone's..."

"I don't think," I interrupted softly. "I know."

Hope gave me a wicked little smile. "Don't worry, darling. I'll make a grand exit."

She breezed past Ellie into the hallway, Glimmer trotting after her as if beach days were the only mission on her agenda.

Ellie stood beside me and paled. "This is insane."

"No," I said, reaching for my jacket. "This is necessary."

I waited a beat, listening as Hope's bright, impossible-to-miss voice floated toward the stairwell. If someone was watching, they'd follow my twin toward the beach.

Which meant I could finally follow the secrets.

"I'll call Rocky. He's FBI." I reached for my phone.

Ellie's voice cracked, sharp enough to slice through the room. "The kidnappers said no cops."

Kidnappers. My pulse didn't spike. It went cold. "He's discreet. He can help..."

Ellie crossed her arms, physically blocking the argument. There'd be no compromise. She had her orders.

"Fine," I said. "Then we do this your way." Better to make my case to Grandma Green directly.

I changed fast into nondescript hiking pants and a loose blouse, then tucked my hair under a wide-brimmed hat, pulling artificial dark tendrils loose around my face.

I handed Ellie another hat, adjusted it low, and handed her a darker lip balm. Subtle changes. Enough to blur memory.

We slipped down the back stairs and exited onto Whittley Avenue. Golf carts hummed past as we diligently avoided visitors clutching maps and iced coffees, until we merged with the pedestrian path and joined a cruise ship tour group funneling along Casino Way. Thirty strangers in matching lanyards and sunburned optimism made for good cover. No one noticed two more hats in a herd.

We moved with them toward the Catalina Casino, its white curve rising against the blue like an Art Deco crown. No surprise, Ellie led me this way. We needed to pass the Casino to reach Hamilton Cove and its gated security. Except Ellie tugged my arm and veered east, away from the Casino's main entrance.

We passed the quiet Catalina Island Museum Dive History exhibit and stopped at narrow doorway, framed in pale stone carved with clean, geometric lines that whispered of another era. The gray door, solid, utilitarian, stood slightly ajar, revealing a dim interior and a metal security gate beyond, as if the building preferred to keep its secrets close.

Ellie produced a key. Inside, a short hallway carried the faint scent of salt and old plaster. At the end, she slid open a railed door, and we stepped into a no-frills freight elevator.

"Where are we going?" I asked as the old lift jerked upward.

"The Casino apartment."

Of course. Sophie had said Grandma would hide in plain sight. But this... this was the most obvious place on the island.

When the doors opened, sunlight spilled across polished floors. We approached the Avalon harbor-facing apartment I'd heard whispers about but hadn't seen during yesterday's behind-the-scenes tour.

Ellie's hand trembled as she knocked twice on the door, then twice again. A signal? A second later, I heard the lock open. Ellie opened the door and motioned me to enter. She didn't follow.

The Casino apartment wasn't grand like the ballroom below. Simplicity better described its appeal. One main room with a small dining nook tucked off a narrow galley kitchen. A metal ladder bolted to the far wall led up to what appeared to be a hatch to the roof above.

The view made up for what the space lacked. An unobstructed harbor view where boats drifted lazily, beachgoers laughed, and music carried faintly in the wind. All below the Wrigley Mansion that watched from the hilltop.

In the corner stood an old Coke machine, its paint faded, chrome dulled by salt air. It didn't fit, and yet it did. There had to be a story behind it, but I wasn't here for tales. I needed answers, and Grandma and her two sisters clustered near the window. All different. All unmistakably related.

Grandma looked exactly like her nickname implied, dressed in a soft sweater, sensible shoes, with her silver hair pinned neatly back. The kind of woman who baked pies and remembered birthdays. Her determined eyes had the look of a mother bear.

The veterinarian, Lady Byrd, suffered from the same height challenges that I did. Her naturally gray hair had been styled into a sharp, modern line, and a pair of exquisite sapphire and emerald bird earrings caught the light when she turned her head. She watched me the way falcons observe field mice.

The third sister, the lawyer, defined polish and posture down to her cream suit and low heels. Not a wrinkle out of place, she seemed as steady as a rock. She didn't bother with pleasantries. "This is entirely your fault."

I didn't take the bait.

"Hardly," I replied, keeping my voice level. "You knew I was coming the moment the Waters' bracelet was stolen."

A look passed between them. Fast but telling.

"True." Grandma's voice turned sharp, cold enough to cut. "But you never would've found us if your dog hadn't dug up Casey's ring."

"Glimmer found it because it ties back to the Waters' stolen diamond bracelet," I said, holding her gaze. "You already knew that."

The slightest exhale betrayed her. So, they'd known about Claire and Lionel. About everything that started long before us. Relief tightened in my chest, edged with urgency. Someone here had answers.

"I've learned something about diamonds." I chose each word carefully. "They reveal the truth eventually. Whether we want them to or not."

Silence filled the space. I let it stretch.

Grandma's fingers tightened into a ball. "Casey's kidnappers have demanded our bracelet as payment for his release."

Her words didn't shake, but I knew there was more by the way her hand trembled.

"And I have the missing four diamonds," I replied evenly. I needed to win their trust.

Three pairs of eyes focused on me.

"You have proof of life?" I asked.

Grandma turned her phone toward me. A video of a young man, obviously related to the threesome, begging for his release played. Lady Byrd turned away. The lawyer's lips pressed into a straight line.

No doubt about the authenticity in their mind. "When is the exchange?" I asked.

"Tonight," the three replied in unison.

No time to waste. I sent the twin message to Hope before announcing, "I only have two of the diamonds. I gave one to the FBI and sent another to a DNA lab in Los Angeles."

"That's five. Where's the sixth?" Lady Byrd asked.

"There were only four in the casino casing," I replied. Chuck and I hadn't missed any. We'd double checked. "Someone else must have it."

Silence swallowed the room. I let fear, anger, and panic cycle through the sisters' expressions. Then I asked the question that had been bothering me since Glimmer had dug up the diamond ring. "Why did you give Casey a diamond from the bracelet?"

Grandma's shoulders sank just enough to betray the weight she carried. "An error in judgment."

That wasn't the whole of it.

"As you've no doubt surmised," she continued, "the bracelet was damaged when Melodie escaped from Mr. Fox."

"He caught her in the Casino," I said, piecing it together. "She managed to elude him with the help of one of the Casino spotters..."

"Yes," the veterinarian sister confirmed. "Mr. Fox caught her as she reached the stairs and demanded the bracelet."

"She was an agile dancer," Lady Byrd added. "She ran out onto the beams."

The lawyer's voice took on courtroom precision. "Mr. Fox was a large man and much slower. She would've gotten away except Melodie circled back to help the spotter and stumbled near the center."

"Where she struck her wrist on a beam and broke the clasp. Seven diamonds dislodged," Grandma added. "Melodie recovered two before he caught up to her."

"By then, the spotter Mr. Fox had injured had regained consciousness," the lawyer finished quietly. "He hit Mr. Fox over the head with something, and they escaped."

Grandma's eyes held mine.

"Then they faked Melodie's death," I said. "And she slipped away on a Canadian liquor ship."

Grandma inclined her head slightly. "And she disappeared forever."

The word *forever* sent a twinge to my gut. "Clearly not forever. She reinvented herself." No one contradicted me or explained. Answers weren't coming that easily. "You said seven stones were detached. I found four. Casey's makes five. There are two unaccounted for."

The lawyer held up an antique cut, round diamond, an exact match to the stone Glimmer had retrieved.

"So, two of you have stones and you…" My gaze settled on Lady Byrd.

"I have the bracelet. We don't know where the seventh is."

"Our mother thought separating the parts was the best way to protect the legacy," Grandma stated.

Each sister had a piece. No single person had the answer. It made sense. What had happened to the missing stone? "What do the two bracelets lead to?" I asked.

The girls shared a look I recognized with my own sister. "We don't know exactly," admitted the lawyer. "Our mother said it led to great wealth and power."

"And it was our sworn duty to see that it never came together again," Lady Byrd added.

"Then why didn't you destroy it?" I asked.

"Our mother…"

"Melodie's daughter?" I asked.

Grandma nodded. "She said that someday someone would come who would know what to do."

My gut jumped under their combined scrutiny. "And you think I'm that person?" Crazy, yes. But I believed her. "Why? How do you all know this? Demi Rosewalt, a clear anagram for Melodie Waters, died before she could have passed on the information to your grandmother."

That look again. I'd missed something. Another double knock

on the door interrupted my next question. I felt Hope's presence even before Ellie opened the door. The three sisters stared. Grandma finally said, her relief evident, "Identical."

"Lionel gave you the clasp," the lawyer announced. It wasn't really a question. Something had changed.

I nodded, answers suddenly falling into place. "If Demi was Melodie, and she didn't die in the San Francisco fire, who did?"

The three sisters shared a glance and a decision. Grandma spoke without hesitation. "Her husband, Dr. Green, died in the fire. Melodie was on the run and had two young children to take care of. She wasn't a college-educated veterinarian, but…"

"She knew how to care for birds. So, she accepted the job at the Catalina Bird Park," the lawyer added.

"Back in 1931, a woman couldn't work at the Bird Park, so she dressed as a man and became her husband, Dr. Green." No disguising Lady Byrd's pride. "I would have done the same."

No doubt she would have.

Hope asked my question. "Her twin sister, Merle, came to live with him/her in 1942?"

The three sisters nodded in unison.

"Did Mr. Fox come after Merle in 1942?" I asked.

"Rather desperately," Grandma admitted. "She was badly injured."

"Melodie knew her sister had been hurt." As I would've known had it been Hope. I followed the thread to its inevitable conclusion.

Grandma gave the smallest nod. "Melodie rescued her sister before Mr. Fox realized what had happened. She knew he'd never stop coming for her. So she disappeared forever."

The timeline finally aligned, mostly. "After that, Mr. Fox and the Teutonic Knights vanished for ninety years," I continued. "Why resurface now?"

The lawyer's half-smile unsettled me. "Twins," she said.

The word dropped like a stone into still water.

Grandma folded her hands. "The heir to the Hohenzollern dynasty is a twin."

"Twin boys," Lady Byrd clarified. "Prince Carl Friedrich and Prince Louis Ferdinand."

Hope frowned. "And we're supposed to know who that is?"

"Kaiser Wilhelm II was the last reigning monarch of a united Germany and Prussia," the lawyer replied, patient but precise. "From the Hohenzollern dynasty."

And just like that, the final lock clicked. I'd been right. The Duette hadn't been society sparkle. It had been a royal secret.

"Who gave the Duette to your great-grandmother?" I asked quietly.

"The Kaiser's wife, Queen Auguste Viktoria," Grandma said. "A week before her death at their home, Huis Doorn."

"After his abdication, Wilhelm settled near Utrecht in Belgium," Lady Byrd explained.

"The Duette wasn't a gift," the lawyer interjected. "We have a legitimate bill of sale. We can prove provenance."

"Maybe." The laws governing royal pieces tended to be vague and better left to international courts to decide. "What happened next?"

"After Wilhelm abdicated, the Knights came looking for the diamonds. But the queen entrusted it to our great-grandmother for safekeeping until..." Grandma continued.

The three sisters recited as if chatting, *"Only when twin heirs —born of one blood and one destiny—do restore with their own hands the broken chain, shall the world remember its proper order and be made whole once more."*

My pulse quickened. Melodie and Merle had been the twins the queen believed ordained to protect it. They had done more than protect it. They'd fractured it. Hidden it. Sacrificed everything to keep it out of the wrong hands.

My instincts hadn't failed me. Twins would end this. Lionel had said the same thing. Was that why he'd hired me? He'd said that he'd done his research. Had he and Claire intentionally set these events in motion?

Practical Hope, immune to monarchy and destiny, broke the silence. "Can I see the bracelet?"

Panic flickered, quick and unguarded, across all three of the sisters' faces. The lawyer recovered first. "That won't be necessary."

"It will," I countered, unwavering.

Grandma's hands curled into fists. Lady Byrd's fingers rose to the delicate bird jewelry at her ear. Her tell. Whatever the sisters were hiding was big.

"She's a professional diamond grader," I said quickly. "The best in the business."

Hope didn't say a word. She simply let her expression settle into professional calm—the one that made auction houses nervous and insurance adjusters sweat. "If there is a way to modify the bracelet to obscure the message, I will be able to do it."

Lady Byrd removed the platinum bracelet from a hidden pouch against her waist and laid it on black velvet in front of Hope.

"May I have the two loose stones?" I asked on Hope's behalf.

The lawyer handed Hope her one-carat round. "The kidnappers believe the bracelet is intact. They don't know about the missing stones."

Grandma removed the ring from a pouch at her side and also turned it over to Hope. "Can you get the missing diamonds back before tonight?" She'd spoken to Hope, but the question was for me.

The three stones I'd kept, maybe, but the one I'd turned over to Rocky that he'd sent to the FBI's Quantico lab...

"No," I replied honestly. "But I'm hoping we can come up with something better."

Hope's *hmmm* offered possibilities. "I'll need to solder, but I can reset the stones and obscure any message the bracelet is meant to convey."

"No one will be able to tell the difference?" the lawyer asked.

"An expert under 30X+ magnification, maybe," Hope said. "The truth is, no one can know the exact diamond order since there's no clear pattern. Even comparing this to the Waters' bracelet, all I see are randomly placed rounds and rectangles, which is not standard Art Deco style."

"You've seen the Waters' bracelet?" Grandma asked.

"Not in person. I've analyzed the GIA report," Hope admitted.

The lawyer cleared her throat. "That's all you can offer?" Silence seemed to hang over us until she continued. "The pattern must mean something. Otherwise, all the sacrifice was for nothing."

Hope shrugged. "Mind if I take pictures? I'm guessing you'll want to reset the bracelet eventually.

"If the message is in the pattern, we may be able to secure the treasure before the Knights," I suggested.

"There is no message. We've tried everything," Grandma grumbled.

"Even Morse Code," the lawyer admitted. "The round and rectangular diamonds resemble dots and dashes."

I'd considered that too. Early twentieth-century spy craft loved the simplicity of signals hidden in plain sight, and secrets disguised as ornament.

"It's nothing but random diamonds," Lady Byrd said. The ladies shared a collective exhale.

Hope couldn't quite hide her anticipation, humming just beneath the surface. This was it. The moment. "What do the bracelets lead to?" I asked.

The sisters spoke in unison. "We don't know."

Not fear. Not deflection. Just... truth, delivered in the three words I'd dreaded. "Your mother never guessed?" I pressed.

"Not exactly," Grandma said. "She had a theory."

My pulse kicked up. "Let's hear it."

The lawyer drew in a measured breath. "She believed it wasn't simply a treasure."

Hope went still beside me. "Then what is it?"

The answer came softer this time. "Something that could bring down governments," Lady Byrd admitted.

Of course. That's why the Knights circled. They didn't want the diamonds—they wanted what the diamonds pointed to.

Silence settled over the room, thick enough to choke on. Glimmer's nails clicked once against the floor. Even she felt it. At its root, this case had nothing to do with missing jewelry.

Grandma didn't soften it. "If we hand over the bracelet to save Casey, the only thing standing between the Knights and that treasure... is you."

I gave a small nod. "I hate to say it, but there's a chance Casey's involved."

Grandma stiffened, her color rising fast. "He is not..."

"I'm not so sure about that." Lady Byrd spoke up. "Casey's been in trouble since the injury. Hanging around with the wrong crowd and that security company problem..."

"I should add," I said, "that someone tried to pickpocket me earlier. She claimed Casey sent her."

Grandma's hand flew to her throat. "Casey would never..."

Lady Byrd stepped in gently. "He's been gambling again. He came to me for money last week."

"Again?" I asked.

Grandma's shoulders sagged, as if the fight had drained out of her all at once. "He started right after his girlfriend left him. When we couldn't find the ring, he felt like he needed to repay me." She turned to her sister; guilt etched across her face. "You didn't give the money to him, did you?"

"I did. He seemed desperate," Lady Byrd admitted. "He said he could handle it, but I didn't believe him."

Grandma closed her eyes, the weight of it settling squarely on her shoulders.

"The security company is part of this," I said. "They have been watching you for a long time."

The room went still. Even Glimmer stopped shifting at my feet.

At last, the lawyer cleared her throat. "Are you suggesting that we don't pay the ransom?"

"She's suggesting we get some help from the FBI," Hope said evenly.

"No." Grandma's voice fractured. "I-I can't risk..." Her gaze flicked toward the bracelet, toward all the old family secrets sparkling in the platinum. The FBI didn't just bring rescue. They brought exposure.

The lawyer lifted a calming hand. "What do you have in mind?"

"I'll deliver the ransom," I said. "After Hope makes the modifications to the bracelet."

A plan came to mind. Rocky wouldn't like it. But if Casey was innocent, I couldn't allow him to become collateral damage in someone else's game.

I expected at least a pretense of resistance. Instead, relief washed over the three sisters so quickly that it caught me off guard.

Hope saw it before I did. Her eyes narrowed slightly. "Don't tell me the kidnappers specifically requested that Hunter deliver the bracelet."

Silence.

Of course, they had.

I'd walked straight into the three crafty senior citizens' carefully arranged chessboard. I lifted the damaged bracelet and angled it toward the light. The remaining diamonds answered with a muted fire—old cuts, softer facets, nothing like the sharp brilliance of modern stones. Still, they spoke to me, hinting at a secret just beyond my grasp.

Chapter Twenty

ALWAYS HAVE A CLEAR EXIT STRATEGY
—WISDOM FROM A JEWEL THIEF

MONDAY, 8 P.M.

The FBI minivan smelled like old coffee and humming electronics. I sat shoulder-to-shoulder with Rocky, the tension between us making the vehicle's other occupant uncomfortable. As expected, he'd been less than pleased with my decision to deliver the ransom.

"The kidnapper asked for me specifically," I said defensively.

Rocky failed to keep his frustration out of his voice. "And that doesn't concern you?"

"Of course it does, but it also means that they can't solve the puzzle without help."

"And naturally, you're all in."

"Not exactly. It makes me wonder if they know I have Lionel's secret clasp. Or just think I can solve the puzzle."

"So, Lionel is involved."

I shook my head. "I don't think he was behind the theft, but my being here isn't a coincidence. He and Claire set everything in motion to make sure Melonie's bracelet was found."

"That's premeditation."

I supposed so. "I'm betting Michael Wise, the current CEO of Wise & Sons Jewelry Store, is in this up to his ears."

"We can't prove anything, yet. The DNA on the diamonds does not have a familial match yet."

"I know." Surprising since we'd all expected a Waters match. Melodie hadn't been the donor. I'd so wanted a Wise family match next. Not a match either. So far, we had no comparison for Christian Weber.

"Which is why I have to do this," I said. "Glimmer's GPS tracker is working." I pointed to the bleep on the screen. Hope, posing as me, had just left Avalon Harbor on the ferry as instructed with my dog. We planned to switch places in Long Beach within the hour. I'd flown ahead to collect Lionel's demantoid-garnet clasp and the diamonds I'd recovered from the Catalina Casino which had been tested through Sophie's DNA lab, and to coordinate the ransom drop with the FBI. Exactly as I'd feared, the diamond I'd handed off to Rocky remained locked down at Quantico. There was no way to get it back in time.

Now, we had our eyes fixed on the live feed streaming across three monitors bolted into the interior wall. The grainy gray building with the rusty fire escape and flickering security lights reminded me that the Los Angeles Diamond District might glitter by day, but it shed its sparkle at night.

We'd parked two blocks from a warehouse the size of a football field, made from corrugated steel and with no signage. A legitimate import/export company on paper. Who-knew-what at night. The pickpocket's tracker had led us straight here—a convenient trail from Avalon to downtown L.A., maybe too convenient. Had I outsmarted the criminals or had I been set up?

"Bad part of town," I murmured, glad I carried my stun gun.

Rocky didn't look at me. "Bad part of the world."

Above the warehouse roofline, two pigeons sat on a crumbling ledge, motionless, watching. They weren't pigeons.

"Military-grade micro drones," Rocky had explained. "Thermal and audio active."

On the screen, one "bird" adjusted its position, its tiny head angling with mechanical precision no living creature could mimic.

It dragged me back to Phoenix when Rocky and I had tracked the Fire Diamond, to the hawk that had tracked my every move before turning the tide in my favor. After this case, I'd never look at a bird and think *innocent* again.

Rocky tapped on the keyboard. The thermal overlay bloomed into color.

"Three heat signatures. Weapons confirmed."

Two sat in what appeared to be a makeshift sitting area furnished with folding chairs, a card table, and temporary crates. One person had been isolated in a smaller room toward the back.

My chest tightened. "Casey's in the back room."

Rocky's jaw flexed. "Maybe. If he's not part of the plan. He worked for the security company covering the Knights' surveillance. That's not a coincidence."

The evidence stacked against Casey, but as Rocky reminded me, it wasn't proof. I checked the time. We didn't have the luxury of doubt now.

"Once the kidnappers confirm that the bracelet's in play, they'll need to move him," I said quietly.

Rocky studied the screen again. "SWAT's staged two blocks east. We'll control the room in under ninety seconds."

"And if Casey's wired?" I countered. "Or worse, cooperating?"

"Then this is bigger than ransom."

The backroom heat signature moved. "Look at his movement," I said. "He's confined. That's stress pacing."

Rocky exhaled slowly. "He's not restrained."

"He might not be tied up, but he's still not in control." I knew that kind of intimidation all too well.

I leaned closer to the monitor as one of the pigeon drones zoomed slightly, infrared sharpening around the back wall and metal door.

"Is Christian there?" I asked.

Rocky didn't answer immediately. "Not inside," he said finally. "At least not yet."

Of course not. Men like Christian Weber never stood in the room where blood could be spilled.

"You'd better get moving if you're going to make the switch with Hope." Rocky's voice remained even, but the warning in it wasn't subtle. "And be careful."

"As if I ever do anything else." I held his gaze a beat too long. "You, too."

The second I stepped out of the van, the night air wrapped around me, heavy with exhaust and marine layer dampness. A tightness cinched behind my ribs. I wasn't the only one walking into danger. If this went sideways, Rocky would be first through whatever door needed kicking in, his badge, gun, and stubborn sense of duty leading the charge.

An unmarked sedan slipped me through downtown traffic to the helipad. No sirens or lights. Just a quiet urgency.

The helicopter lifted in a hard vertical climb, the city dropping away in a glittering grid below. From above, Los Angeles looked almost peaceful except for the red river of taillights frozen along the 110 freeway, proving that the time of day didn't matter. L.A. never truly moved, it idled.

Ten minutes into the flight, Long Beach came into view—marina lights scattered across the dark water, broken by the glow of an approaching ferry. I drew a deep breath. It was time.

Hood up and platinum blonde wig itching against my scalp, I slouched into the ferry terminal like I had nowhere better to be. The act lasted all of three seconds before I located the kidnapper's spotter.

Skateboard tucked under one arm and cheap headphones hanging loose around his neck, the boy's gaze skimmed the crowd without ever looking like it was searching for something. Suspicious didn't begin to cover it.

What kind of operation recruited children to do dirty work? My jaw tightened. I pictured my nieces—bright, stubborn, too smart for their own good. "Spirited" didn't even come close. They would never be pulled into something like this. Not on my sister's watch. Hope might run her house like a Camp Pendleton drill sergeant, but she'd armed those girls with something stronger than fear. She'd taught them how to use their brain. And right now, thinking through consequences was the only thing keeping me from marching over to that boy and demanding he tell me who he worked for.

I took up position in the corner and waited for the ferry to nose against the dock.

We're being watched.

When the passengers began to spill out, I counted. One. Two. Three. On the fourth, I walked into the ladies' room, my stride unhurried. I entered the last stall on the right. I unfolded a clear plastic step, and I stepped up as passengers flooded into the restroom. No one looking under would know I was there.

The bracelet burned against my skin. I slipped it from the pouch hidden beneath my clothes. The diamonds felt warm. They had since Hope had redesigned the setting. Two remained missing—the diamond at the FBI lab and the elusive seventh. My finger traced the length of the platinum setting. No visible pattern. No engraving. Nothing that justified the blood already spilled over it. Which made no sense. I ran my thumb along the underside, and I felt it. A faint ridge. The indentation formed by the stone's placement? I looked closer.

The realization hit just as Glimmer slipped under the stall door with a determined huff. I unlocked the door and Hope slid in, closing us into a space barely big enough for two.

"The message," I whispered, turning the bracelet so the fluorescent light caught the metal. "It's embedded in the platinum underneath..."

"...disguised as the diamond anchors," Hope finished, eyes sharpening as she saw it for herself. "I know what to do."

Of course she did.

She kicked off my favorite blue boots without ceremony and

handed me the blue jacket and backpack. Beneath it all, she wore the same black slacks and fitted shirt I had on. Deliberately identical.

I stepped out of the Keds. In less than thirty seconds, we weren't twins switching places. We were two different people.

Hope touched my arm as I prepared to leave. "Something odd happened when I entered the ladies' room."

I frowned, concerned.

"A blind woman nearly took me out with her white cane."

The words shouldn't have meant anything. But they did. For a split second, I felt my father, like a shadow just out of sight. Protecting me when I'd gotten in too deep. Was it a warning or a nudge?

Then my phone vibrated in my palm. Unknown number. Right on schedule.

Hope didn't hesitate. She fired off a text to Rocky. *Trace it. Now.*

"Do you have the bracelet?" The voice on the other end was distorted—digitally flattened, stripped of age or gender and humanity.

"Yes." I kept my tone controlled.

"Get into the third yellow taxi on the curb. Or your sister will not leave the terminal." The line went dead before I could argue or decide if the threat was real. How could they know Hope stood next to me? Unless the Knights had someone on the inside...

Fear shook me to my core. This ransom handoff just got more complicated. Hope recognized the danger, too. Her composure cracked. "No. This isn't the plan." Her eyes filled, and that hit harder than the threat. "You can't go. It's too dangerous."

"I have to." I slipped the bracelet into a hidden pouch in Glimmer's harness, ready.

Hope grabbed me, arms tight around my neck like she could anchor me in place. She understood exactly what this meant. The rules had just changed. This wasn't a negotiation anymore.

It was a trap. And I was walking right into it.

I sucked in a deep calming breath. I had no choice. I removed the stun gun from my side and shoved the weapon into her hands. I pulled back just enough to meet her eyes. "Go find that blind woman and stick to her like your life depends on it, because it just might."

"What? Why?" Panic edged my sister's voice.

I took her hand in mine. "Trust me. There's more going on here than either of us knows."

Hope's head bobbed. She tried to return the gun. "You need this more."

"I'll be searched. Don't worry, I'm not completely defenseless." I fingered the lipstick tube in my pocket. "Analyze the platinum settings' underside photos. Figure out the diamonds' message. It's the only way to protect me now."

And if I was right, knowing the answer was the only leverage I'd have to survive this night.

Chapter Twenty-One

KNOW YOUR ENEMY'S GOALS
WHEN SEARCHING FOR TRUTH
—WISDOM FROM A JEWEL THIEF

MONDAY, 10:30 P.M.

The third yellow taxi idled at the curb, exhaust curling into the cool night air like a warning I chose to ignore. I opened the passenger side backseat door and slid inside.

"No dogs here." I hardly recognized the driver's heavily accented English.

I hadn't considered that Glimmer would be banned. "No dachshund, no bracelet."

The driver started to speak, but thought better of it when the backseat door opened and a second man climbed in beside me. Too large for the space, shoulders brushing mine. Tall and blond, I'd bet he'd broken his nose at least once, probably twice. He smelled like an ashtray.

"My dog goes with me," I announced, unbending.

His cold blue eyes assessed Glimmer and me. "Hands out," he ordered finally, his vowels clipped and sharp in an Eastern European-accented English.

I complied, glad I'd given Hope my stun gun as a handheld metal detector scanned me.

Of course, it chirped.

The man frowned and motioned toward my ankles. I lifted one foot. The scanner screamed louder. He grabbed the hem of my pant leg and yanked it up, exposing the buckle at my ankle.

"Buckle," he grunted.

"I could've told you that," I said evenly. "That's generally what holds boots on."

He shot me a look and swept the scanner over me again—nothing. This time, he searched my jacket, pulling out the lipstick tube. I grabbed it back before he could say a word.

The wand continued to trace my waistband, then the seams of my sleeves with slow, deliberate motions. He'd made his point. I wouldn't be carrying anything that could help me escape.

Beside me, Glimmer shifted. The scanner wailed again. The man's head snapped up.

"Seriously?" I arched a brow. "She's wearing a collar. Do you want me to take it off of her?"

As if on cue, Glimmer let out a low, rolling growl that didn't belong to a dog her size. It was pure Doberman menace packed into fourteen pounds of fury. The driver on the other side of the plexiglass actually cringed.

The bruiser beside me hesitated. He scanned her collar again, visibly annoyed, then tucked the device into his waistband. "Fine."

He stepped out without another word, shutting the door with a solid thud. I heard the locks click just as I realized there were no handles on the doors. I was trapped. Help needed to arrive from outside.

The taxi eased into traffic. Through the rear window, I caught sight of the bruiser climbing into another taxi idling at the curb. It slipped in behind us a moment later, keeping just enough distance not to look obvious.

Smart. If someone planned to follow me, they'd have to decide which target mattered. Or realize too late that they'd chosen the wrong one.

I watched Long Beach vanish in the rearview mirror as my

driver headed north on the 710 freeway. Streetlights streaked across the windows as we picked up speed on the mostly-clear five-lane highway. I forced myself to breathe slowly, noting the other vehicles around us.

Hopefully, Rocky had been tracking the taxi's movement since it pulled out of the port and wasn't far behind. I rested my hand lightly on Glimmer's back, her muscles tense beneath my fingers. Mine probably were too.

A surge of hope rose within me as we merged onto the 110 freeway ramp, and even better when we exited on 4th Street, only a few blocks from the pickpocket's location. Except we bypassed the building under surveillance and continued into downtown's canyon of dark towers. The pickpocket and the cozy setup had been a decoy.

Few cars passed as we turned north. The street stretched wide and well-lit. Grand Park sprawled on the left, its lit pathways cutting through the dark green shadows.

On the right, towers rose. 2 California Plaza, arguably the tallest skyscraper in downtown L.A., set back from the street. I remembered afternoon crowds on the plaza level and a fountain I'd tossed a coin into. I'd been here many times before, both buying and selling for our Sunset Peak jewelry store. Never after-hours. Even if Rocky was somewhere behind us, following Glimmer's tracker, the tall building could obscure the signal. We were on our own.

Glimmer butted her head against my thigh and looked up at me with her dark eyes as the cab slowed and turned into the underground parking garage.

The driver's phone buzzed. He answered in German. At least I thought it was German until I only understood about thirty percent of the words. Plattdeutsch, I guessed, a northern German dialect spoken in Prussia, the Teutonic Knights' stronghold.

Then he hung up, glanced at me in the rearview mirror, and scanned an entry card. The parking garage gate's arm lifted, and we slowly descended into the building's belly.

The taxi rolled to a stop beside an ominous black SUV with tinted windows so dark they reflected nothing back. No other vehicle was around us until another taxi pulled up beside us. The same bruiser from the port opened my passenger door. "Out."

I stepped onto the oil-stained pavement, Glimmer tucked under my arm. Her nose twitched, no doubt smelling exhaust and damp cement. I located the cameras dotting the ceiling right away. The small black domes watched without blinking.

The bruiser gestured toward an elevator set into the far wall. No signage. No directory. Just brushed steel doors and another keycard panel.

My pulse pounded hard enough to echo in my ears. No visible exits. No obvious blind corners. No comforting sounds of potential witnesses. And no way GPS could bounce a signal with any kind of accuracy in a structure like this. Assuming the Knights hadn't blocked it the moment I'd entered the cab anyway.

Think. I shifted Glimmer to my other arm and scanned the space without turning my head. Two fire doors. Both alarmed. Stairwell access beside the elevator required a badge to access.

The bruiser pressed a card to the elevator panel. The light blinked green, and the doors slid open with a whisper.

I stepped inside. Floor buttons beside another small digital pad mounted below the mirrored half wall.

Of course, I looked like something a cat dragged in. I ran my fingers through my breeze-tossed hair as the doors closed, sealing us in. My mind raced faster than the lift. If the Knights wanted me dead, I'd already be dead.

They wanted the bracelet. Or what it led to. Which meant I still had leverage. I hoped. I adjusted my grip on Glimmer and let my hand brush the inside seam of Glimmer's harness. The platinum bracelet radiated warmth against my fingers, offering strength.

Hope was decoding the message. I could feel her frustration from here. While I had the original, she'd been forced to work with sketches and photos. The truth was still in them. She just needed to put the puzzle together.

Faster.

Her response hardly helped. *Patience. I'm getting closer.*

Not what I wanted to hear as the elevator slowed. I rolled my shoulders back, forcing air into my lungs as I mentally ran through my hostage training. Rule one: stay unpredictable. Rule two: make them underestimate you.

The elevator doors slid open to a dim hallway lined with frosted glass and industrial steel. The bruiser stepped out and glanced back. "Move."

I did. Slowly at first. I needed time to catalog every detail for later use. Because one way or another, I was leaving this building. And if I couldn't find an exit? I'd need to create one.

Brave thoughts as a solid wood door creaked open in front of me. The noise didn't catch my attention. The nameplate did. Diamond Designs, Tash's future husband's company. My pulse kicked up.

Her father's doing... or his approval? Either way, Tash was in it. And her fiancé? Was he part of this, too? And why risk me seeing any of it? The answer hit fast. Cold.

They weren't worried about what I'd seen. Because I wasn't supposed to survive the night.

Plush carpet muffled my footsteps as I entered. The reception area gleamed with glass and chrome. A tasteful understatement meant to signal class without shouting it.

The bruiser directed me toward a side door. I put Glimmer on the ground. She stayed close to my left leg, silent but alert, her body coiled tight as I skirted the immaculate marble desk. Despite the air of expensive perfume, something sour lingered beneath it.

Tash looked up when I entered, her usual confidence missing as her eyes darted like a cornered animal. She wasn't surprised to see me.

Her normally immaculate hair hung loose around her shoulders. Makeup failed to conceal a fresh bruise darkening her cheekbone. One hand gripped the edge of the chair as if she needed it to stay upright.

Or she needed me to think she did. I couldn't decide.

Light glowed beneath another closed door across the room. Low male voices murmured beyond it. We weren't alone.

Glimmer's hackles rose. Mine followed.

"Who hit you?"

Tash stiffened. "It doesn't matter."

I didn't want to care, to be drawn into her drama, but I couldn't help myself. "It does." My voice came out colder than I intended. I hated men who used their strength to intimidate.

I'd seen it before, the kind of power that backed off when challenged. Not Bruiser's style. That man was an equal opportunity bully; his skills were sold to his current employer.

Tash's eyes tracked mine toward the door. "They are some nasty characters," she whispered. "We need to concentrate on getting out of here alive."

Her use of the common "we" concerned me more than the bruise. Did she see me as her savior? "Why are you here?"

"Two men picked me up at the jewelry store this morning," Tash replied.

"In front of your security guard and family?" I asked. "No one stopped them?"

Her gaze slid away. She hadn't been dragged. She'd gone willingly.

"Why?" I asked.

She exhaled. "Bad choices."

Regret? Or performance? It could go either way.

Tash pointed toward the closed door. "They don't trust you."

We had something in common. I didn't trust them either.

"I'm supposed to verify that the bracelet you brought is the real thing." Her composure wavered. "You have the bracelet, don't you?" Desperation rang sharply in her words.

Sophie's warning echoed in my mind. *Tash's worst fear is being irrelevant.*

Was Tash aligning with whoever held the stronger position by choice or fear? Hostage training had a name for it—Stockholm Syndrome, a tactic used by captives to increase their chances of survival by appeasing their captors.

"Like I had time to create a copy," I replied evenly.

She chewed her lip. "Assuming I could tell the difference anyway."

Honesty, dressed up as humility? She'd pushed it too far—turned the whole encounter into a cat-and-mouse game. The only question was... which one of us was the cat?

"I've been tasked with figuring out the bracelet's message," she continued.

Of course, she had.

My instincts sharpened. The game was no longer solely about escape. Information control became the key. "You have the Waters' bracelet?" I asked.

Her eyes flicked to the table beneath the jeweler's lamp.

There it was, laid out on black velvet. Even under artificial light, it glowed with an energy. As if sensing its twin nearby.

The sparkle didn't distract me. The bracelets belonged together. But—not yet.

From the other room, a chair scraped. A man laughed. Glimmer pressed closer to my calf, silent but ready.

Tash swallowed. "They think the answer is in combining them."

"They're wrong."

Her eyes widened. She'd believed it too.

"They need both," I continued softly. "But not like they think."

"So, you know the secret." The edge in her voice betrayed something deeper than fear. Ambition?

"I do not," I replied honestly.

Tash's fingers dug into the chair. Fear or frustration? "You don't understand. You must give them what they want. If they think you're stalling..."

"I'm not." I lowered my voice. "I don't know if an answer is even possible. Melodie's bracelet isn't complete."

"What?" Her shriek drew footsteps to the closed door. The handle rattled. I slid my hand toward my jacket and stepped back, not retreating, repositioning.

Patience. I wasn't getting out of here with both bracelets. Not yet.

First, I needed to decide: Was Tash the frightened cat? Or the one luring the mouse into the trap? Either way, I was done playing polite.

Chapter Twenty-Two

JUSTICE COMES IN MANY FORMS
—WISDOM FROM A JEWEL THIEF

MONDAY 11 P.M.

I recognized Christian Weber the moment the door opened. A silhouette hovered in the light behind him, casting long shadows across the polished floor. A shiver shuddered down my spine as the realization struck. Christian was the henchman, the acquirer. Someone else made the rules. That presence, just out of sight, that didn't move or speak, held my life in his hands.

I tried to look in and confront my judge and jury, but Weber closed the door halfway, not enough to seal it. Enough to keep me guessing.

Weber turned out to be shorter than his photo had suggested. Older, too. Late fifties, maybe early sixties. Thick through the middle, his expensive suit cut to compensate for the weight he no longer bothered to fight. The Knights' signet ring flashed on his right hand.

His face might have been forgettable if not for his eyes. Tash had called them emotionless. Not exactly. I'd call them methodical. Yes, they were green like Tash's, the same shade as the demantoid garnets in the Duette's clasp, and unemotional in a way that gave no doubt to his goals. He planned to the slightest detail.

His gaze slid from Tash to me, then Glimmer, and back again. Assessing. Calculating.

"Ms. Hunter," he said smoothly. I recognized his Midwestern origins in the more nasal, urban quality of his accent. "Thank you for joining us."

Glimmer didn't growl. That worried me more than if she had.

Weber's eyes flicked to the Waters' bracelet resting on the velvet beside Tash. "You understand why we require verification."

"You understand why I require honesty," I replied.

The corner of his mouth twitched. "You are very much your father's daughter."

His words hit me like a sucker punch. I tried to keep my face neutral. I'm sure I failed. "You know my father?"

Weber's exhale might have concealed a laugh. He'd found my weakness. Or so he assumed. "We worked together."

"What kind of work?" I asked through gritted teeth. The possibilities filled my mind. Had my father stolen something from or for him? The man was an acquirer.

Weber's gaze did not waver. "Mutually-beneficial acquisitions."

That told me everything. And nothing.

Tash went perfectly still beside me, the kind of stillness that comes before something breaks.

Weber didn't raise his voice. He didn't need to.

"Your father..." he said, each word placed with surgical care, "...understands that diamonds are power. Nations have risen and fallen over less."

He held my gaze without blinking. I read people well. Micro-expressions. Breath shifts. That flicker in the eyes when they lied. It was part instinct, part training, part survival. Christian Weber had to be the most controlled man I'd ever met. No wasted motion. No stray emotion. If he pulled the trigger, literal or otherwise, it would be because the math demanded it. And I had just become part of his calculation.

I searched Weber's face for the truth. No tells. No cracks. Just composure. For the first time in a long time, I wondered if I'd met my match.

"And the innocent?" I asked. "They're collateral?"

The faintest shift touched his expression, less than irritation, more like disappointment.

"Sentiment clouds strategy," he said evenly. "Your father does not suffer from that weakness."

There it was. The subtle test. *Was I like him? Or would I flinch?*

My father stealing jewels from vaults? Outsmarting insurance syndicates for sport? Humiliating men who thought money equaled intelligence? Absolutely. But dealing with the suffering of children? No.

"My father steals from the greedy," I said, holding Weber's gaze. "He doesn't traffic in human misery."

Weber's eyes honed like a man adjusting a lens. "How certain are you?"

The question slid under my guard. *Am I?* The doubt slipped in before I could shut it down. Had Dad taken a job from Weber without knowing the full reach of it? Or worse—had he known and justified it the way men like Weber did?

Or was this exactly what he wanted? A daughter questioning her father. And for the first time since walking into the room, I wasn't entirely sure whether I was interrogating him or being dismantled by him.

From the shadowed room behind Weber, the shape shifted. Not particularly large, but clearly the real muscle. Weber saw it and refocused the conversation. "You have Melodie Waters' bracelet," he said ultra-calmly. "And you understand its significance."

"I understand you think combining them unlocks something," I replied.

"You disagree."

"I do."

Tash's breath caught. Weber's gaze locked on me. Cold, but curious.

"I'd advise against playing me, Ms. Hunter."

"Not my style." I dared him to challenge me. "Melodie's bracelet is missing diamonds. You're aware of that. I've recovered six. I'd wager you have the seventh."

His expression remained flat, but his lip twitched into a snarl. How fitting. "Two of the four stones I recovered had blood on them," I continued. "They're at Quantico. I imagine the familial match will trace back to you."

No denial. No flare of temper. Just that maddening composure as if we were discussing market forecasts instead of murder. *Fine.* I went for a reaction. "How are you related to Theodor Seitz, the man who commissioned the Duette?"

His pause was so minute I almost missed it. "I am not."

"Then someone in your family was assigned to protect it, because knowing about this..." I gestured toward the Waters' bracelet. "...isn't a coincidence. It's an inheritance." I let my words linger before adding. "It's only a matter of time before the FBI closes in on you. So, tell me why? You're far too intelligent to kill for a bracelet."

His brow lifted slightly. "I didn't kill anyone."

"Yet you have merchandise stolen by a dead man," I added.

"Acquired by an ambitious associate, I'm afraid. Fired for not following protocol. I will, of course, provide the widow's contact information to the proper channels."

"And return the bracelet," I interjected.

"To its rightful owner, yes."

He'd agreed too quickly. I felt the trap closing in on me. "And who would that be?"

"Georg Friedrich, Prince of Prussia and head of the Imperial House of Hohenzollern. The direct descendant of Kaiser Wilhelm II."

Silence settled between us. From the corner of my eye, I

caught Tash studying him. I couldn't tell if she was as shaken as I was... or if she'd already chosen a side. Or worse, both.

"The laws of provenance..." I began.

"...will be decided by *der Landgericht*," Weber finished smoothly. The precision of his high German left no doubt. He'd learned the language as a child.

"The what?" Tash asked.

"It's a German civil court." I knew the rules. I'd testified at a handful of Nazi-era looted jewels cases. Sophie was the expert, though.

"A French spy stole the Duette from a dying queen," Christian added.

No need to disclose the bill of sale in Grandma's possession. "The issue will be if the diamonds were sourced through colonial exploitation."

Weber's lip twitch gave me that answer and an opening. "How did that happen? How did an American diplomat's wife even meet the last Empress of Germany?" I asked.

Weber's disdain surfaced, brief but unmistakable. His first genuine reaction. "Said diplomat attended Eton with the young Prince Albert Victor."

I shrugged. "So?"

"Albert Victor, nicknamed Eddy, was Queen Victoria's eldest grandson. He died before ascending the British throne. He invited his new American friend to ride at Windsor, where he met the queen's German grandson, Prince Wilhelm."

"They were friends?" The realization was a duh moment I'd missed as another puzzle piece slid into place. Eton College educated the British aristocracy, foreign royalty, and the sons of foreign diplomats. Wilhelm, Queen Victoria's grandson and cousin to the future King of England, would have moved easily in those circles.

I chose my next words with precision, studying him.

"The FBI will never allow the two bracelets to leave U.S. jurisdiction," I said evenly. "And you expect me to believe you're prepared to face federal smuggling charges... just to return a necklace to a figurehead king?"

Weber adjusted his cufflinks. "Your father once underestimated how far I was willing to go to attain my goals."

There it was. Confirmation without confession. My stomach tightened, instinct firing before logic could catch up. "And how far is that?"

That shadow in the doorway shifted again. Weber didn't look back. "Enough small talk. Give me the bracelet."

"Not until you release Casey." I held my ground. I had to. The second I turned over the diamonds, I became expendable. "A deal is a deal."

His chuckle sent ice down my veins. "Brave words for a woman with only a piece of her part of the bargain."

Glimmer's rumbling growl alerted me. Bruiser had entered, rubbing his right fist in preparation, his intentions crystal clear.

I stretched my neck. Christian Weber would stop at nothing to get what he wanted, exactly as Tash had claimed. Which told me one thing: This wasn't over. And just maybe, this time I was in over my head.

His voice remained level, but the air shifted. "No one is coming to your aid, Ms. Hunter. Give me the bracelet."

"Not happening." I kept my voice steady. "Until I see Casey."

A flicker, there and gone, tightened his mouth. He inclined his head toward the back room. "Casey."

A young man stepped through the same threshold where I'd seen the shadow earlier. Shaggy head down and shoulders collapsed inward, he moved slowly, but not because anyone forced him to.

And in that single, brutal second, the truth settled like a rock. He wasn't a hostage. He'd been in the room with the shadow I had yet to identify. "Your grandmother will be quite disappointed." Casey had the courtesy to flinch.

Weber's mouth curved faintly. "Now it's your turn."

Fair was fair. I dragged in a slow breath and assessed my chances. The bruiser sealed the entry door, his arms folded, stance planted, the hard outline beneath his jacket advertising exactly how this would end if I tested him. Even if I slipped past him, the elevators and stairwell required key-card access.

My gaze shifted to the floor-to-ceiling windows. Too high to survive the fall. I searched the ledges anyway for the metallic glint of a perched "pigeon," for any sign Rocky's drones watched. Because about now, I could use a miracle.

"I wouldn't recommend jumping," Weber said mildly, noting my glance. His patience thinned, but his control held.

My time just ran out. My eye wandered to the Waters' bracelet. "Why?" I asked. "Why were so many people willing to sacrifice so much to keep these bracelets apart? What do they lead to?"

An almost reverent smile touched Weber's lips. *"Only when twin heirs—born of one blood and one destiny—do restore with their own hands the broken chain,"* he recited softly, *"shall the world remember its proper order and be made whole once more."*

Hearing the prophecy in his voice made it sound less like legend... and more like doctrine.

"You can't seriously believe monarchy will be restored in Germany," I said.

"Not in my lifetime," he said calmly. "But perhaps in my grandson's. Monarchy is the divinely natural order of civilization. Democracy is an experiment. Experiments fail. It is my duty to provide the tools."

"The tools?" I scoffed. "You think a diamond mine is going to replace freedom?"

His eyes narrowed, not in anger, but in recognition. "You do know the secret."

I hadn't been certain until he'd confirmed it, and knowing now didn't feel like a victory. It felt like I'd stepped over a line I couldn't uncross.

Glimmer stiffened beside me, her body coiled tight, gaze flicking between Weber and the bruiser as if she could calculate angles and distance the way I was trying to. The lipstick tube pressed against my thigh from inside my pocket. I needed to get out of here.

One twist. One chance...

Chapter Twenty-Three
GOOD TIMING BEATS THE BEST LAID PLANS—WISDOM FROM A JEWEL THIEF

MONDAY 11:30 P.M.

I took my chances the second Weber's gaze settled on Glimmer. "If she doesn't have the bracelet on her, then the dog has it."

As the bruiser reached for Glimmer, she transformed. My mini dachshund went full badger hunter, her growl low and purpose swift and feral. She darted under his grasp, then launched, teeth snapping onto his hand. Bruiser's howl split the room the moment she caught flesh.

I ripped the lipstick from my pocket, twisted the base, and hurled it past Weber's shoulder. The flash grenade detonated against the wall in an explosion of white light, bone-deep concussion, and a gunshot crack that ripped through the air.

Alarms shrieked all around me. Everyone hit the floor, searching for the threat. I didn't. I lunged forward, snatched the Waters bracelet from the table, and slammed my shoulder into the bruiser's hunched frame while he clutched his bloody hand. He toppled. I wrenched his Sig from beneath his jacket before he could recover.

The weapon's weight steadied me, sort of. I hadn't had time

to grab the key card. So, as the smoke cleared, I needed to be long gone. I already pictured Weber pushing the pursuit with single-minded purpose.

"Glimmer!" My dog hugged my heels as I bolted through the door into the hallway. Enthusiasm was tempered by our reality. Without a key card, we were dead in the hallway. I yanked the stairwell door anyway.

Of course, it didn't budge. I raised the barrel toward the lock... A card slapped the reader. The light blinked green, and the door clicked open.

Tash stood there, hair disheveled, mascara streaked, eyes terrified-wide but resolute. "Come on," she said. "Let's get out of here."

Trust her? Like it mattered. Behind us, Weber's voice cut through the chaos. Loud, not the least bit calm. *Trust the enemy in your sight*, I told myself.

I snatched the card out of Tash's hands. "Glimmer, find Rocky." I swept my arm, signaling her to go down the stairwell. The dog tossed her head and sniffed. She hesitated a microsecond longer and headed up the stairs. *A roof entry? Maybe.* Optimism stirred. "You, too," I pointed at Tash. "I'll distract them."

I shoved Tash back through the stairwell door and slammed it shut in her face.

"Trust the dog," I called, already moving.

I sprinted for the elevators and slapped the key card onto the reader. The doors slid open like they'd been waiting for me. Lucky break. I dove inside and hammered a scatter of floor buttons—anything to throw off a tail. Six lit up in quick succession.

The doors shut before anyone could make a move. When the car stopped, I slipped out on another floor, cut back through the corridor, scanned the key card again, and re-entered the stairwell from the level below. This time, I caught the name on the scanner card.

Tash Wise's access. Not incriminating on its own. She was engaged to the man whose office we'd been in. His role in all of this was the real question. Had he been the second shadow in the back room? Or just another decoy Tash's father had carefully maneuvered into place?

I heard Glimmer's claws clicking fast and purposefully on the steps above me when I returned to the original floor to follow her trail. She continued upward. Didn't look back.

Tash stood frozen in the doorway where I'd left her, eyes wide and unfocused.

"The dog's right," she said breathlessly. "There's another way out. We're on the thirty-sixth floor. If we go up to fifty, there's a freight elevator." She swallowed. "My... fiancé brings his companions in that way."

Of course he did. I didn't ask the obvious question. "Up," I ordered. And we ran.

Two flights below, a metal access door crashed open. Boots slammed against concrete. The chase was on.

Adrenaline snapped through me, and I surged faster. Eight floors left. Then footsteps thundered above and below, heavy, urgent and closing in.

For one reckless second, I hoped it was Rocky. Otherwise, we were sandwiched. And in a matter of seconds, one—or both— would be on us.

Frantically, I looked for cover. The utilitarian corridor offered no mercy, just raw concrete walls and fluorescent lights that exposed every inch of space. I shoved the key card into Tash's shaking hand. "Go to the freight elevator. Now. I'll slow them down."

Her fingers trembled so badly that the card almost slipped.

Steps pounded above us. The pursuers were close now. I stepped back into the landing corner, concrete at my back, and checked the Sig's magazine by touch.

Six rounds. Six would be enough if I didn't miss.

I locked both hands around the Sig and aimed at the bend in the stairs where the first head would appear. *Showdown in a high-*

rise stairwell. I didn't want to think about the tagline on the morning news.

"I told you to go." My calmness surprised me.

Tash hadn't moved. She stood rooted to the step, eyes wide and glassy, fear locking her in place.

"Snap out of it, Tash," I snapped. "Your father isn't going to kill you."

That broke through. Her focus returned, but not with relief. "Not my father." Then she turned and ran, bursting out the door.

Not her father? What did that mean? But pounding steps drowned out my question. Close enough now, I could hear labored breath...

I adjusted my stance. Focused my aim. And waited for the first shadow to appear.

The men from below hit the turn first, bruiser's dark shape surging up the curve. I squeezed off a warning shot. The blast detonated in the concrete shaft, recoil jolting my arms. Sound slammed back at me, deafening until ringing swallowed everything else. No footsteps. No voices. No warning. Just smoke drifting from the barrel and the throb in my head.

Five bullets left...

In the end, I didn't fire another shot. Dark figures stormed the landing like avenging angels. Two defended me while the others finished the job.

It was over in seconds, yet still not fast enough because when the dust settled, and the henchmen had been zip-tied and hauled away, the shadow had vanished.

And not one of them dared to identify him. Tash included.

Chapter Twenty-Four

SOME SECRETS ARE BEST LEFT UNDISCOVERED
—WISDOM FROM A JEWEL THIEF

TUESDAY 8:30 A.M.

I spent the remainder of the night in the FBI field office on Wilshire Boulevard. Suite 1700. The building itself dated to 1969 and was listed on the National Register of Historic Places. A late-modern federal structure constructed with pale concrete and dark ribbon windows that followed the more-functional-than-decorative style of the period. Although the interior had been updated, practicality still ruled. Light tile and gray carpet ran the length of the space, while glass-walled offices glowed under fluorescent lights bright enough to read fine print well into the night.

Through the windows, Wilshire Boulevard's traffic streamed below in steady lines of red and white, and I'd spent most of the night watching it from the same conference room as agents came and went, knowing the answers to the Waters' Duette sat on the table directly in front of me, sealed in an evidence bag, its old-cut diamonds dulled by plastic and flat light.

Glimmer had claimed the chair beside me hours ago. She sat upright with her paws pressed over her ears, huffing every time a door opened or a phone rang. My dachshund required her beauty sleep and made her position on the matter clear.

Melodie's bracelet stayed tucked inside her harness, exactly where I'd hidden it. That one wasn't evidence. It belonged to Melodie's heirs, and I intended to return it—after I understood its secret. And that required both halves of the Duette.

The Waters' bracelet was different. That piece sat on the conference table, sealed in an evidence bag, logged and untouchable. Tied to murder and kidnapping, federal chain-of-custody rules wrapped around it like barbed wire.

Two bracelets. One original necklace. Two completely different legal destinies.

Of course, I needed them together under proper lab lighting and magnification, not available at the Wilshire field office. So, I waited, impatience eating at me, for authorization from someone three floors above us or three states away to move the Waters' bracelet to a facility equipped to discover the truth hidden in the platinum and stones.

I understood that chain-of-custody required documentation at every step. Logged evidence numbers. Supervisor approvals. Transport clearance. The Bureau ran on documentation the way my world ran on instinct.

And my gut said that the clock ticked. Christian Weber had lawyered up. Tash had been deemed a victim and released. And the shadow in the back room? No one saw anything except for me.

Every minute that bracelet sat sealed in plastic felt like we fell further behind.

Rocky worked the process with practiced efficiency. He'd traded his commando jumper for his daily uniform, likely stashed in his office for moments exactly like this. Hours later, he finally shed the jacket, loosened the tie, and rolled up his sleeves.

Watching him move through forms and calls made the divide between us obvious. My mission ended with recovery. His began there, building a case that secured a conviction and survived an appeal.

Different definitions of success. Both deserved respect.

Exhaustion crept in once the adrenaline drained. Every muscle ached from the concussive blast to the sprint up ten flights of stairs. My ears still rang faintly, a high-pitched reminder of how close things had come.

At some point, sitting in that conference chair, I must've drifted to sleep because I woke with a start when Rocky stepped back into the conference room, two Starbucks cups in hand.

"Authorization is complete." He set one of the cups in front of me. "The Waters' bracelet will be released to the agent accompanying you to the lab you requested."

I reached for the coffee like it was a medical intervention. My head pounded in dull, uneven beats.

Glimmer groaned in solidarity and dragged a paw over her face before burying her head beneath both of them. If dachshunds could file formal complaints about mornings, she would've drafted one.

Rocky watched us over the rim of his cup. "You two always this pleasant before nine?"

"Define pleasant," I muttered, taking a long swallow.

Rocky, infuriatingly, looked composed. Tired around the eyes, maybe, but fully alert.

It took a long minute for my brain to catch up with the caffeine. "I'll call Hope," I said finally. My sister had spent the night at the Beverly Hilton. I envied her shower more than the room service.

I also needed to loop Sophie in before we stepped anywhere near a microscope again. This wasn't just gemology anymore. It was imperial history, cipher logic, and colonial ambition layered in platinum. She needed to be part of this investigation. She would see patterns the rest of us would miss.

"Who's the lucky babysitter?" I asked.

"Me."

My eyes snapped fully open. "What about that conflict of interest?"

"I drew the short straw." His brow lifted knowingly. "Rumor has it you're a morning monster."

Glimmer huffed in offense without lifting her head.

"I'm not..." I stopped, yawned, and reconsidered. "Fine. Call it a temporary morning condition."

Rocky almost smiled.

"How about I shower, and we meet at Hope's hotel?" I suggested.

Rocky slipped his sports coat off the back of the chair and shrugged into it. "I'll pick you up in an hour." He motioned toward the doorway. "Ramos will drive you."

Before I could reach for it, Rocky lifted the evidence bag and secured the Waters' bracelet inside a hard-sided briefcase, snapping it shut with finality. Chain of custody. Even from me.

Two espressos and a cold shower later, Rocky picked up both Hope and me, and we returned to the Jewelry District. The low-profile building that housed the lab Sophie preferred had no signage announcing what went on inside. Just frosted glass, reinforced doors, and discreet security cameras tucked into the corners. I knew the place well. I'd used them more than once.

Inside, the lab looked like a medical research facility with white counters, articulated gem microscopes bolted to heavy tables, fiber-optic lighting arms, and spectrometers humming softly against one wall. A DiamondView unit sat beneath a dark hood. Laser inscription scanners. Digital inclusion mapping software open on dual monitors. A perfect setup for our task.

Rocky dismissed the lab-coated techs with a look. The inner lab doors sealed with a soft hydraulic hiss behind us. No cameras in this room. No federal recording devices. Just controlled lighting, sealed walls, and a secure computer feed.

Rocky set the briefcase on the counter and popped the locks. The evidence bag holding Christian Weber's stone came out first, followed by the Waters' bracelet. I removed Melodie's bracelet from the hidden pocket in Glimmer's harness and placed it beside its twin near the computer.

Silence settled over the room.

Alone, each bracelet looked elegant, the old European cuts throwing softer, warmer flashes under the lab lights.

Rocky stepped back as I connected the two bracelets. The moment they touched, my gut jumped. The dot-dash pattern flowed seamlessly across both. File marks matched. Hinge tension matched. Even the subtle curve of the platinum spine aligned perfectly. They belonged together.

Melodie's bracelet, though, looked wounded with three empty platinum settings gaping open. Even with the four stones Hope had reset, the pattern appeared like a fracture set but not fully healed.

"Ah," Sophie's voice carried crisply through the speaker, refined and measured, "they are quite exquisite." No visual, just a voice, the way she liked it.

I touched Rocky's sleeve. "Sophie, meet Agent Rocky Rockman, FBI. And behave. No personal commentary allowed."

"Agent Rockman," she replied smoothly, "a pleasure. I serve as research analyst for Sterling & Sons."

I gave a quiet scoff. "That's the modest version. She's far more important..."

Sophie intercepted my commentary. As ever, she preferred the shadows to the spotlight. "We are losing time," she said briskly. "Shall we proceed?"

"You can trust her," Hope added, leaning over Melodie's bracelet. She carefully set the stone I'd recovered from Christain into the waiting seat.

The effect was immediate. The symmetry corrected itself. I swallowed. The pieces spoke. And for the first time since this began, I understood why people had killed to keep them apart.

Even Rocky leaned in.

"They were never meant to be separate," Hope said softly.

"No," I agreed.

I flipped the Waters bracelet over and ran my thumb along the underside of the platinum spine. The faint irregularity I'd felt last night wasn't wear.

I handed the Duette to Hope. She slid it under the high-powered microscope and adjusted the focus. Her breath caught.

"You're right," she said. "Look at the pattern, Sophie. Hunter thinks it's Braille."

"Braille?" Sophie repeated. "How very progressive for its era. Quite brilliant, Hunter. Let us see if you are right." Sophie continued while she typed. "By 1914, Braille was formally adopted in German institutions for the blind. Empress Auguste Viktoria supported hospitals and education initiatives in that sphere. Its use would have been quite possible. Raised dots beneath platinum would escape notice unless one knew to look."

The lab fell silent, save for the low hum of the equipment.

Rocky braced his hands on the counter, controlled but coiled. Hope stayed locked on the microscope, barely breathing.

I watched the monitor as numbers appeared one line at a time. No one dared breathe. I could feel my pulse pounding in my throat. We had the code. Now we just needed the answer.

"A private message," Sophie concluded calmly. "Designed to endure."

Rocky straightened. "Coordinates?"

"There's no direction," Hope said. "Another cipher?"

Sophie's tone shifted. "If they are coordinates, they may be encoded. Nineteenth-century aristocrats adored layered ciphers. I'll read them in pairs first. Then in mirrored sequence."

I watched the screen, my pulse ticking upward. Nothing made sense.

"We are missing a piece," Sophie stated calmly, as though announcing an overlooked footnote rather than a critical flaw.

I thought about Lionel's piece, the original clasp that made both bracelets into one. "Sophie, upload the clasp."

She did. A three-dimensional replica of the complete necklace showed on the screen. Hope and I figured it out at the same time. "It's a compass rose. The demantoid are the directions."

"Quite right. South and East," Sophie said. "I dare say, ladies, you're holding a map."

The room went very still. "To what?" Rocky asked.

"The Kaiser's long-lost diamond mine in German East Africa," Hope replied.

"In Tanzania specifically," I said.

"The direction is in the Udzungwa Mountains," Sophie began, precise as ever. "One finds terrain empires favor, and outsiders wisely avoid it."

A map filled the screen. Sophie continued. "The range is part of the Eastern Arc. It's rather inhospitable. Sheer escarpments. Dense rainforest. Valleys that swallow roads as quickly as they're cut. Even today, access is limited. In the late nineteenth century, it would have required a deliberate expedition."

"The escarpments contain formations capable of hosting skarn deposits..."

I caught Rocky's frown and qualified the comment. "Skarn deposits are mineral-rich rock zones formed when magma intrudes into limestone or other carbonate rocks. It's not kimberlite, but it could feasibly host diamonds and demantoid in the same area."

Sophie concluded evenly, "If one wished to hide a mine tied to imperial ambition far from trade routes and scrutiny, the Udzungwa Mountains would be entirely feasible."

Trust Hope to translate that into something sharper. "Remote. Inaccessible. Conveniently forgotten. It's the perfect place to fund an insurrection."

"Insurrection of what?" Rocky asked, skepticism unmistakable. He'd come into this diamonds-and-dynasties case midstream and needed it translated into something that fit within a federal statute.

"The Teutonic Knights are *Kaisereichts*," Sophie said.

"Monarchists. They believe Germany's rightful leader is Kaiser Wilhelm's heir."

"Who happens to be a twin," Hope added. "The twin princes' births fulfilled the legacy."

Hope and I spoke the next line together, the words now too familiar.

"Only when twin heirs—born of one blood and one destiny—restore with their own hands the broken chain shall the world remember its proper order and be made whole once more."

"This is about restoring a monarchy in Germany?" Rocky dragged a hand through his hair. I understood the disbelief in his voice.

Germany wasn't a fragile, collapsing nation. It was one of the strongest economies in the world. An insurrection there sounded absurd. And yet... political fractures existed everywhere. History proved that stability could be tested if someone had enough money, enough influence, and enough patience.

"No," I answered. "It's about funding one."

"Allow me to interject," Sophie said, her tone cool and precise. "The bracelets' damage regrettably obscured several defining digits. Locating the mine may prove... optimistic. The coordinates span nearly one hundred square kilometers."

My gut took notice. Melodie had permanently protected the treasure. But the Knights didn't know that. I didn't need Sophie's maps to see the next move. Despite the recent mishap, men like Weber, driven by ideology, didn't retreat; they recalculated because the diamonds were the future.

This didn't end when the message was decoded. It ended when the source and every nonbeliever who knew the answer were eliminated. Because if I didn't shut this down, the Knights wouldn't stop coming until the answers were theirs.

Or someone I loved became collateral.

Chapter Twenty-Five

TUESDAY 10:00 A.M.

Rocky pulled to the curb outside the executive terminal at Burbank Airport. The low-slung terminal constructed of tinted glass and brushed steel on Sherman Way was as quiet as usual. No commercial chaos. No idling rideshares. No lines snaking toward metal detectors. Just one attendant who looked up the moment our SUV rolled to a stop.

Hope slipped out first with Glimmer, leash in hand. "We'll check in," she said, already heading toward the glass doors.

Inside, I knew it would be seamless. Sophie had seen to that. The flight would leave the moment I boarded with no bureaucratic drag.

Rocky didn't say a word, but I could see it in the way his gaze tracked the building, assessing. For a federal agent used to paperwork bottlenecks and jurisdictional turf wars, this had to feel like stepping into another world, one where doors opened because someone anticipated the need.

"If I didn't know better," Rocky said, stepping into my space, "I'd swear you were a spook."

"Occupational hazard," I replied.

His hands came up, warm against my face, thumbs brushing just beneath my ears while his eyes searched mine. "Weber's in custody," he continued. "But we still don't have the shadow in the other room."

He'd believed me. Even without corroboration.

"Why did you release Tash?" I had to ask.

"Footage from Wise & Sons jewelry stores backed her story. She appeared to be abducted and forced to cooperate."

Of course it did. The Wises protected their own.

"Have you found her fiancé?"

"No. She claims he wasn't at the office. Her father is at a trade show in Las Vegas."

"That can be..."

"His alibi has been verified," Rocky said. "Casey's going to do some time for falsifying a kidnapping."

"Don't count on his aunts' cooperation."

"What about yours?" Rocky's thumb traced my jaw absently, distracting and steadying at the same time. "Will you stay and testify?"

A shiver slipped down my spine. It would be dangerously easy to stay here. To let him handle it. To trust federal containment and concrete walls.

"Tash's afraid of someone," I said. "I need to get the information from her."

He didn't challenge my ability. "At what cost?" he asked quietly.

I held his gaze. "That's the wrong question."

He waited for my answer.

"The benefit is what matters," I said. "And that's my family's safety."

Rocky didn't pull away. "Is insurance recovery work always this dangerous?"

"No," I said automatically. I'd lied, and I knew it. The Fire

Diamond investigation had nearly killed us both. And now we chased a colonial mine tied to monarchists and murder.

I exhaled. "Mostly, Glimmer and I go to private homes and find a missing ring in a dusty corner. Or under a sofa cushion. Sometimes a hotel safe or a hedge fund manager's backyard koi pond."

His expression didn't soften.

"Trust me," I added. "I'm well-compensated."

That earned a slow exhale. Not relief—just restraint. The doubt in his eyes lingered.

This wasn't about whether I could handle myself. It was about whether he could live with the risks I took. Despite the attraction between us, when the line was drawn... would I choose him or the job?

His hands still warmed my skin. "You don't have to do this alone," he said.

"I know." But knowing and choosing were two different things.

His forehead hovered close to mine, not touching, but close enough that I felt the pull of him, the almost.

"Why are we always moving in opposite directions?" he asked.

Behind us, the glass doors slid open. Hope cleared her throat. Time for me to go.

Rocky's hands fell away, reluctantly. "Come back."

I gave him the only honesty I had. "Meet me halfway."

I walked into the terminal with the taste of Rocky still lingering on my lips and a look on my face that made Hope zero in like a heat-seeking missile.

"You're an idiot," she announced. Thankfully, no one occupied the leather chairs arranged in small clusters in the waiting area, and the receptionist had the courtesy to check on 'something' elsewhere.

"He's good-looking, gainfully employed, dresses better than most federal agents have a right to, and he's clearly into you. What exactly are you waiting for?"

If I knew that answer... Was I still so bruised from my implosion with Chad that I couldn't risk giving someone else a real chance? Or was I just better at chasing diamonds than holding onto something that might actually last?

The receptionist's return offered me a reprieve. Not a pass. She opened a side door, and we walked straight to the ramp, avoiding TSA bins, gate changes, and crowds pressed shoulder to shoulder. Here, the assumption that your time matters worked.

Surprisingly, Hope didn't grill me the entire flight to Phoenix. She'd made her point and left me to work through the details for now. Protecting the family mattered more than my future.

Chapter Twenty-Six

BE CAREFUL WHAT YOU ASK FOR
—WISDOM FROM A JEWEL THIEF

Finding Tash proved easier than I'd anticipated. When your vanity plate reads **DESERVE**, subtlety isn't exactly your brand.

I parked beside her red Mercedes convertible outside one of Scottsdale's most exclusive spas. The low, modern building constructed of pale stone and floor-to-ceiling glass whispered wealth. I arrived a few minutes before her scheduled relaxation massage.

After her ordeal, a little Zen made sense. Inside, the waiting room exuded a curated calm. Cream-colored walls surrounded oversized linen chairs arranged around slabs of white marble. A wall fountain trickled softly, the water catching the light like cut crystal. The essence of eucalyptus and white tea relaxed with every breath.

I'd reached out to Lionel to secure the appointment. He'd delivered with his usual flair. Of course, a massage slot opened, no questions asked. He'd even scheduled Glimmer for her own blueberry facial.

Perfect. As if my diamond-sniffing dachshund needed another

reason to believe the world revolved around her. Glimmer was already enjoying being fussed over by a groomer in soft gray scrubs when I stepped into the lounge.

Tash was there. She sat in a plush robe that draped just so, a champagne flute balanced between manicured fingers. The robe on me felt like a towel tied for survival. On her, it looked like a fashion statement.

She glanced up, surprise flashing across her features before she smoothed it away. "This can't be a coincidence."

"Afraid not." I settled into the chair beside her.

Almost on cue, the waiting area thinned with the quiet efficiency of a staff accustomed to customer confrontations.

"You must have friends in very high places to get an appointment here on short notice," Tash said lightly, sipping her champagne.

Even in a sanctuary designed for discretion, I had a talent for disturbing the calm. "I know the bracelet's secret."

Her forefinger drifted to her bare ring finger, brushing the pale indentation where her engagement ring had been yesterday. The absence said more than any statement.

"And why," she asked coolly, "should that concern me?"

"You lied to the FBI about the Knights' leader. I saw the shadow in the back room in the office."

The color drained from her face, emphasizing the purple bruise along her cheekbone. "Y-you don't want to go there," she whispered. "You don't want to tell anyone what the Duette means."

"Don't I?" I leaned back, as if we were discussing spa packages instead of possible treason. "I'd consider selling the information. Five million in bitcoin and assurances. A modest investment for the fortune waiting at the end of that riddle."

Tash's gaze turned razor sharp. "You're still missing a piece. You can't possibly..."

She'd said too much. She knew it, and so did I. Deep down,

I'd known she'd been involved; I'm not sure why the realization stung.

"Look, Tash, I don't care if you orchestrated this or got pulled in over your head. It will take the Knights years to reunite the Waters' Duette. Longer to decode it."

She gave a small, measured nod. "Someone will reach out to you."

Of course they would.

She rose as a gray-clad attendant appeared at her elbow, serenity restored on cue. Halfway to the treatment corridor, she glanced back and offered me a Cheshire-cat smile that was all teeth and secrets.

I returned it. She hadn't asked about the clasp. That told me she either didn't know its significance... or she knew better than to reveal that she did. My next contact would be suaver.

Tash wasn't the architect of this. She didn't have the discipline for it. But she knew who was pulling the strings, exactly as I'd suspected. Sophie had been right about Tash. The woman wanted her moment. When it came, I doubted it would be all she'd dreamed it would.

I leaned back as the eucalyptus scent drifted through the lounge again. I stayed for my massage, knowing full well that I'd never get Glimmer to leave before she enjoyed the full experience and the adoration that came with it.

I'm not certain how Tash managed it, but I found a burner phone on top of my street clothing in the spa locker when I dressed to leave. I added the trace before I left the building. Whoever reached out to me would be heard by all.

I picked up my tail as soon as I exited the parking lot. Glimmer confirmed my sighting with a single woof and her eyes on the black SUV. I continued on the Loop 101 toward Sunset Peak when Sophie called. A call at two a.m. London time couldn't be good news. And proved what I'd known all along—the woman had my back.

"What's wrong?"

"A rather unsettling detail has just come to light. The Wises are descended from minor German nobility. Michael Wise II, the current owner of Wise & Sons jewelry stores, is, in fact, the present Baron von Weiberg."

That made Tash the daughter of a baron.

Sophie let the revelation settle before adding, "Michael Wise II also read mining engineering at the *Technische Universität Bergakademie Freiberg*—TUBAF, if you prefer precision. And—do brace yourself—the current Prince of Prussia, George Friedrich, also attended the same school."

"At the same time?" I asked.

"Both the heir and his younger brother spent a semester abroad at the school during the time period in question. One does hate coincidence when it begins to look like continuity."

I cursed. Couldn't help myself, despite the vision of Hope's displeasure.

"I rather doubt a wannabe king befriending an American loyalist is a coincidence either," Sophie said.

"It also means that there's more to Tash's brother than she thinks." Had Tash misread her brother or just pretended?

"In addition to the jewelry store, he will one day inherit the baron title from his father. Another important point: The Von Weissbergs were elevated to royalty for their mining success in colonial East Africa."

Another puzzle piece connected. "So, they know about the diamond mines."

"I would suggest so."

My thoughts scattered. "The FBI confirmed Michael Wise and his son's alibis."

"Yes, well, we are all acutely aware of how difficult that particular balance can be. I shall make further inquiries." A pause. Softer, but no less precise. "And Hunter... do exercise caution. This set is not merely ambitious. They are driven."

Of course they were. And I'd just painted a target on my back and labeled it *obstacle*.

Chapter Twenty-Seven
HELP COMES FROM UNLIKELY SOURCES
—WISDOM FROM A JEWEL THIEF

TUESDAY 8 P.M.

Sunset Peak went quiet after eight. The boutiques below my apartment had locked up hours ago. Streetlamps cast long amber streaks across the sidewalk. I watched the reflection in the glass from my living room. A dark sedan remained on watch.

No surprise. The same vehicle that had followed me from the spa had been parked a block away for hours, a haunting display of patience. Like I was going to run.

Hope hadn't been spared either. Someone had staked out her place this afternoon. She'd called the Sunset Peak police, and a cruiser had chased the vehicle off. That strategy worked for forty-five minutes before the same car returned. A squad car now guarded the entrance to her dog-training ranch. I got the message loud and clear: The Knights could reach anyone, anywhere.

The burner phone rang at eight p.m. sharp.

Glimmer's head lifted from her paws. She wasn't fooled by stillness any more than I was.

I answered. "Hello."

A male voice, distorted by design. "Come downstairs." Click.

No greeting. No negotiation. I closed my eyes and reached out to Hope.

It's time. Our twin telepathy hummed, the thread between us that remained constant.

I know. Her worry brushed the edges of my focus.

Be careful.

Always.

I crossed to my dresser and removed my diamond studs, replacing them with two luminous pearl earrings. Classic and harmless on the surface. Directional micro-charges when needed. Thanks to Sophie and her MI6 contacts, I had a house full of deterrents.

My Glock rested beside the jewelry case. I lifted it automatically, then set it down again; escalation was not part of tonight's strategy.

Glimmer rose as I reached for her harness and slipped Melodie's bracelet into the hidden pocket beneath the padded seam. Invisible unless you knew exactly where to look. The clasp, the true key, remained locked in my safe downstairs in the jewelry store.

Let them think I'd brought everything.

I shut off the last lamp and slipped out of my apartment, taking the narrow staircase down to the street. Glimmer pressed close as I opened the alley door.

A sedan idled at the curb, angled just enough to block my garage. The surveillance SUV had eased into position at the mouth of the alley, sealing off the street view. No witnesses. No exits. That wasn't what caused my throat to tighten. My security camera lay shattered on the pavement—ripped from above the door and tossed aside like it never mattered. No footage. No eyes. No one was watching.

I was on my own.

The sedan's rear window caught the streetlamp's glow, but behind the reflection sat a darker shape. Watching me like a puppeteer enjoying control.

Glimmer's growl gave me half a second warning. I pivoted, unbalancing the shadow that lunged from the alley wall. My arm deflected the grab, my heel swept low. Years of defensive repetition took over where fear might have frozen me.

The attacker's legs went out from under him. He hit the pavement hard, a crack echoing off the brick building, a white rag fluttering from his hand.

Chloroform or something more dangerous? They weren't taking any chances.

Glimmer didn't hesitate. She launched forward with feral precision, teeth finding vulnerable territory. The man howled, curling instinctively.

The sedan door opened.

"Enough. Get in, Hunter."

The voice drifted through the night—familiar, but not enough to place. A chill shimmied down my spine. It wasn't Tash's father or her brother.

Above, a hawk cut across the streetlight glow, wings wide and silent. Hawks didn't fly at night. My heart jumped. It had to be an FBI drone, which meant Rocky was watching. I just needed to survive until help arrived.

"Not happening," I called, keeping my weight balanced, scanning for a second attacker. "If you want the information, you get out of the car and meet me right here."

Hope's voice exploded through my head. *You're an idiot.*

Can't argue with her.

The man on the pavement groaned. Glimmer held her ground, growling low and lethal.

"You'll not get your money," the voice said calmly.

"Some things aren't worth it," I shot back. I made a move to retreat.

Then the rear window lowered an inch. "Let me make it worth your while. I get what I want, and you and your family will never see me again."

I didn't believe him for a second. My words spilled out, instinct taking over. "Threats don't help."

An amused guff, maybe? "You don't disappoint, Hunter. If you have the merchandise, here will do."

Something tightened deep in my gut as the passenger door opened slowly this time. A polished shoe touched pavement.

I forced my breath to steady.

The figure straightened beside the sedan, face still in shadow, posture relaxed in a way that spoke of confidence born of righteousness.

"Your theatrics are unnecessary," he said. "We merely require confirmation."

"Confirmation of what?"

"That you possess the Duette."

My heart hammered. "The FBI has the Waters' bracelet. Your fault when you kill the messenger."

"Careless, I agree."

Glimmer's growl deepened as the man at my feet made a desperate grab for my ankle. I stepped back, my boot heel driving into his wrist. He yelped.

The figure by the car didn't flinch.

"You came armed," he observed.

"Your man underestimated a dachshund."

Was that a scoff or a headshake agreement? The hawk circled once more overhead, then vanished into the dark.

"I will ask once," he said. "Do you have it?"

Melodie's bracelet rested warm against Glimmer's ribs. I swallowed. "Yes."

"Then give it to me."

My pulse thundered in my ears. Every instinct screamed run, but if I did, Hope paid for it. If I turned over the bracelet and I learned his identity, I was dead.

Hope whispered in my mind, fear threading through steel. *Think.*

I was. And that was the problem. There was no way out. I

tapped my leg, bringing Glimmer to my side. "The bracelet is in her vest."

The dachshund growled when the driver moved toward us. He stopped. "If you'll allow me…" I said.

"No quick moves," the voice agreed.

I crouched and unclipped the vest. I made a show of unzipping the hidden pouch. "The problem is that this bracelet was damaged. Even with Christian Weber's stone, the coordinates are incomplete."

"So, you do know the secret."

"I know that the area is an entire mountain range."

"Then you should have no problem giving me the information."

His lack of concern made me think I'd missed something. "You have the miner's logs. You just need the starting point," I said, the realization explaining everything.

"The bracelet, Hunter."

I'd stretched his patience long enough. Time to move. My fingers went to the pearl at my ear. A subtle press against the hidden safety. I lobbed it low, toward the rear quarter panel, close enough to the gas tank to terrify, not ignite.

The flash detonated in a blinding burst of white.

The shadowed figure recoiled, throwing himself sideways, arm up to shield his face. The driver shouted. Glimmer barked.

I didn't wait. I pivoted and sprinted for the rear entrance. The door was three strides away when I risked one glance back. The voice had stepped into the light.

Not Tash's fiancé. Her brother, the second son, the one born to live in the heir's shadow. That tradition needed serious reevaluation. The fury carved into his features wasn't about money. It was personal.

His eyes locked on mine through the drifting smoke, promising he'd finish this here and now. I bolted through the door and threw the deadbolt just as something heavy slammed into the metal from the alley side.

My Glock was upstairs. I had to move. Glimmer tore ahead of me up the narrow stairwell, barking like she meant to take on a battalion. I took the steps two at a time, heart still jackhammering from the flash. I hit the landing and yanked open the interior door... and ran straight into body armor?

Hard chest. Tactical vest. The unmistakable breadth of shoulders I'd once known too well. Even in full SWAT gear, I recognized Chad and the Phoenix police team behind him.

Relief hit first. *Armed backup.* Then questions crashed in behind it. *How had my ex-husband gotten here? And why did it look like he'd come to save me?*

Except... that didn't fit. Chad wasn't the showing-up kind. Not for me. Not anymore. His visor lifted. His eyes found mine. "Out of the way," he snapped. "This is my bust."

And just like that, my gratitude evaporated. Hero wasn't a role Chad played.

Chapter Twenty-Eight
FAMILIES ARE NEVER PERFECT
—WISDOM FROM A JEWEL THIEF

TUESDAY, 9 P.M.

"Come on," Hope said gently, squeezing my arm. "Let the Cad have his moment. Let's get out of here."

Her voice cut through the shock like a setting hammer. I followed her through the hidden passage behind the assayer's office, past the reinforced storage room, and out the secondary exit. The night air hit cool against my overheated skin.

I paused, listening. No gunfire. No shouting. Was the entire conflict already over?

Hope didn't slow until we were inside her SUV with the doors locked. She pulled away smoothly without drama.

"Rocky sent him," she said.

"I saw the drone." I'd known Rocky had been watching out for me.

Hope smiled, satisfied. "That man's a keeper."

In theory, I agreed. The devil would be in the details. I was up for the challenge.

"Rocky's on his way," she added. "He wanted to let Chad have his big bust before the FBI took over."

Of course he did. Glory didn't drive Rocky. Doing the right thing did. I filed that away. A lesson I no doubt needed to learn.

"How did he know I needed his help?" I asked quietly.

Hope's expression shifted. "The FBI found Tash's fiancé's body an hour ago. Rocky surmised you were walking into a trap."

"Without solid proof?" I let out a slow breath. There would be time later to analyze what that implied. For now, I stuck to what I could control. "You let Chad and his team into my apartment through the passage?" It wasn't meant to accuse, but the edge slipped in anyway. "Why would you leave your family? You knew the Knights were watching you."

"My daughters were safer than you," she cut in calmly. "Who is dumb enough to breach a compound that trains police attack dogs anyway? It's harder to get into than Fort Knox. Just ask my daughters. They're convinced they're destined for spinsterhood."

Despite everything, I laughed. I loved those little troublemakers. "If a few dogs scare the boys off, their standards are too low."

"My thought exactly." She glanced over. "So. Who was the shadow?"

"Tash's brother."

Hope's jaw tightened. "That entitled..."

"Not the heir apparent," I said. "The forgotten second son."

Understanding dawned. Every kid needed to be loved equally. "What a family," she muttered.

I reached across the console and pulled her into a quick, fierce hug at the next stoplight. We had each other. Always.

As Hope drove out of town, I leaned back against the seat, adrenaline finally ebbing, Glimmer climbing into my lap like she'd personally won the war.

"When are you going to return Melodie's bracelet to Grandma and her sisters?" Hope asked.

"I'm not sure. The sisters are meeting with Lionel and Claire later this week." A reunion a century overdue—somehow, that part felt right. "My guess? The bracelets will be reunited permanently and donated to the Charlottenburg Palace to be folded into the historic Hohenzollern collection where..."

"...they belong." As usual, Hope finished my sentence in complete sync with me. "With a few..."

"...modifications," I agreed, rubbing the back of my neck. "The Wises have the original mining records, but even with the Duette's coordinates, finding the exact mine will be next to impossible."

Hope didn't miss a beat. "Nothing stays hidden forever."

"True." I squeezed her hand. "When someone finally does find it, let's hope the people of Tanzania see the reward. Not just whoever gets there first."

Hope broke the sudden silence between us. "You were right. Twins began this adventure, and twins finished it. So, what's still bothering you?"

Of course, she knew. Our twin radar never failed. "Dad."

Hope went still. "What about him?"

"I don't know how it's connected or even if it is, but both Lionel and Weber know Dad."

Tension radiated in Hope's long pause. "Dad knew them both?"

"Yeah. The coincidence is statistically..."

"...impossible." Hope verbalized my fears.

"Lionel admitted to meeting him at an embassy event. And Weber wouldn't say how he knew him."

"You think Dad ran a job for Weber?" Hope asked.

"I don't know." That was the problem. With our father, not knowing was the most dangerous place to stand. The Fire Diamond had been, in part, about my father's revenge against the man who'd killed our mother. Had the Water Diamond been another personal vendetta? I didn't want to believe it, but...

Hope's exhale seemed sharp, unwelcome. "Remember the blind woman at the Long Beach ferry? The one you told me to stay close to?"

I nodded, slower this time as a thread of unease pulled tight in my chest.

"She said something that I didn't think was important until now... like she knew we were up to something."

My gut twinged. "What did she say exactly?"

Hope held my gaze. "Just that things aren't always what they seem."

Silence settled in. Because suddenly it didn't feel like a warning about us.

It felt like a warning about him.

We exchanged a look—one of those silent, twin-bound exchanges that said too much to ever be spoken aloud. Doubt had crept in where certainty used to live. All our lives, we'd cast our father in a single role: the thief. The man who'd left us. Maybe we'd been wrong about him. Or at least... not entirely right.

Hope's expression softened, but the question lingered between us, sharp as a cut stone. Had he been part of the hunt for the Water Diamond? Or had we been chasing shadows shaped by our own childhood fears? Either way, guessing wasn't enough anymore. It was time to learn the truth about our father.

A hundred-year-old mystery had led us here—straight to the edges of something far more dangerous, far more personal. And for the first time, I couldn't tell where the past ended... and his story began.

"Not today," I said quietly, more to myself than to Hope. There would be a next move. There was always a next move.

I pulled out my phone and dialed Sophie, not worried about consequences. When you recover hundred-year-old diamonds and shut down a monarchist's plot, even I'm willing to get up at the crack of dawn for that story.

Besides, Sophie would have answers. Or at least a direction. Somewhere out there, the man we thought we knew was either waiting for us to find him...or hoping we never would.

Either way, the hunt had just begun.

THE END

* * *

Be sure to follow Glimmer the Diamond Dog on her quest to keep her human safe. You can find her on Facebook and Instagram.

Facebook: /GlimmertheDiamondDog/
Instagram: @glimmer_the_diamond_dog

* * *

Join Hunter and Glimmer in their next adventure...

Every diamond has a story... this one is carved in ice.

When the legendary Ice Diamond is stolen from a sealed suite inside the famed Hôtel de Glace, diamond recovery specialist Taylor "Hunter" is called to Quebec City to solve the impossible: a locked-room heist with no entry, no exit... and too many suspects.

The guest list is elite—and dangerous. A powerful maple syrup syndicate with something to hide. A world champion ice skater whose flawless performance masks deadly precision. And a trail of secrets frozen beneath centuries of power, wealth, and control.

But a colder truth closes in: what role did her father play—if any? The legendary thief known as the Silver Fox has always been untouchable... until now. Because the evidence isn't just whispering his name—it's pointing straight at him.

As the case begins to crack, Hunter and her diamond-sniffing dachshund, Glimmer, follow a trail buried in ice, illusion, and ambition. But in a world built on frozen perfection, the smallest rise in temperature can erase everything.

Because this time, the truth isn't just hidden...It has to be found before it melts away.

Acknowledgments

While writing may be a solitary process, the finished book is always a team effort. I'm grateful to my incredible cheerleader crew—Ann Goldfarb (JC Eaton), Douglas Seedorf, Ruth Rotkowitz, Dee Kaler, Pam Wright, Becky Witters, Regina Kotkowski, and Darlene Dziomba—who listened to my wild ideas and gently reined me in when needed. I truly couldn't do this without you.

And to Lori Roberts Herbst—your guidance has made me a stronger, better writer. Thank you.

This book wouldn't exist without all of you. Special recognition to Sharon Jacobson and Mia, the sweet inspiration behind Glimmer.

Thank you to Mary Haller for her invaluable insight into Catalina Island, and to Jason Clay for introducing me to the "real" Catalina. Chuck Lenz, thank you for being part of the adventure itself. I hope you smile about this for years to come.

A heartfelt thank you to Tash Foti for graciously allowing me to use her name and for her generous support of women's education through the Desert Foothills Women's Club.

I'm deeply grateful to Sergeant Jeff Daukas of the Glendale, Arizona Police Department for his expertise on police procedures —you're a true hero and friend. Any remaining errors are mine alone. Thank you as well to retired FBI agent George Daniels for helping me understand the challenges he faces daily.Melissa Martin, thank you for keeping me sane. And finally, to my husband Rocky—your unwavering patience and support make everything possible.

Award-winning author CB Wilson writes the Gem Hunters Mysteries and the Barkview Mysteries—two series that blend intrigue, heart, and unforgettable animal companions. A GIA-trained gemologist, she brings authenticity and insider detail to her fast-paced stories of stolen jewels, hidden histories, and high-stakes recovery.

Her breakout novel, *The Fire Diamond*, has resonated strongly with readers, launching the Gem Hunters series with a compelling mix of adventure and intrigue. The story continues in *The Water Diamond*, following diamond recovery specialist Taylor "Hunter" Hunter and her diamond-sniffing dachshund, Glimmer, as they unravel a mystery that reaches back generations. The next installment, *The Ice Diamond*, is set for release later this year, taking readers into an icy world of secrets, danger, and international stakes.

CB's Barkview Mysteries offer a lighter, Hallmark-style escape into the dog-friendliest town in America, where each story highlights the charm, quirks, and realities of life with beloved canine companions.

When she's not writing, CB draws inspiration from horseback riding through the Arizona desert, playing pickleball, and her lifelong love of animals. Her stories reflect her passion for blending cozy mystery warmth with adventure-driven suspense— where every clue sparkles, and every diamond has a story.

Awards:
CIBA 2026 First Place
Bookfest Gold Medal
Readers' Favorite Award Gold Medal
Silver Falchion Finalist
Dog Writers of America Finalist

To connect with C.B. Wilson:
www.cbwilsonauthor.com

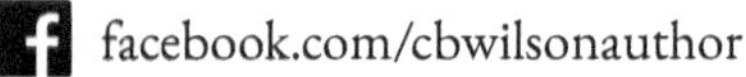

facebook.com/cbwilsonauthor
instagram.com/cbwilsonauthor
tiktok.com/@author.cb.wilson
bookbub.com/profile/c-b-wilson